JANE BAILEY is the author of *Promising*, *An Angel in Waiting* and *Tommy Glover's Sketch of Heaven*. Her first novel was shortlisted for the Dillons Prize and she received a Royal Literary Fund award. She was born and brought up in Gloucestershire where she now lives with her two daughters.

Constable & Robinson Ltd
3 The Lanchesters
162 Fulham Palace Road
London W6 9ER
www.constablerobinson.com

This edition published by Robinson,
an imprint of Constable & Robinson Ltd, 2006

A copy of the British Library Cataloguing
in Publication data is available from the British Library

ISBN 13: 978-1-84529-340-6
ISBN 10: 1-84529-340-1

Printed and bound in the EU

1 3 5 7 9 10 8 6 4 2

MAD JO

Jane Bailey

ROBINSON

London

With thanks to The Royal Literary Fund
for supporting me in the writing of this novel

1

At the age of five I ran into a wood, and nearly two years later I walked out of it and into the nearest house. I was covered in filth, shoeless, with leaves and plant stems matted in my hair. My mother – or the woman I would call my mother, Gracie Burrows – found me curled up on her armchair beside the fire. I did not say where I'd come from, because I did not speak.

For a long time I lived mute with Gracie Burrows and she, for her part, was quite happy to be ignorant of my origins in case anyone should reclaim me as their own.

Imagine the scene. On that very day in 1927 Gracie had buried her father, the clockmaker Edmund Burrows, and last remaining member of her family. There had been a small gathering back at the house afterwards. A pitifully small gathering: three half-dead neighbours, in fact, who'd had nothing better to do on a Thursday morning. Gracie had washed up the last plate of crumbs and covered the pyramid of uneaten paste sandwiches with an upturned bowl. She had most probably fought back tears of anger at her wasted life, just as she had always kept her emotions in check through years of duty and restraint. And the newly orphaned, lifelong childless spinster was about to yield to some fierce unfettered grief at last, when she unlatched the parlour door to find me, a fetid, grubby gift of fate.

We both played our parts so well: she not wanting to know, and me not willing to tell. It was a fine act. We thought we could keep it up for ever.

2

It was a long, long time since I'd been in a house, and the being there brought a rush of chaotic ghosts. The smell of carbolic soap, paraffin and vegetable leaves; the sooty smell near the range and the linen warming above giving off a powdery cooked-cotton aroma. The sweet, oily smell of the pantry, laced with the trace of cheese and mould and bread and vinegar and everything that had ever been stored. The insides of old wood cupboards, tarry and camphoric: the echo of a chair-leg scraping; the space, the dryness, the silence, the warmth.

The garden was damp and sulphurous with cabbages, little white insects floating around them like thistledown. A stone path led down to the lav and robust clumps of nettle.

The front garden was altogether different. Just a few feet from the road, it was bursting with colour: marigolds, roses, lavender. It was the lavender which had struck me on that bleak September day. Its few remaining florets rose high on their stems, soft and grey with only a hint of mauve. The familiarity of that dignified mist toppled me back to another time, when sitting in its tall stems meant healing and calm.

I had seen a cat by the side of the road – a black and white cat with a pensive, intelligent face. Black and white was good. Dark and light. Balance. It rose and put its tail straight up, as if beckoning me to follow the little mast. I followed it breathlessly across the road, through the outrageous, uninhibited lavender, and in through Gracie's front door, which was ajar. It welcomed me into the parlour where two comfy chairs stood by the range. It took one, and settled into a snug curl on the cushion, showing me what to do on the other. She – for she introduced herself with her eyes – explained that this was a good house for me. Contented and exhausted, I fell asleep.

Grace Burrows was a tallish, big-boned woman who walked as if she were wading through a very deep river. Her face was wide and soft, and on each side of it, covering her ears, she wore a little brown bun.

From the very first moment I woke to see her, I felt I had arrived. The armchair opposite hers by the range seemed to have been waiting for me, its dense old cushion curved already into my shape. I was allowed to explore in any room, and I could touch anything I liked. The only exception was a beautiful porcelain shepherdess on the mantel above the range, because that – although it might not look like it – was a 'nair loom'. I respected her wish. In any case, I was suspicious of something that pretended to be a shepherdess but which was, in fact, something else altogether.

I loved the picture of her parents on the mantel. They were kind, loving people, she said. I liked the way they looked so old-fashioned, and the advice they used to give, according to Gracie: 'Never trust a woman with more than two handbags,' 'A bird in the hand isn't worth anything unless you can eat it,' and 'A man who wears shop-bought socks is a gentleman.' They peered out of their silver frame with remarkable goodwill, and I felt a twinge of regret that I hadn't known them.

*　　*　　*

The bed that Gracie put me in that first night was so cool and deep and soft that I wanted to weep. But I was not used to sleeping alone, and she was not used to sleeping in the double bed in the front, so after several visits from her, checking on me, stroking my forehead, kissing me tentatively, I made my own way to the front bedroom and curled up in the soft curve of her, and fell into an easy sleep at last.

I always slept with her after that, pressed up against her wide back or cupped in the warm cotton of her nightgown. And I knew I had always slept with someone. The sappy woodsmoke smell of Nipper, the musky, shadowy smells of long past, and the warm cake smell of Gracie's soft skin, these all smelt of security. There was nothing that terrified me more – truly terrified me – than a cold, empty bed, with no one but myself to fill it. I did not choose to ask myself why. I slept with Gracie until I left home, although as far as anyone else was concerned, the back room was my room. In it I kept my few clothes, and spent time looking out of the window at the hills, or talking to myself in the mirror.

Views out of windows were dangerous for me. They were a reminder of being inside. But the view from my back room was a good one. It was a long view, taking in the hills in the distance, with sheep that grazed and were going nowhere. I liked the sheep for staying on the hill. Their progress was slow, and when they weren't there, they were somewhere else. But they never, ever disappeared for good, and I was grateful to them for their consistency.

Because I arrived so soon after her father's death, Gracie saw me as a gift. She named me 'Joy' and told people I was the orphan of a distant cousin who'd died of a tubercular cough. Owing to my mouth being permanently ajar like an idiot, and my tendency to say very little, I was soon known as Mad Joy by my classmates at Woodside School. There was no bullying involved; it was purely descriptive. They had all sorts at that school, and mad was just one in a spectrum of words to describe the ragbag of children we were. Others were Stinker, the boy who sat on my right in class, Weasel, the girl who sat on my left, and Spit Palmer, the sweet-natured girl in front of me whose neat parting and pigtails I gazed at for most of the day and who had a slight lisp.

Mo Mustoe was a few months younger than me, and emaciated. Most of the children in Woodside were thin because our diet was so poor and we ran around a lot. But Mo Mustoe looked as if you could pick her up and put her in your pocket. Mo's older brother was Stinker (or Robert) and her younger brother – who was two but weighed more than she did – was called George, and thought he was a sheepdog as long as I ever knew him.

From the moment she patted the empty seat beside her, I saw little Mo Mustoe as an ally. She seemed perfectly content with my silence, and chattered away to me as if my grateful looks were replies. I must've always said the right thing because she was always delighted with me.

Other children were not so safe:

'She mad or what?'

'Bit touched, ent she?'

'She got a tongue or what?'

Once Mo put her hands on her hips with pride and said, 'She only speaks to me.'

They laughed at her, and I could see a worried frown appear. Her confidence was so frail and I began to see it was something new she had invented for herself: for a moment her special powers had made her interesting. This playing dumb lark was not so easy as I'd thought. The trick was to make no connections and therefore risk no hurt or derision. But if you overplayed it, you became too interesting. And now this thin runt of a girl had drawn attention to both of us, and I had to make a decision. I could stay mute and watch them laugh at her, or I could play along.

I waited for her to test me out. She looked at me helplessly, as if she'd been caught out trying to be someone when she was, in fact, worthless. I looked back at her, willing her to make me speak. I would, I decided, say something short if she asked me to: a yes or a no. That wouldn't hurt. But she said nothing, just looked crumpled and defeated.

Suddenly I lunged forward and put my hand to her ear. I could think of nothing to say, so I whispered 'Yes.'

The children, who had started to turn away, turned back.

'What she say, then?'

Mo seemed to grow and glow with my one small action. 'She got a spell on her!' Mo breathed, her face alight with excitement. 'If you want to speak to her, you best ask me.'

I had done that. I had made little Mo happy and important. And she for her part had let me fit in. She had given me a role – and a place beside her.

We sat there in class all day, learned nothing and were very happy. It seemed a far better place than the last school I could remember. Here at Woodside, Miss Prosser loved us as if we were her very own, and gave us each a quarter of an apple on Fridays. We had a kitchen garden to plant and dig, logs to play on, songs to sing and triangles and tambourines to make a nice racket on. We thought we loved Miss Prosser with all our hearts. We loved her headphone hairdo, her downy face and her dingy brown handbag; but although we knew she was lonely, we prayed she would never get married in case we lost her for ever.

Nothing much really happened in Woodside except the seasons, and I was happy enough with that. But no one ever went anywhere. If they walked to the next village they'd get homesick and if they had to go to Gloucester or Stroud for market they'd come back full of complaints about the place, consoling themselves they were glad they lived in Woodside. It seemed to me they had no aspirations and no curiosity. They got up in the mornings and went to work in the fields and grew so bored that they invented days to celebrate.

A few weeks after I arrived there was 'Apple Day' in October. I remember it well because there was a smell of ripe apples in the air, and just before I was put to bed Gracie rapped on her back window at some people taking apples from the orchard down beyond the end of her garden.

'Tiz them bloody gypsies again,' said Mrs Mustoe from next door. She walked right on in whenever she felt like it, and gave her two pennies worth. 'Steal the ruddy shirt off our back, they would. Greedy beggars.'

'Only take what they need,' I ventured.

This sudden utterance drew such surprise from Mrs Mustoe and Gracie that I thought they were pleased I was speaking. But then Mrs Mustoe narrowed her eyes at me suspiciously, and Gracie shuffled me off to bed, at pains to change the subject. Later when she tucked me in she looked at me with a mixture of anxiety and tenderness, and opened her mouth to say something. But, of course, she didn't want to know too much, so the matter was left floating. If only she had asked, I could have told her I wasn't a gypsy, and saved her a lifetime of worry. Instead I rolled on my side, paddled my limbs in the coolness of the smooth cotton sheets, and remembered.

3

I remembered running in a wood. It was damp and chilly and leaves stuck to my shoes and my breath smoked. I had bare arms; I remember the wet leaves flicking them and soft ferns drenching my socks. Was I running towards something or away from it?

Running. Out of breath. Completely unknown pathways. I think I was running away, for what came next seemed like being caught. There was an almighty snap, the bite of a ferocious animal at my ankle. I can't remember the pain, but I know it must have hurt, because I howled, and when I looked up I saw him standing there, right next to me, fixing his eyes on mine, almost as terrified as me.

He must have been very brave, because he didn't run away. He would have been seven or eight, a couple of years older than me, but he had the presence of a wild animal.

I hadn't heard him coming; he seemed just to be there, standing silently in the ferns. His face was as still as a deer, and he watched me a long time, motionless, with his dark green eyes. Then he knelt down at my feet and parted the undergrowth, so that I could clearly see the iron teeth that had sunk into my left ankle. He released the trap, and gently put my arm around his shoulder.

It was the first time I had smelt a human since . . . The smells came at me suddenly from his neck and arms and clothes, drenching the air. They were disturbing. I was shocked and fascinated, tasting them on the back of my tongue. My pulse thumped and my head began to swim. But woven in with these siren smells were calming ones, tugging gently at my memory.

I went with him in a trance, and he took me to a clearing in the woods. That was how I came to meet Alice Snow, and I would share a pillow with her – or her relations – for the next four seasons, in her caravan or out of it, under the stars.

I missed Alice in the simple luxury of my feather bed. I missed the easy warmth of her through the night, I missed the smell of her, the raw musty whiff of her neck. But it didn't do to talk of gypsies too much at Woodside. People loved them well enough when they wanted illnesses healed, but that was in private. In public they were mere thieves and liars who ate hedgehogs, and sent their children to school when the fancy took them. Even so, there was a mystique about gypsies which Mo from next door was the first to impress upon me.

No one ever listened to Mo because she was too small and insignificant to be bothered with. So I was quite a catch for her.

'See that big house up there?' she said to me one day as we were building a den. 'Just see it hidden in the trees . . . that's cursed, that is.'

I murmured something in idiot fashion to show I was interested, and she knelt down and turned huge stealthy eyes on me: 'Cursed by a gypsy woman!'

I looked puzzled. The gypsy women I'd known had been gentle folk. But anything to do with gypsies intrigued me. I longed for news of Alice. Mo looked about as if we might be overheard in the middle of nowhere and lowered her voice to a whisper.

'Swear you won't tell no one.'

I nodded and spat three times on my hand to shake hers.

'Eurh!' She looked at my spit and then continued in hushed tones. 'He wanted a boy so's he could leave all his land to him. But his wife's only ever had a girl. And every baby she's had since have come out all bleeding.'

I looked suitably shocked.

'*And*,' she continued through suddenly slitted eyes, 'she's very very very scared of cats.'

I nodded gravely and somehow managed to agree that we should seek him out and try to lift the curse by fair means or foul.

'I seen lots of people go in an' out. I never seen him, yet.'

I looked curious.

'We'll know him when we see him, mind. Our mam says he wears his heart on his sleeve.'

'Eeeurch!' I managed.

'Tiz 'orrible! No one knows why!'

We both tried to imagine the organ strapped by some sort of belt to his arm. He certainly would be hard to miss.

Although it seemed perfectly natural that I should be referred to as 'Mad Joy', it is surprising that I didn't contest it, given that most of the population of Woodside seemed clinically insane.

Violet (or Vile It as we called her) was the resident tramp. There were many tramps passing through the village, but Vile It made her bed at the memorial cross or the bus shelter and her living room was the main street and village green. She spent her days telling people to clear out of her house, and since she smelt of stale cider and wee, they usually obliged. Mo said she'd lost her husband and all her four sons in the Great War, but I couldn't imagine anyone marrying her so it must have been made up. Once, when we were about eleven, we asked her and she said, 'Fuck off you fuckers,' and Mo was cross because we both knew real mothers didn't speak like that and therefore she *was* probably wrong.

Then there was Swallockelder. It took me years to realize that she was Miss Wallock Elder, and the older sister of Miss Wallock, my piano teacher. Swallockelder was truly barking mad. Every time you saw her she was pushing a pramful of lambs about. As the lambs grew bigger they looked even dafter, and by winter she was forced to carry one fat sheep at a time. She did not lay off mothering them until the following spring, when some more lucky lambs were shown off proudly, bleating at the top of their voices for her generous bottles and trampling carelessly on the lovingly crocheted pram blankets.

Mr Bearpark was the most famous cyclist in Woodside. He wore bicycle clips that displayed mustard-coloured socks, hand-knitted by Mrs Bearpark. Every day he could be seen pushing his bicycle. He pushed it down the hill to work in the sawmill and back up again at dinnertime and teatime. He pushed his bicycle to church on Sundays and to Libby's grocery stores on Saturdays and even to Stroud and Gloucester and Cheltenham. He wasn't afraid of hills, he had 'a fine pair of lungs', he said. On Sunday evenings he could always be seen on his front step with a piece of rag, tenderly rubbing the sacred machine and polishing the chrome handlebars, oiling the chain, adjusting the tyres. And when he passed the top year boys slouching on walls with their cigarette butts, he would always say something like 'You need some exercise, you do. Wanna get a bike, you do. Work those limbs – that's the trick!' No one ever saw him astride his bicycle. But no one – not even the bad boys – ever pointed this out.

It wasn't long before these people seemed perfectly normal to me as well, and they were always somewhere in the back-ground, gently going about their oddball lives in a world that never changed.

*   *   *

Mo's advantage over me came to an abrupt end three months later when Miss Prosser came to visit Gracie and announced that I was not mad but deaf. A little stay in hospital would sort it all out.

My 'little stay' was a shock to Gracie. I screamed at the nurses and spat at them and had to be held down. I spat at the nurses because no one understood that I didn't want them near me. I didn't want to be left in a place where women wore tight smiles, a determined look in their eyes and starched white veils clamped to their heads. I didn't like the way they sported syringes and smelt of nursey chemicals probably designed to knock you out. I had a terror of the rows of iron bedsteads. I felt locked in. I felt alarm. In the end they let me out early, and the fact that Gracie came back for me, like she'd promised, made me love her more than ever.

I had had my adenoids out and my ears syringed, and the world transformed itself overnight. I no longer had any excuse not to speak, but at least now I knew the story I was supposed to tell.

Not that speaking was an easy business by any means. Now that I had a tongue in my mouth, people expected the worst language to come out of it. I remember going into Mr Tribbit's, the grocer's, to get something for Gracie. I had a sore throat and a cough and didn't feel much like talking.

'Aren't we going to hear that lovely new voice of yours?' said Mr Tribbit.

I looked at the soap I was holding out to him. 'A cough,' I mumbled.

He looked outraged. 'I beg your pardon? *What* did you just say?'

'What did she say?' asked Mrs Tribbit, coming up from behind him.

'I couldn't possibly repeat it,' said Mr Tribbit. 'Told me where to go. And,' he said, jabbing his finger at me, 'you can go straight home to Miss Burrows, you can. No one speaks to me like that and buys my produce!'

Speaking was quite a dodgy business, then. You could offend people without knowing it and come home without any soap. Language was a dangerous thing.

4

Gracie and the Mustoes lived in two little stone houses in a row of four. Opposite was a spring and a field of sheep penned in by a lichen-covered stone wall. To the left was the church and graveyard and to the right was the pub. Further up the road in this direction – about half a mile – was Buckleigh House.

It was a fine-looking building, if you made the effort to get right up close and look through the iron gates and between the trees. There was a grand driveway leading up to a golden-pillared porch, and the tall windows were the same on both sides. Its symmetry was part of its beauty, but the way the drive approached almost from the side seemed to add to its mystery. There would be no full view of this house unless you were standing squarely in front of it, inside the grounds.

Mo and I could not leave this house alone. We were fascinated by it. As time went on we invented even more gruesome additions to the stories we had heard, and since I was no longer mute, Stinker became interested in our games too, and joined us in ever more daring feats of voyeurism.

We had a good excuse for playing up the road beyond the church, because that was where Mrs Emery lived.

Mrs Emery had a reliably short temper and a husband who

worked nights. We didn't know where he worked, only that in the daytime he was sure to be sleeping. We took a shameful delight in trying to wake him, not because we wished him any harm, but because our attempts drew out Mrs Emery like rain drew out the lady with the umbrella on Gracie's hall barometer. And Mrs Emery's temper thrilled us. We never stayed around long enough to hear a word she said, but the sight of her standing beetroot at her gate and gabbling furiously sent us flying up the road to hide, breathless with exhilaration.

It was always up the road we ran, because of the slight bend. Down the road we would be seen, but up was all hedges and trees and, if we ran far enough, the imposing gateway to Buckleigh House, totally invisible from the village.

The road was good here, and the yellow gravel of the drive entrance so impacted by car wheels that you could bounce a ball on it. The boys liked it because from time to time you got to see a car drive in and out, and we girls liked it because we very occasionally got to see the beautiful Mrs Buckleigh with her incredible changing outfits. If there were too many of us or if we came too close she told us to clear off, but mostly she allowed us to admire her. This she did by ignoring us completely while the driver opened the gates. She tantalized us with her matching coats and hats and feathers and her long trail of dead babies that had come out bleeding.

Once, loitering by the iron gates, we saw a man striding across the lawn, and we squealed and scattered in all directions. He came right out of the gates and told us to clear off, but Mo said it was only Mr Rollins the gardener. Another time we saw a face at an upstairs window, and Stinker said for certain it was Mr Buckleigh, but no sooner had we seen it than it was gone. The next time we saw the face we all looked much more carefully, but it was a long way off and we couldn't see for certain the heart on his sleeve or any blood or anything.

Our interest never waned though, fuelled as it was by the little bits of information we all contributed to keep it alive. Spit Palmer said her mother had said he was a philanthropist. Stinker said he'd thought as much and we'd better watch out, because they did terrible things to children. George said he had a room full of guns, which was most likely true. I said I'd heard he had a hook for a hand, which wasn't true at all but seemed to fit in with the general picture.

Often Mo and I would play on our own, and then I had to be Buster Keaton and she would be Mo grown up. I think she somehow knew I'd come from the woods, because we always had to be lost in the woods which she found terribly romantic, and I just knew it was cold and damp so I tried to make us find a cottage. Mo insisted the cottage was always deserted, although it miraculously had plenty of fresh food and a warm fire blazing.

'Look! A cottage!' I would say, as soon as I'd had enough of the woods.

'It's deserted!' she would discover, the instant she stepped into some bushes. 'Let's warm up!'

'I'll light a fire.'

'Oh, Buster! There's already a fire – but I need warming up.'

I would go and rub her skin and she would fall limp in my arms. 'I'm so tired.'

Then I would have to find a bed, and there would strangely only be one in the whole house. We would button up our coats to make a blanket and snuggle up underneath. I had no idea who Buster Keaton was, and so found it hard to stay in character. Fortunately, before we progressed any further, we were usually bogged down with details: how big the room was, what sort of food was in the pantry and how long it would last, what she was wearing and so on.

Sometimes George would wander over and want to join in. Usually he would be a doctor called out to examine some injury or other which required the lifting of my dress or jersey. I was quite happy with this turn of events, but Mo wasn't. She would throw him a stick and say 'Go fetch' and usually he would.

5

Just before Christmas a gentleman came to our door. I knew he was a gentleman because he wore a tweed suit and removed a very fine hat when he came in. He didn't smell of the sawmills or sheep fields. He smelt of woodsmoke – beech with a little sappy hint of pine. He wafted in like a breeze, and spread his manliness to every corner of the room. I hid behind Gracie and clung on to a chunk of her skirt. She offered him a seat, and I could feel her fluster, although she spoke calmly enough. He looked about him at the room, and then at me and Gracie in equal measure, but intently.

He had a gentle face: eyes brown and glistening as if they might be half full of tears.

After the greetings and the kettle going on, he fumbled his way through some sentences. He had a deep, tender, almost apologetic voice.

'I heard about the girl . . .'

I felt Gracie go rigid under her clothes. 'Run along out the back, now, Joy. Fetch some wood, will you, my love?'

But I could not fetch wood. I ran as far as the back kitchen, and stood with my cheek on the cold stone wall, listening by the door. They were speaking in low voices, and the kettle was rumbling, and I only heard fragments.

His voice:

'She's my responsibility . . . I promised I would take care of her . . . I assumed . . . it seemed . . .'

Then Gracie:

'. . . my second cousin's child . . . a coincidence . . . mistaken . . . understandable . . .'

The kettle began to whistle and the voices muddled and died and I was dizzy with fear. Then Gracie shouted for me, 'Joy?' and I came in, and it was obvious I'd been nowhere but the back kitchen, and he said, 'Joy, is that her name? What a lovely name,' and Gracie smiled and poured tea, and I sat by her feet.

They sat looking at each other for a long time, sipping tea and saying nothing in particular, except he said he was sorry a lot for the intrusion, and she said it was no bother at all.

She breathed in and out very deeply once, and he stared into his tea leaves as if holding his face in place to stop it wobbling. I looked at his socks. They were dark green and shop-bought. That was another reason I knew he was a gentleman.

When he left there were lots more apologies, and when the door closed Gracie held me very, very tight, and almost suffocated me.

'Am I going to be taken away?'

'No. You're going nowhere, my darling. You'll stop here safe with me, if that's all the same with you.'

'Yes.'

Then she sat like a stunned rabbit, and gazed at the window-sill for a very long time.

When the gentleman left there was a doll. I remember it in particular because, although it was second-hand, it was an exceptional toy for anyone to give away. It was an articulated doll with real hair. When I say real, it wasn't painted on, but made of some substance that looked like hair. And apart from a slight frizz on one side where it had become matted, the little cap of ginger locks was in perfect condition. Her eyes, unlike the modern ones which opened and closed, were painted on. This gave her a slightly unnerving fixed stare, but since the look was wide-eyed and innocent there was nothing sinister about it, and everyone who saw her exclaimed what a darling, happy face she had. And it *was* happy, too. Her lips were shaped into a beautiful cupid's bow which turned up at the edges with what seemed genuine pleasure. She had a blue dress with daisies on it and a slight tear in one sleeve.

I called the doll Conceptua. I didn't know why I chose that name: it seemed to choose itself. If I had told her, Gracie would have said it was a beautiful name, but no one knew her name except me.

I took Conceptua everywhere with me when I first had her. I sat her next to me when I did colouring with some newly acquired crayons, and I looked at her watching me. She watched me with that beatific smile, happy with everything I drew. And when I sat down to eat, Conceptua would sit at the table too. Sometimes I would try to feed her cabbage, but she simply smiled and wouldn't take it. Gracie thought this was amusing, and used to say, 'It's no use, she's just not hungry.' Or sometimes I would tuck the corner of a hankie into her neckband and pretend it was a bib, and Gracie would smile. But once, I remember, Conceptua wasn't interested in my lentil soup. She showed no interest as I put the spoon of khaki liquid to her lips – just sat there smiling her candid little smile. I pushed the spoon into the groove of her lips more forcefully, trying to make her take it.

'Eat up!' I said in my head. 'Eat it up, or else!'

But Conceptua stared ahead, helplessly smiling her stupid smile, so I rammed the spoon in hard and, since there was no mouth to enter, the contents spilled over on to her spotless blue dress.

21

I could see Gracie was upset by this, but I couldn't help it. It was because I wasn't very nice. I was bad, but I wasn't sorry.

My ambiguous relationship with the doll lasted for a few weeks – maybe more. I wanted her with me at all times, enjoyed her hopelessness, but at the same time there was an unease about the little thrill I always felt when I considered how easy it would be for me to hurt her. Gracie forgave me, convinced that my impromptu cruelties were mistakes, sheer moments of clumsiness she somehow linked with my having been largely mute.

In so many ways I loved that doll. I adored her angel face – truly I did. Those wide blue eyes meant no harm to anyone, and even though the smile did seem slightly too contented, she did look, at times, almost lost.

What motivated me most, though, was her inability to respond to my cruelty. I wanted her to feel it, to show it by crying or howling. Even just a little wince would have done. But no matter how hard I tried, Conceptua just grinned her hapless grin: angelic, harmless and utterly, dangerously, provocative.

One morning I took her down the garden and into the shed. I removed her clothes and laid her on a small, gritty shelf alongside some empty flowerpots. I took a small mallet from a rusty metal grip on the shed wall, and I examined it. I thought Conceptua would be feeling frightened by now: so exposed and uncertain. But she didn't bat an eyelid. Just went on smiling. So I raised the mallet and hit her on the head with it. More smiles. I hit her very hard indeed, raised the mallet high above my head and smashed it down on hers. I didn't stop until the face was broken up, and the smile in so many tiny fragments it no longer smiled. I thought I heard the faintest scream – I wasn't sure. It just showed how far you had to go to get a reaction.

I wasn't pleased with my experiment. In fact, it had been something of a failure, for now the doll was gone. Gracie couldn't believe what I'd done, and kept suggesting other possible reasons for the doll's demise, but I made it clear it was me. After that she must have thought I really was mad, but she didn't ever tell a soul. Just kept on loving me.

6

The Mustoes were intriguing neighbours. Mr Mustoe worked at the manor house, and when his hours dropped with the recession, rather than help around the house, he took to trying to learn the piano. He did this because he thought he might become a pianist and earn lots of money. When he gave up, a few months later, with 'Twinkle Twinkle Little Star', he sold the piano and bought an old harp (much to Mrs Mustoe's disgust, who had hoped to see some benefit from the sale of their family piano). Strings were the thing. He would be all right if he could pluck. It was the black and white keys that were holding him back.

When he gave up the harp after a few weeks, he sold it and bought a trombone. Wind was the thing. He had always wanted to be in the Woodside Brass Band, and it had a social side to it as well, which was good for a man's soul when his hours were cut. And so as the months and years went by, we heard an entire orchestra of second-hand instruments honk and wheeze and wail through our parlour wall.

Mrs Mustoe seemed a haphazard housewife. She was forever finding things to do in the middle of doing something else. Her washing line was always full, her laundry never done, her children wild and unkempt. She was forever running out of sugar or bacon or milk and having to borrow, yet her cakes were flawless and her pies mouth-watering. She may have appeared careless as she slapped the ingredients together and into the oven, but they always came out as small masterpieces. She called her children by the wrong names and forgot their ages, but for all that she brought up five happy children who adored her. If George thought he was a dog, that was fine by her. She got him to eat his greens by throwing him scraps. And if Tilly thought she was a boy for the whole of one summer, that was fine too. She gave her shorts to wear, and let it pass. (And it did, soon enough, for Tilly was only trying to get the same privileges as Stinker who stayed out late and smoked, and it didn't work.) To the outside world Mrs Mustoe looked a clumsy, incompetent, irredeemable mother. To me she was a perfect one.

Gracie, by contrast, had had no practice in motherhood. She had no confidence in the simplest of tasks. She forgot what she was preparing for supper, burned cakes, left the iron on white sheets until it scorched brown marks. Her vegetable growing was a disaster: the beans she trained beautifully up poles turned out to be bindweed; her Brussels sprouts didn't sprout; her seedlings withered and keeled over. Her pies were too dry, her carrots too soggy, her tea always stewed, and her nooks and crannies laced with fine cobwebs.

She had but one vanity which, when she wasn't knitting, she pandered to in the evenings by the fire: embroidery. Gracie Burrows was the finest embroiderer in Woodside – if not in Gloucestershire. Every year the church ran a competition for the best embroidered prayer cushion (an unchristian idea to boost prayer cushions) and every year it seemed you could knock Miss Burrows over with a feather, so shocked was she that she had won it yet again. Even though she spent every free moment perfecting 'Faith, Hope and Charity' in pinks and reds and greens with the most intricate interwoven floral decoration, even though she knew she would self-destruct if anyone else came first, she would always declare, 'Me? What, *me*? *Again?* Good Lord above!'

Her needlework was so perfect it belied her character. Each stitch was so exactly placed, each piece of work so wonderfully creative and vibrant that jaws dropped in astonishment. It seemed that, despite the chaos of her life, every atom of her skill came together in that one activity: the ability to stitch colours together flawlessly into an astonishing feast of delight.

I talked in the mirror because that is what girls do. I practised my different selves, each new emerging possibility needing to be tried and practised before it could be approved and un-leashed on the world at large. Sometimes I talked on the radio, sometimes I was a singer or an actress or else I held up a bar of soap and marvelled at my complexion and sang the praises of Lux. In the mirror I solved difficulties with Mo or Tilly, I gave instructions to a class of children who hung on my every word, I dealt with the attention of unwanted suitors, I explained a new invention to an audience of thousands, I told my own children how to behave, I defended gypsies to Mrs Mustoe, I gave Mrs Emery a piece of my mind, I was interviewed for newspaper articles, I turned down offers for screen and stage. I learnt how to be coy, savage, heroic, wise, coquettish, indignant and brave. And because she always pretended not to notice if she caught me talking to the mirror, I knew Gracie would be loyal for ever.

I thought I had Gracie pretty well worked out: apart from this little vanity with the embroidery, her sole purpose in life was to look after me.

Then one day she surprised me. It was when we were in Tribbit's the grocer's and Mrs Buckleigh came in. Mrs Buckleigh hardly ever went into village shops on her own except to buy chocolate or Turkish Delight. On the few occasions I had seen her, she always expected to be served first, regardless of the other customers, and requested that any animals should be removed. Mr Tribbit always replied politely that he had no animals, almost genuflecting in her presence and rushing to his meagre display of sweets. On more than one occasion I had heard a kitten mewling, to the horror of Mrs Buckleigh and the abject terror of Mr Tribbit. Such was her fury that she only came into Tribbit's shop under great duress, when the need for something sweet outdid her will to drive into town.

I became as obsessed as everyone else with the mystery, until I discovered that the phantom cat was Gracie. She was standing behind a display of tins, and I caught her miaowing furtively to a can of corned beef.

I studied her intently, and she stopped when she saw me with a curtailed little mewl. We never spoke of it, but from that day on she became considerably more intriguing.

7

I knew from the gentleman caller that people were still looking for me. I knew they'd been looking for me anyway, because of something bad I had done which I did not wish to remember. But even if I didn't remember that bad thing, I couldn't forget the men who were after me, because that was why I was here: if it hadn't been for them, I would never have lost Nipper and Alice.

Alice Snow had seemed old to me when I met her, although looking back, she can't have been. Her last child, born late to her, had died some years before, and she suffered from a weak chest. This, with her papery hands, sun-grooved face and lucky charms, was a pretty elderly mixture as far as I was concerned, and I instantly imagined her eating hedgehogs and brewing magic potions.

There was for certain something magical about her, but she was not a woman to be feared. From the moment the boy took me to her, I was enveloped in a thick comforting smell that wrapped me in nostalgia and warmth. I was at once excited by its familiarity – exposed suddenly from under layer upon layer of memory, singled out miraculously from the new onslaught of so many other smells – and calmed by its hypnotic, soporific perfume. It was lavender.

She set about taking care of me straight away. She bathed my ankle in water and told the boy to fetch down some flowers and herbs hanging in a row in the corner of her shadowy home. Then I was lying back, supported by the boy and the powerful smell of lavender that filled the little caravan. I yielded completely. Strange but comforting words were being muttered by Alice. I could smell people. My nose reached out to the frenzy of smells from the boy, delicious and disturbing, and to the soft, powdery scents of the woman, but all the while it was being lulled by the lavender into sleepy submission. I had reached a new and uncertain place, but I felt safe.

After a few days, when I had recovered enough, the boy had shown me how to catch a hare. He circled it slowly for some half an hour, getting gradually closer to it. At length the hare sat next to him, mesmerized. It was only then he threw his coat over it and took it home. I never did see what happened before it arrived in our stew, but the men always made sure that our food came to us, and that was the only way to eat animals. If they didn't come to us, then we weren't supposed to eat them. A mesmerized hare, a tickled trout, these were the finest foods a man could eat, not shot or chased or hooked or trapped.

The gypsy boy disappeared just days after I arrived. People seemed to come and go in the woodland camp, and another boy, Nipper, became my friend, not at all bothered that I barely spoke a word.

It was a small band of gypsies: just five vehicles and as many piebald horses. Only Alice and a very elderly couple had the well-known wooden 'vardo' caravans, the other three were 'benders', a bit like cowboy wagons only more intricately made. I never did work out the relationship between all of my gypsy friends, but I soon became part of their close-knit group of Romanis, and learnt to respect the ancestors and the spirits of trees and plants and animals. Nipper taught me how to talk with the trees and to listen to their whispering. From that day to this I have never taken a branch or a flower without first asking its permission. And some days – even now – when woodcutters are about, I hear trees scream. None of these things seemed odd, for I was at an age when thinking and speaking animals and plants seemed perfectly natural. And it soon became blindingly obvious that no gypsy had set the trap which tore into my leg. They would never catch an animal by such barbarous means.

We always ate in daylight, around a fire, so that no dark spirits could attack the food. This way we had cleaned every-thing up by nightfall, and could go to bed with the pots all neatly stacked. And they *were* clean too. Alice washed everything in separate bowls. A bowl for men's clothes, a bowl for women's clothes, a bowl for pots. Nipper and I always helped, but once a month Alice would not cook for a week and we did it all. This was because once a month she was full of magical forces which might affect the food.

Each season we moved on, but to a spot they already knew from previous years. The year was a journey, Nipper said, and we must move on. It was bitterly cold in winter, and must have been hard for Alice and the elders, but for me it was an enchanting life. I remember the summer nights best of all, because they seemed to draw out the stars, and Nipper and I would lie out all night under a blanket, just listening and gazing and journeying in our imaginations until we drifted off to sleep.

One night, in the spring before that summer, we had been joined by two other caravans. They stayed for three days and brought with them some children and a chovihano, their gypsy healer. One of the men must have gone to seek him out, for Alice was very ill. Her cough had become intense and there was often blood in what she spat out.

The chovihano did all sorts of chanting and moving, and people sat round in a circle chatting and laughing. One of the children, a boy of about my age, came over and showed me a whistle, and began to play it for me. Nipper immediately stomped off to the vardo and brought out his grandfather's fiddle, which he proceeded to play quite badly. Then he stood up and drew me away behind a bender, stuck his hand in his pockets, and said very solemnly:

'You're my woman.'

It seemed a most natural outcome, so I smiled. 'Okay, then.' Marriage seemed too far off to worry about, but Nipper was a determined boy.

When we returned to the circle, the boy with the whistle had slunk off and joined two other children pulling funny faces at a fat worm which the chovihano was holding up. We watched as the healer transferred Alice's sickness to the worm, and then hung it on a bush.

The following morning, the worm was dead, and the healer and his family departed.

Alice did seem to get a lot better that summer, but when the autumn came, she grew suddenly very ill, and one of the men went off in search of the healer. As the days passed and no one came, Nipper and I found a worm and did our own healing session. We tried to imagine the worm as Alice's illness, and we hung it on a bush like the healer had done. But Alice kept on coughing.

One morning she went out and came back with a basket so full of apples she was staggering. It was a good sign, she said. An angry man had caught her taking apples, and another kind man had come and said she could take as many as she liked, because they were his apples. He was the kindest non-Romani she had ever met, and even offered to get a doctor to see about her cough. She refused this, of course, because all that sort of medicine was misguided, but she remained deeply respectful of the man, despite the suspicions of the other gypsies.

It must have been early that autumn then, a month or so

before Apple Day, that the police came. Nipper and I were out collecting nuts when we heard a commotion in the trees behind. Then I saw a row of silver buttons and a dark helmet, and it was coming towards us.

They were probably coming to tell the camp to move on, to tell us we were on private land. Or perhaps they had a particular gypsy in mind they were going to haul in for thieving. Nipper would have seen all this before. But I hadn't. As far as I was concerned, these men in blue were coming for me.

I knew they would be looking for me one day. I simply hoped they had lost interest by now. It seemed so long ago since I had run into the woods, and we had moved on several times since then. But I felt certain, as I saw the uniform glinting through the leaves, heard the pant of a heavy dark-clad man, that they had come for me.

I dropped the nuts I had collected in my skirt. 'Run!'

And we both ran. But Nipper must've forgotten all about our betrothal, for he ran in a different direction to me, back to his family in the vardo.

All this I could remember, but my memory stopped at the far side of the woods. I still couldn't let myself see beyond it.

8

Christmas came and went and I felt settled and safe with Gracie Burrows. In the New Year we sang a wassail at school. I went home practising it:

> 'A-wassail, a-wassail all over the town,
> Our toast it is white and our ale it is brown,
> Our bowl it is made of the white maple tree,
> With the wassailing bowl, we'll drink unto thee.'

Gracie smiled and joined in.

'It's different,' I said, without thinking.

'Different to what?'

I wasn't entirely sure. Somewhere at the edge of my memory, a little fragment of the past had gone floating by.

'We used to . . . it was . . .' It was like waking from a dream. I tried to grasp at it, but no sooner had I touched its tail than it slithered away downstream. I was left with an atmosphere, a feeling, and even that I couldn't hold.

Of course you could say I didn't really want to remember, and this was largely true. But sometimes curiosity was greater than my fear, and I just wanted to know a thing myself, like a child kicking over a heavy stone with the tip of a shoe and then jumping backwards.

Gracie often told me stories about her own childhood, which sounded wonderful. Every birthday her mother made her an elaborate cake, and everyone would come to see it, and then all her friends would have a piece. No one made cakes like Gracie's mum. They were covered with white icing and sometimes made in the shape of an animal or a log. One year there were squirrels on it, and another year little jelly sweets. Every year her name was written in coloured icing and there would be miniature candles to blow out. What's more, her parents always gave her a present. Other children were lucky if they got sixpence or an apple, but Gracie's parents always bought her the best present they could afford.

I had never had a birthday cake.

'We'll have to make you one for your next birthday,' Gracie said. 'When is it?'

I couldn't remember ever having had a birthday.

'What time of year is it?'

I couldn't remember. The only happy time I could remember for certain was sitting in a lavender bush.

'There was lavender,' I said, hopefully.

'July or August, then. Let's say late July. I shall make you a cake on 25th July! How about that?'

'Is it soon?'

'No. How about we make a practice one now?'

And so Gracie made me a cake with a candle in it for me to blow out. After a lot of clattering about in the kitchen, hours of consulting the cookbook, and flour flying in all directions, the various ingredients turned into a Victoria sponge. She squirted some icing sugar on the top from the corner of a bag and she told me it said 'HAPPY DAY'.

I was so proud of it I asked if Mo could come round and have some too. Mo said, 'Yum yum! Who's HARRY DAG?' and

Gracie chewed her lip and said it was only a quick thing she'd rustled up on the spur of the moment.

I blew the candle out and Gracie lit it again so that I could have another go, and then so that Mo could have a go too. Gracie was all pink-faced and pleased. I didn't say thank you because I had no manners, but I was bursting with joy and she could see from my face how she'd made me feel.

The helpful thing about having lived with gypsies was that it was a good substitute for the past, for everything that had come before Gracie. But I knew there was more, I knew there was a past behind that one, and that Gracie wanted to bury it, and I wanted to bury it, but that it was still there. I knew also that it threatened Gracie in some way, and that therefore it threatened us. We both had pasts we needed to forget: my own, because I couldn't risk losing her, and hers because she longed to have lived it so differently, and her recognition of what she'd lost hung over her like a bereavement. But Gracie, at least, had found solace. I blew in with an easterly September wind and defied fate.

For me it was different.

One night, a year or so after I'd arrived, I wet the bed and woke up suddenly, screaming, 'Come back . . . come back! Please, please don't leave me! Please . . .'

'Who's left you?'

'He's not looking back! . . . Please!'

'Hush now! You've had a bad dream, tiz all. It's just a bad dream.' And I had believed her – or let her think I believed her. What was truth and what was untruth became a blur. All I can say for certain, looking back, is that I was happy to think it had all been a bad dream. I wanted her to be right, and since grown-ups usually were, what harm could I possibly be doing in colluding with her?

For many years I had a recurring dream that I was seriously wounded in some way. I would wake up, terrorized, and say things like, 'I've been hurt! I've been badly hurt!' I would've been shot by a mad woman or bitten by a tiger or crushed by a lorry. But really, on reflection, it was what I said that was significant.

9

One day I did something that clinched the 'mad' bit of my name for good.

Once a week, on a Thursday, we made a bus trip into town. Along with half a dozen or so other women, we waited tentatively in Vile It's stone bus shelter by the edge of the green, and would pick up our bags and shuffle forwards every time a motor engine was heard, or just pick up our bags and shuffle if Vile It herself appeared. Eventually, its green nose would appear around the brow of the hill, and we would bristle with the collective excitement of explorers setting out on an expedition.

Sometimes the bus was already full when it reached Woodside, having passed through several villages in a loop before it arrived. Then we would stand up in the aisle, holding on to the upright steel posts, or the handle on the edge of a seat. If we were sitting down when it became full, Gracie would always offer her seat to an older person; I had no manners so I didn't, although I soon learnt through her nudging to offer my seat to anyone older than myself, even if they looked stronger than me. I never minded because I liked to be thrown from side to side by the sway of the bus, but on one of these days, when the bus was full to bursting and the conductress reminded us that she was exceeding the limits out of the kindness of her heart, I broke my own limits and did something that would never be forgotten.

I was sitting with Gracie in the front seat, and she was craning her neck to check that the elderly women who had just got on had been offered seats halfway down the aisle. The aisle was already almost three-quarters full when it stopped at the next village, and the conductress rolled her eyes and beckoned on two elderly ladies and a nun. 'Go on then!' she said, waving them in as if they were children awaiting a fairground ride.

Gracie and I stood up for the old ladies, and I was standing right up against the metallic-smelling conductress with her shiny leather bag and ticket machine, until she squeezed past me to collect more fares, and I was left sandwiched between Gracie and the nun.

There was no door on the bus, and the wind swept in as we sailed downhill, and the nun, right next to the entrance, kept pressing down her habit with her free hand. Her other hand was gripping the same steel post as mine, and I kept finding myself swaying into her as the bus veered slightly around curves in the road. I watched her sinewy hand tighten its grip on the bends, its blue veins forming ridges through the neat white flesh. There were no red knuckles like on Gracie's hands, no flaking skin from hours of scrubbing and hot water. I resented her for gripping so tightly when the bus swung about. God didn't seem to be helping her out here, then. I felt I had caught her out being human, when she was pretending to be something better. I looked up at her face, soft and pouchy where the wimple seemed to squash it all up together, and it looked harmless enough. She wore a bland, beatific half-smile, and I fixed my eyes on it suspiciously, reaching out a hand to grip Gracie's coat sleeve.

'Hold on with both hands, my love,' said Gracie.

At the same time the conductress shouted, 'Hold on tight!' from somewhere deep inside the bus.

The vehicle swung us all to the right, and then back to the left. I was forced into Gracie, and then into the nun. I felt her yielding flesh and saw, unmistakably, the eyes screw themselves up at the jerking of the bus. The smile disappeared and the mouth grew rigid and thin; the brows frowned ferociously and the nostrils flared. I was certain that this angry gargoyle of a face was meant for me, and just as it began to calm itself, a fresh jerk pushed me into her again and the face reappeared, teeth clenched and stony.

I began to sweat. I could see the road ahead was anything but straight, hear the 'Hold on tight!' again and I clutched at Gracie in panic.

'Hold on!' she said. 'Don't hold me – we'll both be over!' And we swayed from side to side again. Each time I lurched into the nun with my shoulder, and soon I was pushing her harder than I needed to. That soft, spongy nun-look hardened again. Her nostrils grew and her lips shrunk; her eyes squeezed tight with the concentration of staying upright, looked so full of spite I could feel my palms grow sticky as I clasped the pole next to hers. Her nails, so neat and clean on their snowy fingertips, seemed to grow and curve and twist into talons. I could feel my breath failing me: great gasps of air barely lasted a moment and were no sooner exhaled than drawn in again, desperately.

When the bus took the next corner I rammed her. She toppled sideways and nearly fell down the step out of the bus. 'Joy! Steady on!' I heard Gracie say, but I wasn't listening. The towering face of the nun seemed pitted against me: red, panting and full of frown.

The idea came to me before I could register it. It came so naturally it was more of a reflex than a decision. With the next stagger into Gracie and the corresponding swing the other way, I pitched into the nun with the whole weight of my body, shouldering her down the steps and out of the bus. She toppled like a baby bird, spreading wings of raven black as she flew into the wind, and everyone on the left side of the bus saw her knickers before she flopped into a heap somewhere back up the road.

It's all a bit foggy after that. I think the bus stopped, but I can't remember if the nun was badly hurt or not, whether she continued her journey or was helped into a nearby house or what. I don't know to this day whether she told anyone I'd pushed her, whether any of the passengers saw me push her, or if Gracie saw. Gracie didn't say anything to me. I often caught her studying me after that. I would look up and she'd have a face filled with curiosity. But if she had seen me do it, she didn't say. She never said a thing. Just kept on loving me.

10

Miss Wallock was the one who first made me realize that Gracie had a secret too.

If Swallockelder was as batty as a fruitcake, the younger Miss Wallock was perfectly sane. When I was a little older, Gracie started sending me a few doors down to Miss Wallock's for piano lessons on Tuesdays. I went straight from school, which meant Gracie had a bit more time at the dress agency where she worked, or else could catch the bus back a bit later from shopping in town.

Miss Wallock was something of a rival to Gracie, it always seemed. They had known each other from girlhood and took pains to compare every detail of their lives.

'You've got a linen tablecloth, I suppose,' Miss Wallock might say.

'Yes, I think we have one – for best, though.'

'Ah! For best. Of course. Now is that embroidered?'

'I think so – maybe lace-edged.'

'By Gracie, is it?'

'I'm not sure.'

'Probably not. She knows her sewing, doesn't she? She never was much at lace-making, though. Tried, of course. Always did work hard.'

And whenever I got back home, rather than questions about my lesson, there would always be a little inquest.

'Were those *new* lace curtains I thought I saw in Ivy's front window?'

'Don't know.'

'Hmm. Ask her next time.'

Or 'Sherbet lemon, is it, for doing well? Where would she've got them from, I wonder. Thomson's, is it?'

I was well aware of my position between the two of them, and over time I learnt to play the situation better than the piano. If I wanted more attention off Gracie, I would give her a little tweak, and if I was fed up with Miss Wallock for over-working me on the scales I would feed her a little nugget of jealousy to last the rest of the lesson.

I realized now, of course, that she would be a prime source of information, and fed her compliments to get her in the mood.

'What an exquisite vase,' I said, admiring a dull-looking clod of ceramic on the sideboard. 'We've got nothing like that at home.'

'Really? No vases?'

I sighed, ruefully. 'Oh, we just put flowers in jars. I wish we had beautiful vases like you.'

Miss Wallock simpered in an over-modest fashion.

'I'm surprised Gracie isn't more like you. You must've known each other since you were young, back in olden days.'

Miss Wallock smiled. 'We've known each other since I can remember. We went to school together.'

'I bet you both had a string of boys after you. And men.'

Miss Wallock gave a high-pitched giggle, and sounded just like a girl.

'Heavens above! We had no such thing. Mind you, I had my fair share – I was quite a beauty, some say, when I was young.' She sighed, got up from the piano stool, and wandered over to the sideboard.

'And what about Gracie? I don't suppose she had any young men, did she?'

I knew she would respond to this provocation. She took something out of the sideboard drawer and turned bright eyes on me. 'Gracie? Lord, no! She never had any luck . . . look . . .'

She stood next to me and showed me a dog-eared photograph. A row of girls were standing dressed in white and in the centre was a girl wearing a crown.

'Is that you?' I pointed at the May Queen.

'No, that's me.' She pointed to a passably fine-looking girl, and I responded ecstatically.

'How beautiful!'

Miss Wallock inhaled a deep lungful of satisfaction.

'Which one is Gracie?'

'Have a guess.'

I scanned the photograph. They were a motley crew, it had to be said, with every kind of physical defect known to man, and mostly they looked completely surprised to be wearing pretty white dresses. I was sure I would find Gracie, because I'd seen pictures of her at home. And there, the eyes had it – there she was but . . . what a face! What a startled, smiling, youthful face! And the eyes, the old sad eyes I was so familiar with, now they sparkled prettily out of the picture from under a gloriously wide-brimmed hat. The same eyes. The very same, but transformed.

'There – there she is.'

'That's right. And here's . . .'

Miss Wallock wittered on about every single girl in the line-up: who they married, where they were living now. I let her get on with it, then I said, 'Wasn't Gracie ever even in love? Not once?'

Miss Wallock giggled again. 'Heavens above, Joy Burrows! You do ask some questions!' But it was clear I'd hit upon a topic she was interested in, and a wicked, conspiratorial look came to her face. 'Well . . . there *was* someone . . . once.'

'Who?'

'Well . . . I couldn't possibly say . . .' She folded her lips together tightly and replaced the photograph in the sideboard drawer.

'Was it a gentleman?'

Her eyes widened. Yes, I definitely saw them widen. 'Who-ever told you that? My goodness, wherever did you hear that?'

'It's true, then?'

'Did Gracie say that?'

'No. It *is* true, then?'

She parked her wide behind next to mine on the piano stool, and looked at me full of secrets. 'You'll have to ask Gracie. I can't go telling you things like that.'

'Oh *please*, Miss Wallock.'

'Certainly not. She'd never forgive me. No. If she got one sniff of it . . . one sniff . . . Some things are best left unsaid. Now find all the policeman Cs for me.'

I gave her one last forlorn look, and played all the Cs on the keyboard.

'And all the doggie Ds.' She licked her finger to turn a page in the music book. What with the smell of her metallic breath, her soapy cardigan, and the overenthusiastic layer of polish on the piano, Miss Wallock's was always a very odoriferous experience.

At least I knew now that there was something Gracie hadn't told me. I had caught the scent of mystery, and I was determined to track it down.

11

It was in the summer of 1931 that I first began my own affair
with the mysterious Buckleigh household, because that was
the summer I first met Celia. It was one warm June evening
after school – I was about eleven at the time – and a crowd of
us were playing up by the gates: me, Mo, Tilly and Spit
Palmer. Mo was still small and skinny, her younger sister was
taller and more robust, and Spit was as sweet and quiet as
ever. Spit stood with her back to the high dry stone wall and
we lined up facing her:

> 'Queenie, Queenie, who's got the ball?
> Is she fat or is she tall?
> Or is she thin like a rolling pin?'

Spit stood on one leg and chewed a plait, considering us.
   'Joy – handth.'
   I brought my hands round from behind my back, palms up.
More chewing.
   'Mo – legth.'
   Mo parted her ankles, but no ball fell out of her knees or her
thighs.
   'Wider.'

Nothing.

'Tilly—'

'She's thin like a rolling pin!'

We all looked up to the voice and Spit turned to look up too, but we could see nothing.

'Thin like a rolling pin!' came the voice again. It was coming from behind the wall.

We looked at each other, thrilled and wary. Spit backed away from the wall and came to stand with the rest of us.

'Who's there?' asked Mo.

After a short silence, as if the voice were considering what to do next, came the answer, 'Me.'

As we stood bewildered, a head appeared slowly above the upright stones at the top of the wall. It was a girl our age with the fine features of a porcelain doll and one long toffee-coloured plait.

'I'm Celia! Tell me your names!'

She seemed so pleased to meet us that we all did as we were told, and chimed our names out in unison.

'Golly! Steady on! Let me see . . . Rose—'

'We call her Spit.'

'How dreadful! Poor Rose. I shall call you Rose . . . Tilly . . . Mo – I suppose that's short for Maureen and . . .'

She put her head on one side and considered me. I felt a mixture of disappointment that she hadn't heard my name and gratitude that she should gaze at my face for so long.

'Joy,' I supplied.

'Mad Joy, we call 'er.'

'Joy . . .' The girl repeated it wistfully, as though it pleased her. 'Why mad?'

The others looked confused, as if they had been asked a tricky question in class.

'Just is,' shrugged Mo.

Celia took a satisfied deep breath in. 'Oh well, I shall soon find out. I'm coming over!'

'Watch out! There's glass!' I was foolish enough to imagine she didn't know that her own walls were covered in broken glass to deter intruders. But Celia had disappeared, and reappeared a few yards further down the road outside the wall.

'It's okay, thanks. I have my own secret way out!'

Now she was standing before us and we could see her full perfection. She wore a dropped waist summer frock with glorious red poppies on it, and red shoes with a bar and button. None of us could think of anything to say. We just stood there gawping at her.

'May I play?'

We nodded, but didn't move.

'What shall we play then?'

We looked at each other, terrified.

'I've seen you playing on a see-saw you made, over there by the field. Can I have a go?'

We would have to make it again; it consisted of a split trunk the boys had lifted on to an old broken sheep trough. But we couldn't run fast enough, and between us we rolled the log up on to the crumbled stone, but it swung in all directions, giving an unpredictable lateral ride as well as a vertical one.

'What about your lovely dress?' asked Tilly, when Celia straddled the filthy old log.

'Oh, don't worry! They're only play clothes! Whoo . . .!'

She was flung about in all directions, and shouted lots of wonderful words like 'Golly!' and 'Cripes!' which we immediately adopted as our own.

When we were called home for bed she made us promise not to tell anyone about her playing with us. We shook our heads solemnly and skipped home on air.

'You look pleased with yourself,' said Gracie as she tucked me up.

'Golly! Do I?'

She frowned at me, then shook her head and blew the candle out. 'Whatever next!'

My thoughts exactly.

12

The summer had emerged with its usual trickery: canopies of green unfurling overnight, trees heavy with leaves you might not notice until a slight breeze shook them into a thrilling frenzy, or the late sun transformed them into translucent shimmering emeralds. The clod of blank sky that had sat over us all winter was now a screen of moving shapes. Summer was here and so was Celia. The two seemed to have arrived together, with a new moon, and that made her pretty magical stuff.

The four of us, Tilly, Mo, Spit and me, made the Buckleigh House entrance our regular playground now. George would sometimes tag along because they had a dog called Zeus that he wanted to befriend. Stinker didn't play with us any more because he was about thirteen by now and into more manly pursuits. He and the other boys smoked fag ends collected from outside the pub and did a good deal of loitering. We completely forgot about Mrs Emery, and her husband must have slept peacefully for a while, until the other children. It wasn't long before our new playground sparked interest in other children, who made their way up out of the village too. But Mrs Emery's had the same magnetic pull it had had on us, and very soon she was fuming at her gate again, waving her arms and threatening to call the police. What she actually did was march down to the school, for soon all the parents were warning their children not to play 'up past the church'.

This scuppered our new games for a while.

We mostly played families and adventure games. Celia liked to be in a poor family, and we all wanted to be in rich families. I didn't mind being poor though, if it meant I could be Celia's mother or sister and roam about penniless and ragged and forlorn with her, arm in arm or starving under bushes. Mo and Spit didn't see the disadvantage in living in a castle and never getting to touch Celia at all. George didn't count because he was never human. Tilly sometimes gave me a wistful glance, and asked if she could be poor too. Then Celia would invariably make her our starving cousin who was locked in a dungeon and we had to save her. If I noticed the unfairness of this I was too selfish to mention it, for I was too busy enjoying my death-defying feats of bravery with Celia, the proximity of her cotton lawn dress, the coolness of her palm, the touch of gentility.

One day up at the house, George said in a sudden spurt of undogginess: 'Why don't we ever play in *your* garden?'

We all stared at him, and then at Celia, and then at our feet. We would never have asked it ourselves, but it seemed a fair question. Celia pushed a strand of hair behind her ear and sighed. 'Well! If you all come the gardener will see and tell you all to clear off. And he'd tell my mother and we don't want that . . .' We didn't ask why that would be so unthinkable, but we all knew: the wall separated two different worlds, and whilst we had allowed her into ours, we were not allowed into hers. 'There might be a way . . .' She pulled her plait around to the front and slowly brushed her cheek with it. 'I'll take one at a time. I'll start with Joy. The rest of you close your eyes. You mustn't see where I take her.'

'What about Joy? How come she can see?' asked Mo.

Celia glanced at me. 'I'll put my hands over her eyes.'

'When's it our go, then?'

'Later. Wait here.'

I closed my eyes and let her lead me down along the wall.

'You can open them!' she whispered, and we clambered behind a bush and up a piece of crumbled wall. On the top of the wall were lichen-covered stones broken to reveal the yellow yoke of their insides. We scrambled over them, free of glass, and jumped down under some yews. I stood and looked. The great house with its golden pillars, a long glass-covered building next to it full of greenery, a lawn before it so neatly cut it looked like felt.

'This way!' she hissed, and grabbed my hand.

There were three sheds: a 'potting shed', a 'tool shed' and a 'den'. It was to her den she took me, a small musty-smelling hut full of girls' comics and a variety of sports bats and sticks. We must have stayed there for half an hour, with her pushing me into a corner every so often and hiding me in an old rug so that the gardener wouldn't see me.

He wouldn't have done anything anyhow, for he was Mr Rollins, whose three boys were at school with me and used to play in the grounds when the Buckleighs were on holiday. I didn't mention this in case Celia didn't know. Also I was rather enjoying this game of subterfuge, which was still fraught with the danger of seeing Mr or Mrs Buckleigh.

We tiptoed to the glasshouse, and I was struck by the muggy warmth as we went in.

'Wait here!'

Celia disappeared with the efficiency of a spy, and came back with two glasses full of drink.

'Mother's away shopping. Here . . .'

'What is it?'

She sat on a stool by a tall umbrella plant, and I saw her lips through the bottom of the glass as she drank it down. 'Barley water!'

I sipped it. It was good. But however far I tipped back my head, I couldn't match her unbearably attractive insouciance, and had to wipe the half moons from the corners of my mouth.

'What about . . .' I hardly dared to mention his name after all these years of spying on him.

'My father? He's out. And my brother's on some sort of camp to do with school, and Mrs Bubb is having a doze in the kitchen. So you see, we've got the place to ourselves!'

I hadn't time to digest the fact that they had a housekeeper. All I could think of was the lie I had lived – we had all lived: Tilly, Mo, Spit, Stinker and myself – for so long.

'You have a brother?'

' 'Course!' She put her glass down suddenly and widened her eyes at me, smiling, so that I almost thought she was teasing me. 'You know, Joy, I think you'd like him . . . actually, yes! I think you'd like him a lot!'

She pulled me forcefully by the hand so that I had to put down my glass unfinished. It was that way she had of assuming the supremacy of her slightest whim. A part of me felt belittled by it, and an equal part of me was enthralled. Even then I knew that at some point the balance would have to tip one way or the other, and that then I would be changed; weaker or stronger. But I did not want to think of these outcomes because for now the enthralment was too wonderful, and I was riding high on the thrill that was Celia.

She led me through a black and white tiled hallway, past little round tables whose only purpose was to hold one statue or one potted plant. She led me up a twisting staircase with carpet and brass rods to a wide, imposing landing. White panelled doors with crystal doorknobs beckoned in every direction. She showed me her mother's room with its many wardrobes and mirrors and busts of ladies supporting hats. She showed me her father's room with its wide brass bed and African elephants and masks. The way she displayed them it seemed perfectly normal that a husband and wife should not share a bed if they could have one each. She let me peep in a bathroom – something I had never seen before. I didn't want her to see my amazement as I peered into the patterned lavatory bowl and gazed at the porcelain bath on its ornate claws. I was ashamed of my awe as I reached out to feel the four heavy towels hung upon a wooden towel stand, and sniffed the soap with a little sigh of ecstasy. But Celia was delighted with her new-found wizardry, and took me into her own bedroom with a flourish, studying my face intently for these interesting new reactions.

The walls were the colour of butter and flooded with sunlight. She too had multiple hats, but they were pinned to the wall in a sort of display. Her drapes and bedspread were a flawless cream, and she had her own gas lamp above her bed so that she could read. And that was another thing, she had books – with the sort of print that grown-ups read – propped up on a little carved shelf beside her bed. On the back of her door was a large brass hook and a mauve dressing gown in what looked like crêpe de Chine. And there, on an Indian-looking rug beside her bed, was the dearest pair of beaded mauve slippers.

'Oh!' I said, forgetting to say golly or gosh. 'It's . . . it's just . . . perfect!' I walked towards the window and looked out. There were the lawns stretched out below us, and at the very end, beyond the shrubs and yews, was the wall behind which she had met us.

'What about the others?'

'Heavens! They'll be gone now! There's another room to see yet.'

She yanked me out and across the landing. 'There's loads more rooms downstairs and on the next floor up, but that'll have to wait for next time. Mother'll be home soon.'

I was gladdened by the idea of a next time, but uncomfortable at dismissing the others although they almost certainly wouldn't have waited this long. But now we stood in another room, a room that felt wholly different to the others. The walls were the palest green, and every nook and cranny was filled with something. There were feathers, coins, bird eggs, a telescope, drawings, stones, and on the wall was a huge oar and a sizeable tree branch. I looked at Celia, and she was doing her wide-eyed thing, waiting for my reaction.

'There! You see? James's room. My brother. What do you think?'

'I like it,' I said, truthfully. And there was something about it I preferred to her room, although I didn't say this.

'James,' I repeated, and felt a little thrill as I caught sight of his cricket bat leaning against the wall. I breathed in deeply – a rising smell of manly things – and bent to examine one of his drawings (a wagtail) with a wicked sense of trespass.

'Scruffy, isn't he? Come on then . . .'

I didn't want to leave. I wanted to find out more about the brother no one knew about. I was hooked on this sudden find, this little enclave of unruliness in a spotless dolls' house.

We slipped out into the garden again via the glasshouse, and scampered down the lawn like thieves, although Mr Rollins saw me and waved to me and I didn't tell Celia because I didn't want to spoil it for her.

Over the wall she sent me and into the bushes, a good hour since we started. We forgot to hide my eyes, forgot everything but each other and the feelings we had made each other feel.

And then I saw them. Mo, Tilly, Spit and George, all standing in a row, just as we had left them, all staring up at the wall. George even had his eyes closed. They didn't move, but their eyes followed me as I made my way back to the gate. And for a moment I saw them just as Celia must've seen us the first time.

'What about us?' asked George, opening his eyes.

The others said nothing. The silent questions in their eyes

shamed me. I had crossed from one world into another and back again and now I had to tell them that it was my privilege alone. And when I did I knew they were already slipping away from me.

13

It was the following evening that Gracie spoke to me. She stopped me before I went out to play and sat me down by the range with a mug of milk.

'You know Mo's all upset, do you?'

She looked into the fire. I raised my eyes in slight surprise. 'Mo?'

'Izzie reckons it's something to do with you.' She played with her wristwatch, a delicate gold-plated affair given to her by her father. 'I hope you've not been unkind, sweetheart.'

'What's the matter with her, then?'

More fiddling. I knew Gracie was uncomfortable telling me off about anything, and I hated to see her this way. It would have been so easy to lie to her, to put her out of her misery, but I knew she knew more than she had let on at first.

'Izzie reckons . . . well . . . she reckons you've all been playing up by the Buckleighs' and with the Buckleigh girl.'

I folded my lips tightly together and studied my milk.

'She reckons you went into the Buckleigh house to play and left Mo and the others outside. I said it didn't sound like the sort of thing you'd do at all. I said, Izzie, that doesn't sound like my Joy to me.'

I could see she was trying to give me a way out, willing me to live up to her expectations. I also knew she would find out one way or another, even if I said nothing. Even now she was studying my embarrassment, gauging my awkwardness.

'I did go with her – Celia *invited* me. But she invited all of us one at a time and then she just forgot about the others. It wasn't fair. It was cruel.'

There was already something frightening in Gracie's eyes that was more than anger. It looked almost like panic.

'You must *never* go near there again. Do you understand?'

'But—'

'*Never!* Promise me. Promise me you will never go inside that house again or play with the Buckleigh girl. Never!'

'I—'

'Listen to me.' She took my milk from me and put it on the floor. Then she held both my hands and squeezed them in hers. 'Joy, my love, this is important. Just believe me.'

'But I don't understand. I like Celia.'

'You said she was cruel.'

'I don't think she meant to be. I think she just—'

'Please, Joy. Just promise!'

Her eyes were imploring now, and the tone changed suddenly from reprimand to mystery. I promised solemnly, and in that moment I meant it, but Gracie had done nothing but enhance the intrigue of Buckleigh House.

14

The following day was hot. The morning sun was so bright that it lit up crowds of busy dust specks in a great shaft across the parlour. We had barely cleared away the breakfast things when there was a knock on the door.

Gracie went to answer it, and I heard a man's voice: educated, official-sounding. Even now, after all these years in hiding, I could feel my pulse accelerating. I hurried into the kitchen and stood by the door, listening. But it was all right. She called him Howard. I heard the kettle clank on the range, heard them exchanging awkward thoughts about the weather.

I turned the tap on to fill a jug with water in case Gracie asked me to, and to make it sound as though I was busy. I didn't want to hang around. I was pretty sure this man was okay, but you couldn't be certain with gentleman callers. And he *was* a gentleman, I could tell from his voice. I didn't recognize him from some years before. I stood poised by the door to the parlour, listening with the jug in my hand, trying to make out the louder words which would link the muffled words into sentences.

'. . . just a thought.'

'. . . her life . . . whatever she wants.'

'Don't think . . . take her from you.'

Then there was a silence. I pushed my ear to the door and heard nothing. And then:

'Grace!'

More silence.

'It doesn't matter now . . .' Gracie was saying.

'But I've always . . . you know . . . can't believe . . .'

'What . . . matter any more?'

'But . . . you were married.'

Then there was a silence so thick and unyielding I found myself pushing open the door to break it.

'Joy? Are you Joy?' The gentleman stood up and reached out a hand to me. I placed the jug on the table, wiped my hand on my dress and shook it timidly, feeling quite grown up. I wasn't sure if it was safe to admit to being Joy, so I looked at Gracie for guidance, but she was staring at the window, her face golden with the morning light and haloed in wisps of gleaming hair and dust.

I looked up at the man: he was very tall and lean, and he looked as though moving his limbs was a game whose rules he wasn't quite sure of. His shoes were enormous – like Olive Oyle's – and as polished as horse chestnuts. He addressed me with kind, troubled eyes:

'I was hoping to see you, Joy. In fact . . . I was just saying to your . . . to Grace here . . . Well, I hear you're doing very well at school.'

He raised his thick dark eyebrows and smiled earnestly. I smiled too, and he smiled gratefully back.

'What I was wondering was . . . well, would you like to go to a really good school to continue your education? Would you like to go to a school like Celia's?'

At the mention of her name I almost gasped. I looked at Gracie again for direction, but she seemed statuesque in her stillness.

'Celia's? How could I?' I managed at last.

He sat down on the arm of the chair he had risen from, and then almost fell off it.

'Well, you could sit a scholarship exam. I'm sure you'd do well. And then any remaining fees I'd be happy to cover.' I didn't understand what he meant by covering fees, so I looked at Gracie again, but he continued, 'Do you think you might like that?'

Gracie looked up at the mantelpiece as if I might find the answer there. But the sun was too bright by far, and the figurine and the cuckoo clock and the miniature copper ornaments and the silver picture frame of her parents and the embroidered 'Home Sweet Home' and the brass date and month holder looked far too loud and cheap and suddenly seemed to say 'This is all I've got for you here,' and she turned her head to look at me and her eyes said it was nothing but trash.

'I . . . I'll tell you what. Why don't you think about it?' he asked.

'The same school as Celia?'

'Yes – if you want. Will you give it some thought?'

I nodded, and he picked up his hat and made for the door.

'Only one thing – don't say anything to Celia about this yet, will you?' I shook my head. 'Not until it's certain.' He smiled and shook my hand again. 'Goodbye, Grace!' he called over my shoulder.

Gracie rose from her chair and came to stand behind me, 'Goodbye, Howard,' but her voice was weak and dragging its feet. There seemed to be nothing left of her but that thin voice.

The day after the gentleman called, Gracie did something odd. Apart from the miaows, it was the only time she had ever done anything which didn't make sense.

I was doing some colouring at the table after tea, and the wireless was on, as usual. Gracie came in, lifted the kettle off the range, and reached up on to the high mantelpiece above it. She took down the shepherdess figurine and went into the kitchen. Then I heard the back door swing to, and an almighty crash in the garden.

I ran out to see what had happened, and there was Gracie, standing by the back door and breathing hard. She was staring at the lav at the end of the garden, and looked as if she were out of breath.

I followed her gaze to the broken fragments of shepherdess and ran towards the stone wall of the lav. I crouched down and picked up the larger pieces: a lace bodice, half a crook, a hollow head. I was wondering if they could be glued back together, but the rest of her was in such tiny fragments I could see it was a lost cause. Sadly, I looked back to inform Gracie, but she was gone.

I found her back in the kitchen, going about her business as if nothing had happened. Her ordinariness terrified me. Fleetingly, I remembered how it had felt to smash my doll; I should have understood. But Gracie wasn't someone you had to understand. I didn't like this reversal of things. Her brisk smile in the face of such evident disaster made the floor wobble beneath my feet, and nothing seemed certain any more. That was the first time I felt truly excluded from her world.

15

I went round to see Mo. She was still sulky with me about Celia for a bit, then perked up and suggested we went off to play 'newlyweds'. This was a game in which we would find somewhere quiet, button our coats together, and lie underneath them pretending to be a newly married couple. The interest in the game lay in choosing unlikely characters from the village or from our class to be the main protagonists. On this particular day, up in the beech wood, Mo was Mo grown up, and I was Buster Keaton.

'So, you wear false teeth – I didn't know.' (Mo grown up)

'Yes – I'm sorry, my love, I also have a wig.' (Buster)

'Don't worry, darling. I adore that gummy look. It reminds me of my old granddad. Mm, I'm hungry. Can you make lardy cakes?'

'No, sweetest.'

'Right, the marriage is off!'

'Now you've spoilt it!'

'Is this still the game?'

'No, you've spoilt it!'

'I haven't. You've got to beg me to stay. Say you'll do anything . . .'

'Okay. Darling – don't go. I'll do anything.' I got out from under the coat and knelt wringing my hands next to the marital bed. 'Please – *anything* – I'll do anything.'

'Anything at all?'

'Just name it, dearest Mo!'

'Well . . .' Mo was thoughtful, and then looked me right in the eye. 'Take me with you into Buckleigh House.'

I knew straight away we had stopped playing, because she stopped doing her posh voice.

I stopped wringing my hands and started to fiddle with the tag of her coat.

'I can't. I promised Gracie.'

'Just *one* time, that's all I'm asking.'

'She made me *promise* never to go there again.'

'Why? She ought to be pleased you've made friends with toffs.'

I was puzzled myself. 'I know, it doesn't make any sense. But I think it's got something to do with a man that came round.' I hoped to deflect Mo from her determined plan by introducing some romance into the picture. 'Gracie called him by his first name and he knows Celia. I thought it might be Him but he was too normal.'

'I *thought* there was something—'

'Yes, and I tried to ask Gracie about it and she went all cross and grumpy.' I decided not to tell Mo about the offer to educate me with Celia. 'She made me promise never ever to go near Celia or Buckleigh House.'

'But we've got to find out, Joy. We've got to solve this mystery!'

Mo's eyes grew wide in her bony face, then she started unbuttoning the coats as if there was no time to lose.

Just as I was wrestling with what to do next, we heard a familiar voice calling:

'Joy? . . . Joy? . . . Where are you all? . . . Is anyone there?'

We both looked at each other and made our way quickly from the edge of the beech wood to the Buckleigh House gates.

Celia seemed a little annoyed. 'Where've you been? I've waited here every evening and you haven't come.'

Mo tugged at her bottom lip, clueless as to what to say. I was awkward too. I didn't like this new, ice-edged Celia. But it was Mo who came to my rescue.

'She's not allowed.'

Celia let out a breath of laughter. 'Not *allowed?*' She caught my eye and almost smiled. 'By whom?'

I loved this 'whom', even if I hated her tone. Only Celia used words like 'whom'.

'By Gracie,' supplied Mo.

'Gracie? Who on earth is *she?* How come *Gracie* gets to decide what you do all of a sudden?'

She was staring right at me, her little toffee plait draped over the top of the wall, and her rosy bottom lip so hurt it began to protrude slightly. I felt my resolve slipping away.

'Well! Jolly well play with Gracie, then, if she's so special. I don't care!' and her head disappeared.

I could hear my pulse in my head, pummelling me into action, but I felt powerless.

'Stop her!' cried Mo.

'Come back!' I yelled. 'Celia! Please! Wait! It's not like that! Celia!'

'Celia!' shouted Mo.

'Celia!' I shouted.

The dear head reappeared. It said nothing, and seemed to find something of interest to study on top of the wall. I had no idea what to say, but I didn't want to feel again how I'd felt when that head of hers had vanished.

'Celia . . . Gracie is my . . . mother. She made me promise not to come here again.'

Celia's face sprang into action. '*Why?*'

I started to swing my coat on its tag, and looked at the buttonhole stitching for an answer.

'*Why?*' Celia was furious.

'I can play here, it's all right. It's just . . . I can't go in.'

'I don't think you've heard what I've just said: why? Why doesn't your mother want you in our house, for heaven's sake? Lord above, it's not as if we're beneath her!'

I swallowed. 'Do you know her?'

'Of course I don't!' Her voice was full of disdain. I hated it, and resolved to stop it, as if by appeasing her I could shut down a whole side of who she was that I didn't want to see.

I glanced at Mo. She seemed to have lost her nerve, and was biting her nails under hunched shoulders.

'Can we come over, then?' I asked.

Celia sighed. 'At *last!*' She bobbed down from the wall and made her way to our secret entrance, where we stood to meet her.

I climbed the section of topless wall and leant back to take Mo's hand.

'Hang on! I didn't say *she* could come, did I?'

'I thought—'

Celia had that voice again, parched and cruel. She narrowed her eyes at me and said slowly and decisively, 'One at a time.'

I stopped climbing, my elbow on top of the wall. 'No.'

She raised her eyebrows.

'I'll only come if Mo can come too.'

Celia's face became very dark, and I was certain I'd gone too far. I was ready to take it all back. I was ready to renounce Mo if that was the only way to transform Celia back to the girl I adored. But Celia's face changed suddenly, for no reason I could understand.

'All right, then.' She smiled, a little strenuously I thought, and beckoned us both down behind the yew trees.

16

'We'll have to be jolly careful. It's a million times more dangerous with the two of you. If Mrs Bubb sees us she'll tell Mother, and Mother will have forty fits if she finds out.'

We were following Celia across the lawn to the glasshouse. I watched her confident step, which seemed totally unlike any other girl I knew. It wasn't the way she placed her feet – she was still untrained in deportment – but the way she held her spine: her head was very high and her behind very pushed out, as though she were in a constant state of alert, an animal ready to pounce.

'If anyone sees us, you've just come to get your ball,' she said to the hall ahead as we entered the house. 'Now, follow me. I've something to show you.'

She turned and beckoned us upstairs, her eyes resting on Mo and drinking in the obvious adulation. Mo said nothing but kept looking round at things, utterly fascinated. For some reason this irritated me. I wanted her not to be there, despite my rigorous defence of her coming. I wished she would stop noticing things and nudging me. I wished she would be less awestruck. Her being there simply magnified my own vulgarity in the eyes of Celia, and I could feel my status as her special friend slipping away.

She led us to her bedroom, walked over to a vast wardrobe on the far wall and flung open the doors.

'What do you think?' She unhooked a few coat hangers and held up dresses for us to see. One was a dark green velvet shift with a scalloped white collar and cuffs, another was in a cream silky fabric with a bias cut and fashionable uneven hem. A third was in a beautiful blue printed cotton with gathered side panels.

'They're beautiful.'

'Oh!'

We both stared at the dresses. She dropped them on the bed and dived back into the wardrobe for some more.

'Go on,' she said, turning round. 'Try them on.'

Mo gawped at me. I stared at Celia for help. 'Oh . . . we couldn't!'

Mo didn't bother to look at me for approval. She already had her frock over her head and was reaching for the cream silk. The speed of her actions made me snatch at the green velvet, and before long we were both pacing up and down in front of Celia's long mirror.

'What a perfect fit,' said Celia, arms folded and smiling like a generous aunt. 'I was afraid they might be a little small – they're last year's.'

Last year's or not, they were more spectacular than anything we'd ever tried on before.

'A perfect fit,' said Mo giving a twirl, although her little frame was quite clearly swamped in the yards of cloth.

Then came Celia's moment of glory.

'Take them,' she said. 'If you want.'

Mo and I stared down at our gorgeous dresses and then at Celia. 'Take them?'

'Take what you want.'

'Are you sure?'

'Don't be a couple of goofs. Take them.'

'Oh, Celia,' marvelled Mo. 'Oh, Joy – what will people say?'

She beamed at herself in the mirror, and I realized then that we could never wear them. Gracie and Mrs Mustoe would know straight away what we'd been up to, and even if Mrs Mustoe wasn't averse to a bit of charity, I could never, ever risk Gracie knowing we'd been here.

'I'm very sorry, Celia,' I said solemnly, 'but we can't.'

'Joy!' Mo turned her ferociously wounded eyes on me. 'What you bloody playing at?'

'We can't. Gracie'd kill me.'

'Well, you bloody ent gunna stop me!'

Celia unfolded her arms and furrowed her brow.

'What is all this nonsense about "Gracie"?'

I unbuttoned my beautiful dress, but she beckoned me over to the window, and I couldn't resist the confidentiality of the gesture.

'I think you'd better tell me what this is all about.'

I looked out of the window and swallowed hard. I too wanted the dress I was wearing, as much as Mo wanted hers, and when Celia continued silently unbuttoning it for me it was more than I could bear.

'It's Gracie. She made me promise never to come here again. I think it's something to do with love.'

'Love?'

'I think she was in love with someone here once. A long time ago.'

Celia stopped unbuttoning, slipped the dress off my shoulders, and a little smile came to the corners of her mouth.

'Someone who's still here, then?'

'I . . . suppose.'

I was down to my vest and a pair of knickers with the elastic knotted and reknotted on the outside.

'Well . . . let's see . . .' She studied the view from the window, and, as if on cue, into it walked Mr Rollins. 'It must be someone who's been here a long time, don't you think?'

I hugged my elbows awkwardly.

'I s'pose. At least twenty years or so.'

She walked over to the bed and tossed my dress over to me. 'There were a couple of stable hands ages ago – before we had the car. The horses have gone now, of course. Terribly messy creatures, that's the beauty of cars: they're so wonderfully clean.'

I put my dress on hurriedly, feeling suddenly more naked than I was. Mo was still wearing her cream affair and showed no signs of intending to take it off.

'When did they leave?' I asked, holding Mo's own dress out to her. 'And do you know what their names were?'

Celia still had that little curve on the edge of her lips, as though smiling at some inner joke. 'Oh gosh! That's a difficult one. I do just about remember them, so I might have been three or something. Lord knows what they were called, though. Ned or Ted or Sid or something.'

I didn't like the way she was talking about them. If one of them had been Gracie's lover then they should be shown more respect. And in any case, I had been doing some calculations in my head, and it all seemed pretty unlikely. 'I don't think it could be either of them.'

'Why ever not? Mrs Bubb always says one of them was a first-rate looker.'

Mo chipped in: 'Have you *seen* Gracie Burrows? She's old!'

Steady on. I knew it was because she was grumpy with me about having to get changed, but I frowned sternly at her, and Celia, thankfully, did not answer her, but went to sit in the window seat and stretched her arms out to grip the ledge on either side of her.

'Is she ugly now?'

'No!'

'How long ago was this love affair? Do we know?'

All the awkwardness of the clothes scene and Mo's sullenness seemed to evaporate. In that one little 'we', Celia had suggested a complicity that had lacked any real substance before. Yes, she had offered us her beautiful clothes, but that could be seen as charity if you wanted to be horrible about it, and yes, she had shown me around the secret corners of her house while her mother was out, and she had let me play in her shed, and all sorts of friendly things, but now we were an item, she was uniting with us to solve a mystery – my mystery, and she was going to give up her precious, Celia-time to do it. If I had the impression that she hardly cared whether Mo was in on it or not, and even that Mo's presence irritated her, I tried to brush such thoughts aside. She must have read my mind, because she suddenly addressed Mo whilst looking out of the window.

'So, Maureen, do you think *Gracie Burrows* . . .' (she said it emphatically, as if it were humorous or unusual – I couldn't quite think why) '. . . could have been in love with our Mr Rollins?'

Mo looked at the back of Celia's head and spoke to her plait: 'Mr Rollins! But Mr Rollins is married. Sid and Walt go to our school.'

Celia turned slowly to look at us, her eyes wide and knowing. 'Ah, but he wasn't married twenty years ago, was he?' Mo and I looked at each other uncomfortably. 'I believe he's worked here all his life, because his father was gardener before him.'

I wanted to be pleased for Celia, for her clever solution to the mystery, but I felt cheated by it. For one thing, if the mystery was solved, then we were no longer a team trying to solve it, and for another – far more importantly, I think – I found myself indignant at the suggestion of my dear Gracie with crusty-faced Mr Rollins. It wasn't that he was too old for Gracie (in fact, he was probably in his late thirties, whilst Gracie was forty-six) or that he was a gardener, or even that he was the father of Sid who farted a lot in class and Walt who wiped his snot on the underside of my desk. It was more that I wanted the mystery to be romantic. I wanted it to continue, and I wanted to spend forever with Celia trying to unravel it.

I shrugged. 'We haven't shown Mo the rest of the house. Won't your mother be back soon?'

Celia got up from the window seat and fetched an old canvas bag from the bottom of her wardrobe. Then she carefully folded the two dresses we had liked, the cream and the green ones, along with two more she chose at random. She put them carefully into the bag, and slung it on her shoulder like an explorer. 'Follow me!'

We followed her, and to my delight we did a quick revisit of all the rooms she had shown me before. I lingered in James's room, while she continued the tour with Mo.

There was something different about it this time, and I found myself unable to leave the room until I worked out what it was. I stood rooted, and looked about. The walls were still of the palest green, and the oar and the branch were still on the wall. The coverlet on the bed was untouched, and the cricket bat was leaning where it had leant before. I walked slowly around, as though if I disturbed the air, I might knock something off balance. I studied a row of coins leaning against a bookshelf: they were foreign mostly, and I didn't recognize any of them. There was a cup full of feathers. I took one out and saw that it had been made into a perfectly carved quill. I examined its tip, and felt a wave of pleasure at its perfection. Replacing it, I saw a book of stamps, which I opened carefully. The pages were plastered in colour, each stamp carefully placed on its folded stamp paper so as to produce a rainbow effect, or a grouped colour pattern. There seemed to be squares of colour, circles, triangles, flowers. There was no indication whatsoever of any grouping according to country, and the titles at the top of each page, 'People's Republic of Mongolia' or 'British Commonwealth in Africa', had been completely ignored. I closed the book and looked at the little bureau for the wagtail. But the picture had been replaced by another bird, this time a chaffinch. I caught my breath. Not only was it beautifully drawn, but since I had been here last, Celia's brother must have been here and drawn it. I placed my hand on the chair and imagined him sitting there. It gave me an odd feeling. I could hear Celia calling to me from across the landing, but I wasn't ready to finish my trespass. And just as I was about to go, I turned from the bureau, and as I did so I saw a pair of shoes on the far side of his bed. I approached them. They were large – much larger than I expected – and stood together but at a slight angle. Not ten to two, more twenty past eight. I bent down and knelt beside them. They were made of a very polished brown leather with an intricate inlaid pattern on the toe. I touched the inside leather: it was soft. I picked up the right shoe and smelt it: a delicious leathery smell fought with another pungent, overwhelming odour. I sniffed again. I looked inside: size eight. Of course, at fourteen he would be a grown man, but I hadn't expected it. I inhaled again, and then again.

'Joy! Wherever are you?'

I placed the shoe beside its partner and rose to my feet. Oh, what a thing is a pair of shoes! I stood there looking at them, as if they *were* the feet of a young man, the ends of his legs, the mysterious James who drew so carefully and stuck stamps too carelessly, and who played cricket and wore size eight shoes and smelt of man.

'Oh, here you are! You like this room, don't you?'

I smiled meekly. 'It's different.'

'I'll say it is. Thank goodness we're not all as messy as James.' Celia, buoyed up by Mo's adulation, looked flushed and happy. 'Come along, I'm going to show you both the living room. We've just got time, I should think.'

And so we saw the grand living room with its high ceiling and exotic plants on tall stands. We lapped up the drawing room and its funny furniture with curly wooden claws, we gasped at the chandeliers and gawped at the crystal, the door-knobs, the carpets, the electric light, the telephone. And then we scampered across the lawn, past the wretched lovelorn Mr Rollins with his rake, into the yew trees and over the wall, Mo clutching our canvas bag of delights.

'Joy!' whispered Celia, grabbing my arm as I got down last from the wall. 'You will come again, won't you?'

I looked desperately into her clear turquoise eyes, 'I can't – I don't think I—'

'I've got something important to tell you!'

I clambered down before Mo could notice. She was brushing the chalky stone off her frock and spitting on her scuffed shoes, and I didn't think she'd heard.

We didn't know what to do with the dresses. When we got back home we hid the bag deep in Gracie's coalhole.

17

We had other places to play which lent an air of grandeur to that summer.

Mr Mustoe worked at the Really Big House, Upton Manor. Although his hours were cut, he was almost Head Gardener, and given that the head gardener was bent double with arthritis and unable to kneel any more, Mr Mustoe felt certain he was heading for better things.

The key thing about Mr Mustoe's job was that whenever the occupants were in London – which was most of the time – only a skeleton staff remained, and he would let us children roam free in the grounds.

We lorded it up, Mo, Tilly, George, Robert and myself. We played croquet on the lawns, lounged about in deckchairs and made ever more gruesome scarecrows in the vegetable gardens. Our exploits were made even more exciting by the terrifying prospect of meeting one of the fleshless skeleton staff.

Prompted by the abundance of roses and the packed flower-beds, we held scent-making competitions. Mr Mustoe declared Robert the overall winner with a product named 'Utter Pong'. It went without saying that we helped with the upkeep of the gardens by polishing off the raspberries, the strawberries and some of the gooseberries. We roamed freely in the conservatory and the potting sheds, and felt obliged to pilfer a few pots. Similarly, when we were allowed through the scullery to an indoor lavatory, we couldn't stop ourselves – confronted with stacks of neatly cut soap and white laundered hand towels – from collecting a few. It wasn't that we needed flowerpots, and heaven knows we generally avoided soap like mustard gas, but the fact that it was there, stacked up so neatly and abundantly, made it irresistible.

It wasn't long after that, that Mr Mustoe was sacked from his position for stealing, and so was the poor girl who had been kept on to preserve the summer fruit. I felt terrible. Mr Mustoe would never make it to Head Gardener now, his dreams of bettering himself were all in tatters, and he and the girl were out of work just as a great Depression was descending. And it seemed to me that we had caused the great Depression ourselves and were entirely responsible for it. We had ruined the careers of two innocent people – as well as most of the population of Britain and America – for some bits of old soap and a few gobfuls of berries. The guilt of it hung over me for years, until Mo told me blithely one day that her father had been pilfering the silver tableware, and the servant girl had walked off with a string of real pearls.

Coming home from the really big house one day, we found a rabbit in a hedgerow. It lay very still, its head smeared in blood. George said it was dead and became very interested in it, poking the belly with a stick. But I could see it was moving – a little tremble, that was all, but moving.

'Stop it! It's alive!'

'S'not.'

'It is! It's shaking.'

We all looked carefully, and each of us saw a wobble, and

then a distinct shudder. I picked it up and held it close to me. It was warm. Through the metallic whiff of blood it had a deep musky smell in its fur. The others were showing signs of disgust, but I walked home purposefully, hugging the soft creature against me. They all followed, eager to see what I might do, but advising against whatever I had in mind. 'Best to put 'im out of 'iz misery, look,' and 'Head's all mashed up – ee'll 'ave no brain,' 'Best make a pie of 'im.'

I felt confident Gracie would support my plans for its revival, but when she saw me with the bloodied creature she threw up her hands in horror. She said if it lived it would be in great pain, and it would be kinder to kill it. She would not make a pie of any animal whose cause of death was uncertain, even if it did look like a failed trap to her. So we waited for Mr Mustoe to come home, and in that time I cried and cried, and watched the rabbit tremble and open one eye to look at me, terrified. I held it close and kissed it and they all saw I was mad as a donkey, and when Mr Mustoe came home he slaughtered it with a big stone on the head and I couldn't look. Gracie said I should have left it to die, and so did Mr Mustoe. I didn't know if they were right or not. I didn't know whether it would have got better if I'd looked after it, or whether I would have just prolonged its misery. I still didn't know at bedtime, and it bothered me. I wasn't being senti-mental. I had eaten rabbit lots of times, and with Nipper in the woods I had helped to mesmerize them. I don't know how he killed them, for I never watched that part, but I knew it was quick, and with the animal's permission.

Sometimes you just can't know what the right thing is. And sometimes it can be the difference between a life or a death, or between a life lived in pain or peace at last. And I was troubled by that open eye. Did the rabbit see me as its rescuer or, in the split second as the stone came down on its skull, did it see me as a murderous traitor? But what really stopped me sleeping was this conundrum: at what point can you tell that an injured creature is unrescuable? How much pain can you put it through in order to let it live? How did Gracie and Mr Mustoe know? And if they didn't know, did they have the right to guess?

18

It was the third week in August. Gracie had not mentioned the gentleman's offer and neither had I. School would be starting again soon for us, and we were ready for it, in a troubled, excited way. It seemed right, just as nature was thinking of closing down for the year, dropping its fruits, waving its weary leaves and gathering the birds to chatter about leaving, that we should have the chance of new beginnings. The start of a school year, with a new upgraded status for each of us, was a compensation for the end of the summer. There would be no surprise at seeing each other again, for we had spent the long summer days playing in the quarry, building fires, baking potatoes, making potions, digging for treasure, swinging from trees and gates, exploring old sheds, exploring ourselves – our scuffed knees, our friendships, our hurts, our roles in each other's lives. We had made dens, got married, divorced, died horrendous deaths, murdered, kissed and spied on each other. When we looked at each other across the rows of desks, it was just another role we were playing, just a change of scene.

But before that day arrived, I resolved to see Celia one last time. I had battled with my fears because Gracie had been so adamant about it all, and there was nothing that terrorized me more in the world than losing Gracie. This, I reasoned, could never really happen. Nothing could surely turn Gracie against me to such an extent that I would lose her. This was about some love affair she didn't want uncovered. But I wasn't planning on telling anyone. Her secret would be safe with me. And in any case, she need never find out. One last meeting with Celia, that was all. She *had* said there was something she had to tell me. It would have been wiser to wait a few weeks, to put Mo off the scent, but once school began I knew I would be easier to trace in the dull routine of the days.

I set off for Buckleigh House at around ten. We were building fires in the quarry to try and melt down old lead we had found. I said I needed a wee and hotfooted it back across the village and up the hill.

Celia wasn't there, but climbing the wall in the secret place, I could see the car was gone. The garden was completely empty and still. I waited for about ten minutes, and then grew afraid Mo might come after me, so I climbed over. Cowering in the yew trees I waited another ten minutes, and then I saw a face come to an upstairs window. It looked directly at me. From where I was I couldn't tell if it was Celia's or someone else's, and it disappeared almost straight away. I began to panic. If I was caught climbing the wall I would look like a burglar, and also Mo might even now be coming up the hill or wandering about on the other side. I started to run towards the sheds. No one would find me in the den, Celia had said so herself: no one ever went in there except her. I pushed the latch and dived towards the chest of old comics. There was no room in there for me, so I hid behind it as best I could, crouching in the musty corner, my nose in a pile of mildewed curtains that were rotten to the core.

Outside I heard footsteps thumping on the grass. The metal latch rattled as the door was slung open. I tried to stop my heavy breath, but it was impossible.

'Joy! Is that you?'

I raised my head and closed my eyes in relief. 'Celia!'

'Gosh, that was brave! Wizard timing though! Mother has just gone out to town – but you knew that, you've worked that out by now, haven't you?'

I sighed, my pulse still racing, and took in her peachy cheeks and the little dip in the centre of her lips. She was wearing a violet-coloured dress with a huge white collar.

'You don't mind, then?'

'I should say not! We can't really go inside though, Elsie is doing the rooms and Mrs Bubb is clucking around her.'

I was more than happy to stay with Celia in the shed, and we sat there exchanging bits of news like old friends. I loved to hear her speak, the easy way in which she put words together and made them sound so elegant, her bizarre phrases which belonged to the realm of posh people, the way she held her back so straight – even when sitting on a sack – and the cleanness of the little white curves across the tips of her nails.

'How is your mother?' I asked, hoping that she might get ill and die and then Gracie could marry Celia's father and Celia and I could be sisters.

'She's quite well, thank you,' said Celia. 'Although she does *loathe* it here, and it plays on her nerves.' She lowered her voice suddenly and touched my arm. 'She has a *lover* in Monte Carlo!'

I said nothing, stunned by this announcement, and not quite sure what it meant for Mr Buckleigh.

'Does Gracie have a lover?'

I was shocked. 'No!' As soon as I said it, it seemed to make Gracie somehow inadequate.

Celia was studying me, smiling with one half of her mouth. Then she sighed and said with renewed enthusiasm, 'I can't wait to have a lover, can you?'

Suddenly she lay down, put her wrists together and asked me to grip them. I did as I was told. They were remarkably solid for someone who seemed so elegant.

'Tighter!' she commanded.

I gripped tighter.

'Harder!'

I gripped tighter still, afraid of hurting her.

'Harder!' she hissed. 'Hurt me!'

Reluctantly, I tried to seem like I was gripping tighter, without actually hurting her. Her face was pink now, and she was panting, almost in exasperation.

'Come on! Hurt me! Tell me you'll have me one way or another!'

I felt ridiculous. It was far worse than being Buster because I didn't know if I was supposed to *be* anybody, except myself. I mumbled the words to the floor, then she wriggled free and slapped me on the face.

I let out a muffled howl, which I instantly disguised as a cough. My cheek smarted so badly I could feel my eyes welling up and I furiously willed the tears away.

Celia was radiant.

'That's what they do at the pictures,' she beamed. 'I've always wanted to know what it was like.'

I hadn't.

'I hope I didn't hurt you,' she said.

I shook my head.

'You hurt *me* quite a lot actually. But it was worth it!' Then she sat back on her heels as if nothing had happened. 'Mo's very quiet, isn't she?'

'Well, she was a bit, when she was here . . . it was all a bit . . .'

'Hmm! Tell me, what's it like being poor?' I couldn't believe for a moment that she meant me. 'You don't mind me asking, do you?'

'Well . . . Mo and me, we're not what you'd call poor – we're sort of . . . just medium.'

'Oh, I know. I don't mean you're starving. I just mean what's it like not being able to have lots of clothes – that kind of thing?'

'Well . . . you don't really notice it, like . . .' I wasn't sure whether I was irritated by her assumption that I was poor (if she wanted poor she should see the MacNallys or the Hoggards or the Crumptons) or whether I was flattered to be asked my opinion, in a position to teach her something. 'It was lovely to have those dresses. But if we hadn't've seen them, then we wouldn't've never noticed not having them, sort of . . .'

'Mo was clearly so thrilled with that cream dress, wasn't she?' She tossed her head back and smiled, and I noticed how white her skin was, all the way down, without a trace of suntan. I wondered when she was going to tell me her important piece of news, or if she had forgotten.

'We're very grateful – it was ever so kind of you, Celia – I loved my dress too – oh, it was so . . . oh . . .'

'Please, don't be such a goof! I told you, they're all going out, anyway. And even this one (which is new, by the way – do you like it?), even this one will hardly be worn, what with school and everything.'

I studied the soft folds of the cotton as it draped over her knees. 'Too nice to wear to school, I s'pose.'

And then Celia laughed. She laughed in a way I somehow knew she would. It was a laugh that was so nearly excusable, so nearly just a surprised laugh. But that little trace of – what was it? authority? contempt? – was still there.

'School? Heavens, I have to wear a dreadful uniform with a horrid green tunic and a horrid green hat and stockings the colour of pea-soup.'

I felt foolish for not realizing that Celia did not attend a school anything like my own. I had seen children in uniforms when I went shopping in town with Gracie, and I had always hated the way they hung around in clusters, talking too loudly with pigtails too tightly woven and piping around their blazers. I had hated the way they never met your eyes, as if you weren't there, as if the town belonged to them and the shops existed solely for them to buy buns and chocolates.

'Still, you can always wear it at the weekends,' I suggested.

She put her head on one side and considered me sympathetically. 'I shan't be coming home at weekends. I'm boarding. That's what I was going to tell you.'

'Boarding?' I began to feel my heart quicken again. 'Are you going away on a ship?'

'No, silly. Sleeping in a dormitory. It's supposed to be fun, but it sounds dreadful.'

'A dormitory . . .' I found myself breathing fast – panting, almost, in panic. 'Does that mean you won't be coming back?'

'Not till Christmas.' She looked me in the eye as she said it, as if testing its effect.

'Christmas!'

'Well . . . there's half-term, of course. And exeats. I shall have two exeats but Mother might just come to me and we might stay in a hotel and shop or something. I'm not awfully sure yet.'

'Oh, Celia!' It was a jerky utterance, and she must've heard the emotion in my voice.

'Oh, Joy! I'm going to miss you terribly!'

Then she got down on her knees, with no concern for the pretty frock, and put her arms around me. I wasn't sure what to do, so I put my arms around her too, hoping she didn't mind, hoping she wouldn't slap me again. She smelt of posh soap, and felt as soft as Mrs Mustoe's new baby. I was surprised to find that she was warm though, and that her neck, deep in the forest of her plait, smelt as oily and musky as a woodland animal.

We stayed clasped together for some time. My temples ached with the tears I held back. I felt I was breathing in something of what she was, and for some reason I wanted plenty of it. I didn't realize it at the time, but she was doing the same to me.

*   *   *

We stayed in the shed and played shops for the next hour or so, but we were too old and too sophisticated just to buy comics. Instead we were lovers, buying clothes and luxury items for our honeymoon. It allowed us to call each other 'darling' and to dream up interesting purchases: orange-flavoured toothpaste, banana and fig marmalade, see-through dressing gowns, diamond-studded knickers. With a definite role I was on familiar territory. The shopkeeper was invisible, and we took it in turns to speak for him or her, but we used real wallets and purses, old ones which had belonged to Celia's mother and father and which, like everything else old but in perfectly good condition, had been thrown out.

'That'll be one million five thousand pounds, please, sir,' said Celia, in a very deep voice. 'Cash, please.'

I opened my wallet and slid my fingers into its luxury soft pocket, but I had run out of the notes we had made from cut-up comics.

'Hmm,' said Celia, unruffled. 'I'm afraid the gold-plated swimsuit will not be Sir's, after all.'

'Wait – I have something.' I could feel some paper through the lining of the pocket, and eased my fingers into the slight tear in the taffeta. 'I've got it!' A little white corner emerged and I tugged gently. 'I can pay!'

But as I drew out the rectangle of paper, my elation turned to curiosity, for it was not a piece of comic at all. It was a photograph. And it didn't take me long to realize where I had seen the person in the photograph before. Celia leaned over and took it.

'Gosh. Whoever's that?'

'It's Gracie.'

It didn't matter how hard Celia tried to convince me this must be Mr Rollins' old wallet – and yes, she could remember it now, he had given her his old wallet – I knew people like Mr Rollins didn't have wallets like these. I knew, and what made it worse was that I knew – from the way she flustered and flushed and panicked – that she had always known, and that the Mr Rollins idea had been a red herring, and that she had known right from the moment she selected me from the line-up in our ball game outside the wall. That was why I had been the chosen one.

My nose was very much put out of joint. I certainly didn't consider murder as a revenge, but things have a way of getting out of hand.

First I had a few questions to ask Gracie.

19

Gracie wouldn't tell me. She wouldn't say if she'd ever been in love or whether there was something going on between Celia's father and herself. Instead she gazed at the mantelpiece and told me a different story.

'When I was a little girl my parents gave me a valuable and beautiful figurine: a shepherdess. They told me it had been my mother's, and before that my mother's mother's, and so on, and that one day it would go on my own mantelpiece. Well, I suppose they weren't wrong there. I suppose this amounts to my own mantelpiece now. But, you see, I had envisaged a change. I thought, all the while I was growing up, that one day that little shepherdess would stand smiling on a fresh mantelpiece, one that I dusted every day while my husband was out at work. That's what they led me to believe, and that's what I thought.'

The importance of handing it down to her own daughter was also emphasized. This was another thing that made her own, separate mantelpiece and the accompanying husband a certainty. 'And if I was still in any doubt, there were the umpteen little trinkets, deemed of great value by my parents, which were to be "kept in the family".'

A small bugle, for example, which was of no use to anyone,

was feverishly guarded when a boy down the road wanted to learn the instrument; a second sewing machine – which was never used because the bobbin was broken – was considered a secret in case a neighbour borrowed it and never gave it back; a wooden tractor that could've made many a little boy happy over the years, was policed by her father in the spare room cupboard; a perfectly good wireless set, endless clocks and watches, mountains of unimaginative antimacassars crocheted by ancestors, chipped china, a set of pistols, moth-eaten cashmere rugs, her own used baby clothes that might once, long ago, have been of use to one of our poorer neighbours – all these, shielded from the world at large (clearly clamouring for this bounty) had to be kept in the family. Because one day it would come in handy for her own children.

'But they didn't stop there. They kept me in the family too, like one of their precious trinkets. It didn't seem to occur to them that in order to hand on these treasures I would have to have a husband, and to have a husband I would have to meet a man.

'All the time I was growing up there was never anyone good enough. Even when I was very small, the children I played with were "too common", and when I invited a little boy round to play he was told to "stop trying it on with folks like us", and sent packing to the little half-door shack he lived in up by the pub. Eddie Dunn, his name was.

'No one much wanted to play with me before long. Only posh girls and boys were welcome here, and they didn't want to play with the likes of me. Soon, there was hardly anyone come round. Just me on my own. I couldn't understand it. I was sure my parents knew what they were doing.

'Then this boy from the post office got a bit sweet on me. Walter, he was. He was a good boy, Walter. He had brown curly hair and bright smiley teeth. He used to whistle when he was out delivering. All sorts of tunes . . . "If you were the only girl in the world" . . . "You are my honeysuckle" . . . always happy, he was. I didn't realize I was sweet on him too, until Father told him to clear off one day. Just hollered at him like that, for no reason: "And *you* can clear off!" he says. "Sniffing around my daughter! If you think you're walking out with her, you've got another think coming!" And that wasn't the worst of it. Then he said – without any say-so from me – without even *asking* me, he says, "She wouldn't touch you with a bargepole, our Grace." And that was it. He hardly dared look me in the eye after that.

'Then another time there was a dance on the green. Whitsun, it was. We were all dressed up in white – we used to do that then, before the war, dress all in white – white shoes and all. Lovely, it was. They don't do that now, see. Still, it was one Whitsun – I must've been seventeen or so – and we were all dancing, and the young men joined in later – you know, the young men from hereabouts. Well, I was having a whale of a time, as you can imagine. All sorts of dances we did. *The Waves of Tory*, *The Nottingham Swing*, and one we always called *The Woodside Polka*. Probably no different to any other polka, I suppose, but we had a few little extra steps of our own. Anyway, there I was dancing with some lovely gentle boy called Albert. Tall, big brown eyes, really handsome. I'd never *had* such a good time. Then all of a sudden, up walks my father and breaks us up. The fiddles still going and everything and he just breaks us up. Just like that. Says it's nine thirty and all respectable girls should be in bed. He practically pushes poor Albert away, and he drags me by the arm. I was that angry. I was fuming, I was.

'I cried myself to sleep. Now I think of it, I felt a lot like that little tractor in the cupboard in the spare room. And I *was* like it, really. I wasn't even allowed to be of use. I couldn't even make a meal, or do the washing up. See, if I made a pie, Mother was sure to say it was burnt, even if it was only a little bit too brown. And if I defied her advice and made a cake ("Oh, don't go making a mess in the kitchen," she'd say), then there'd be something wrong with that, too. If I washed up, I'd always've missed a bit on some plate or other, if I tidied up there'd be an inch of dust left on something or other, if I polished shoes I wouldn't have got the proper shine, if I weeded the garden, I'd've left a dandelion likely to "spread a million seeds".'

And all of it, the burnt cakes, the speck of food on the plate, the undusted surface, the not-shiny-enough shoes, the single remaining dandelion, were all proof of her utter incompetence. Better to leave it all to them. They knew best. She couldn't begin to compete. And all those tiny mishaps were exaggerated by this special way they had at mealtimes.

'They'd always start by praising me up, saying how hard I'd tried and everything. Then Father might scratch his neck or sigh or Mother might raise her eyebrows in a hopeful, kindly way, and one of them would say, "It's lovely, Gracie," and look at the other one with a little mock smile, "Isn't it, dear?" and the other one would give the faintest little smirk and say, "Lovely!" And that would be their way of making sure I didn't go trying it on again. I was not allowed to be useful, because if I was useful I could manage on my own. And if I could manage on my own, I wouldn't need them any more.

'Of course, I didn't see that then. I thought all married couples lived just for their children. I didn't realize they were supposed to love each other as well. By love I mean, you know, romantic love. I just thought we were a kind of unit, the three of us. Without me, they wouldn't exist.

'Well, it's all right to think that when you're little, isn't it? But as I got older I should've felt trapped by it, but I just felt frustrated and ungrateful. *Ungrateful!*

'And then they did something really terrible.'

She looked into the fire.

'Really terrible. I didn't even know how terrible until last week.'

She looked at me.

'I suppose . . . I should've given that shepherdess to you.'
She gave a deep sigh, but she didn't tell me what they'd done.
'Still . . .'

20

It may have been the last week in August – I can't quite remember – that we killed the Buckleighs' dog. It was called Zeus (or 'Zooss' as we children used to say). We didn't know what type of dog it was, but George called it a 'tartan' dog, because it always seemed to be dressed in little tartan garments, even in the summer. It was shortish, woollyish, and yapped like something deranged. It was obviously some sort of pedigree, we concluded, because of its extensive wardrobe, and there was nothing we liked more than to get on its very delicate nerves. In many ways this resembled the Mrs Emery game. We did it because the thrill of causing a stir – whether it was a tantrum or a barking fit – reminded us that we had power, that we could affect things. And because this fact took us by surprise – being, as we were, on the cusp of childhood – we needed to be reminded of it as often as possible.

We were playing in the field opposite the Buckleighs' – me, Mo, Tilly, Spit and George – when Zeus came scampering towards us, yapping. We stopped the death-defying contraption we had made (half see-saw, half evil catapult of torture) and looked at him.

'Thought they was on holiday,' said Tilly.

'That's what Mr Rollins said,' said Mo.

'Woof!' said George. 'Grrr . . .'

'Must've got out over the wall. Here, boy!'

Zeus put his head on one side and considered us. He seemed to be saying that being stuck with Mr Rollins for a week was no party, and that even for a neurotic, mollycoddled dog like himself, playing with us looked more interesting. So George approached cautiously and they sniffed each other, then we put Zeus on our wild see-saw and he really got the hang of it, barking his little head off in glee.

He came to see us for a few days after that, and we always gave him a go, because he seemed to enjoy it so much. We swung him round, we chased him, and let him chase us. George made a den for him and hid in it with him. He was really not a bad little dog when you got to know him, and we were certain he hated his tartan togs as much as we did.

One day things got a bit out of hand. It wasn't anyone's fault. We had piled up some rocks so that we could jump on the contraption and catapult things into the air. Mo and Tilly and George were collecting ammunition, when Spit and I thought we'd do a height check. We jumped, and the other end of the see-saw flew up magnificently. It would have propelled stones, clods of weed and other ammo wonderfully into our 'goal' area, but what none of us had noticed was that Zeus had trotted up quietly (no need to yap at us any more – we were friends) and gone to sit on his usual seat for his usual ride. The first we knew of it was when he flew above our heads, and landed with a mighty thlunk on the grass. He wasn't dead, because he rolled over and started to yelp, but he had come down right in front of Prince, the carthorse who pulled the milk cart. Prince took exception to the live ammunition, and reared up at the little yapping bomb. It was a terrible sight: Zeus against Prince, deity against royalty. Prince tossed him in the air. With one thud he was down, and completely silent. George rushed over and shooed Prince away. Prince trotted off like a lamb, a little embarrassed at what he had done.

And that was how we killed Zeus. And we realized very quickly that it wasn't us who would get the blame but Mr Rollins, whose job it had been to tend the gardens and keep an eye on Zeus.

Then we saw Stinker riding home on his bike for dinner. We stopped him and told him everything, and he had a plan which, for Robert Stinker Mustoe, was a remarkably good one.

We hid Zeus in George's den until the following evening, when Stinker reliably assured us the Buckleighs were returning home. Then, at dusk, we crept over the Buckleigh wall: Mo, George and me, with Zeus wrapped up in an old blanket. I stayed as lookout by the wall, while the others hid in the yew trees by the side of the driveway. Then Stinker arrived, pedalling fast from the train station to say they were coming. I took up my position with the others. He climbed over the wall, and streaming with sweat, he crouched beside me in the shadows.

'Give us the dog,' he hissed. I could see the sweat glistening on his face, and the hot biscuit smell of him enveloped me as he whispered in my ear, 'This'd better be worth it, Joy Burrows. I'm on'y doin' it for you!'

We crouched there for an age, our legs buckled and aching, waiting until the sound of a taxi puttered down over the hill. At last the car came to a halt and the taxi driver got out and opened the gates. Stinker was stinking next to me, and breathing very heavily. As the car came in through the gates George started to yap loudly and Stinker hurled the dead dog in front of the car. It hit the bumper and flumped on the ground. The taxi swerved to a halt.

We waited in silence as the taxi driver, followed by members of the Buckleigh family, got out and beheld the deceased dog.

Mrs Buckleigh could be heard wailing. Mrs Bubb came running out of the house. Someone told the taxi driver it wasn't his fault, and it took forever for the whole drama to be played out while we waited in agony. I was certain the dog had yapped beyond the time of death, but George was so emotional he weed in the bushes and some of it sprayed out and hit my dress. I never did find out what Stinker had meant – not for a good few years, anyway.

21

I left school when I was fourteen, along with everyone else in my year. Miss Prosser told my mother I could go to the High School, and Gracie was all for it, despite the fees. But I didn't want to go. I went to Griffens with her instead, and stayed there five years making dresses and coats and mending trousers. I wanted nothing to change: just me and Gracie, beavering away together, listening to the gossip as people came in, putting the kettle on the little range at the back at mid-morning, going to the pictures with Mo on Saturdays.

As the years went by I almost forgot about Celia. She came to me in dreams sometimes – or rather, her brother came to me. I was often in James's bedroom and James would walk in and find me there. Then he would take me in his arms and tell me he had been watching me for years and had always loved me. I usually looked far more pretty: hair more like Celia's, clothes like Betty Grable, and an accent just like I imagined his to be. I was not so foolish as to be unaware that James fulfilled a function for me. In the absence of any romance in Woodside, with my failure to be aroused by the clumping, neolithic clodhoppers that posed as young men, I needed a man to stand in for my burgeoning fantasies. I couldn't substitute film stars, like Mo and the other girls. I had never understood hero-worship in any of its forms. Mo cutting out a picture and pinning it on the wall or keeping it in her diary seemed senseless to me. Was she ever going to meet Bing Crosby? Was he ever going to get on a boat and a train and a number 38 bus and get off at Woodside and say, 'Hey, Mo, darling! Let's go round the world together, honey!' No, he wasn't. It was no good dreaming about it, because I could tell her right away it wasn't going to happen. And she knew it. Yet she still drooled over his films and touched his photographs and practically wet herself when he came on the wireless.

James, however, lived in Buckleigh House – at least, I understood he did. It was highly unlikely that he would ever push me up against a tree and kiss me, but it wasn't outside the realms of possibility, like Bing. And it was that tiny loophole of possibility that made him so intriguing.

As with all things we long for, sooner or later, if they are remotely within the realms of possibility, we find ourselves giving fate a little helping hand. And so it was that in the summer when I was seventeen, when my fantasies about James had reached a peak of obsession, I found that I walked past Buckleigh House on several occasions for no reason whatsoever, and took furtive sidelong glances through the tall iron gates. I even found myself walking past Celia's school when I was in town, haplessly imagining that of the hundreds of inmates I might see Celia spill over the pavement in one of the little green-clad gangs.

In the end it was in Cheltenham that I saw her. I had just come out of The Daffodil after seeing *King Kong* a second time through. Mo had gone after the first showing because she wanted to buy some stockings. I emerged into the glaring light of day and was shielding my eyes on the pavement, when Celia spotted me.

'Joy! Heavens! It *is* you!'

'Celia!'

'Joy, this is my friend Dee. Were you just in there? What did you think?'

'Oh . . . it was lovely.' I couldn't take my eyes off them, now that I had adjusted to the light. Celia wore her hair in a curly pageboy, perfectly executed with tortoiseshell side clips. Her friend had the same hairstyle, and they both wore hats with matching clutch bags, and bright red lipstick which made Celia look about twenty-five.

People were jostling past us, and there was an awkwardness in the air. It had something to do with the way Celia's friend was eyeing me with a fixed smile, as though I were a specimen she hadn't come across before, and something to do with the way Celia and I had left things between us so many years before.

'How's . . . your family?'

Celia, who had been standing by the kerb, dodged a passing bicycle and grabbed me by the elbow. 'Oh . . . gosh, they're fine. Hey, look – it's *so* good to see you—' She beamed suddenly over my shoulder, and I became aware that two young men had joined us: they were clearly with Celia and her friend.

'Simon, Henry, this is my old friend Joy.'

Both men shook my hand courteously, and one kissed it and did a little bow. 'And is the lovely Joy accompanying us tonight?'

I coloured and looked down at the pavement uncomfortably. Before I could think what to do, Celia said, 'Oh, that's a smashing idea. Hey, Joy, what are you up to tonight?'

'Well . . . nothing . . . I—'

'How do you fancy coming to a party?'

'Well, I . . .' It all seemed so easy for them, making arrangements at the drop of a hat. I couldn't just go to a party. What would I say to Gracie? What would I wear? How on earth would I get there and back? 'I don't think so . . . I'd better not, look—'

'I'm sure we could find a nice young man to take you,' said Henry or Simon, winking. 'Bertie's not seeing anyone, is he, Dee? He's got a car.'

'Or Maurice! Yes . . .' Dee started to giggle. 'Oh, dear . . . Maurice! Just imagine! Oh, yes, Celia: Maurice!'

I felt like a ping-pong ball being batted to and fro. I couldn't imagine for a moment that these people would want to make fun of me, but there was something in their manner that made me wary. I drew my cardigan closely around me.

'Look, it's very kind, Celia. But I really don't think—'

'I've got it! James! You always did like James, didn't you? And he'd be crazy about you if he could see you now!' She was all teeth beneath her crimson lipstick. So pleased was she with her decision that she actually clapped her hands together decisively. 'Right! That's it. James and Joy. It'll have to be next Saturday. Let's not stand on the pavement any more. Who's for tea at The Queen's?'

I made my excuses – said I had to meet Mo at the bus station. But Celia wouldn't let me go without an assurance that I would come to Buckleigh House at seven thirty on Saturday evening.

I walked to the bus station with wings on my heels, but also with a sly foreboding.

Celia came to the dress shop on Wednesday afternoon to take me off for tea. Gracie looked up from her machine in astonishment, and when she turned her eyes on me they were full of curiosity and fear. I wished Celia hadn't turned up like this. She couldn't have forgotten that I wasn't supposed to play with her in the past. Or did she think it was all water under the bridge, now that we were grown up? Evidently so, for she beamed at Gracie, and even let slip the bombshell of Saturday night's plans. To my shame, I hoped Celia wouldn't notice Gracie's old pinny with its mismatching buttons and the blackberry stain that wouldn't wash out. I hoped she wouldn't see the thick fawn stockings rolled down to the knees for comfort. I wished Gracie would look less awestruck at Celia's clothes, and I hoped and prayed that she wouldn't open her mouth and breathe a single, burry Gloucestershire word.

'You don't mind if I take Joy out now for some buns, do you, Miss Burrows? I know a lovely little place in Painswick.'

'Oh . . . well . . . no – of course not.'

I knew Gracie was doing a shepherd's pie for tea: she had bought the meat from the delivery van that morning. But somehow we were both powerless before the easy confidence of Celia Buckleigh.

'Jolly good. I'll be borrowing her again on Saturday night – you won't mind that, will you? Might be a bit late back.'

Gracie looked dumbfounded. I couldn't meet her eyes because I didn't want to see the hurt there might be there. Gracie and I shared almost everything, our own giant secret like a pod we nestled in together.

'I wasn't expecting . . .' I said, going to fetch my coat. Celia was already ahead of me. I folded it over my arm and peeped back in the workroom. 'Cheerio, then, Gracie . . . you don't mind, do you?'

She looked up and smiled, and there wasn't a trace of hurt in it – 'Don't be daft. Have a good time!' – only fear.

Celia took me to an intimate teashop with lace tablecloths and bought us a pot of tea and fancies as though she knew the menu by heart. I fiddled with the sugar lumps and she jokingly slapped my hand.

'Oooh, Joy! Look at those nails! We'll have to do something with those!' Then she looked into my face, circling it with her eyes. 'You know, you could be quite pretty with some make-up.'

I rolled my eyes.

'No — really — you could!'

I was devastated, but all I managed was, 'I'm sure anyone could look quite pretty with make-up.'

'Oh, I don't mean it like that. You would look stunning. You are pretty in a natural, country girl sort of way, but there's a ravishing beauty in there somewhere just waiting to come out!' At this she leant over and touched my hair, pushing a piece behind my ears. 'Your hair! The things we could do with that! Gosh, I can't wait! You won't know yourself!'

The waitress plonked a pot of tea on our table, with matching jugs of water and milk. I felt embarrassed, because I recognized her suddenly as Olive Truss, who used to go to our Sunday School. I smiled, but she didn't meet my eyes.

'Celia . . . I'm not sure about all this. Can't I just come as I am — I mean, with nicer clothes?'

Celia breathed in deeply and sat back in her chair. She was quiet for a second or two, and then she said, 'You know, James really likes you.'

'James? How on earth can you say that? He's never met me.'

'Ah — but he's seen you.' The table seemed to float away. A lady on the next table was telling her companion that she wouldn't employ Derek again if he came begging. A woman's shout drifted in from the kitchen like an echo: 'Table four!' Hooves clopped loudly outside the shop window and a horse's flank stopped inches from where we were sitting, steaming.

'Where?'

Celia sighed patiently. 'Well, on Saturday for a start.'

'Where, on Saturday?'

'In town, you goof. Just after you left he came out of the cinema and asked who you were.'

I stared at the tea she was pouring out. She had forgotten to put in the milk, but I was too intrigued to point it out. 'What did he say, then?'

'He asked who you were. He said, 'Who was that lovely girl?' – or something like that.'

'So he just saw my back. He might think very differently if he saw my front.'

'No, no, he's seen you before.'

'Where?'

'Oh, Joy! I don't know. He just has, I can't remember. We were driving through the village once and he saw you come out of Griffens.'

'So he knows I'm a seamstress?'

'Yes.'

'And he doesn't mind?'

'Why on earth would he? Milk?'

'Yes, please.'

The 'fancies' arrived: a little two-tiered affair with Peek Freans on the bottom and tiny iced yellow and pink cakes on the top. Normally I would have wanted to try them all, but I had no appetite. Celia ate one after another – very delicately chewing with her lips closed – and made arrangements for me to be picked up on Saturday. I said I would prefer to come to them. So it was agreed: seven thirty at Buckleigh House. I could hardly breathe.

'Do you think I could take one or two of them home for Gracie?'

Celia sighed. 'We'll buy some on the way home.'

I fiddled in my coat pocket for my purse, and awkwardly placed two threepenny bits on the tablecloth, which was all I had. Celia picked them up and grinned. 'That's an awfully big tip – you are a sweetheart!' Then she plonked half a crown on a plate as we left, and ignored Olive Truss who said, 'Thank you, madam' to her back.

22

When I got home, Gracie was sitting by the range, her knitting in her lap. She was looking at her hands in astonishment. It was as if they didn't belong to her at all and she had just happened to notice them, this very moment for the first time, at the end of her arms.

'What is it?' I asked.

'When did this happen?' she said, flexing her fingers. As she did so, the skin puckered into little mountain ranges like the ones on the maps hanging in our classroom. 'Whenever did they get like this? I used to have lovely hands. Everyone said I had lovely hands . . . slender . . . that's what they said . . . Look at Gracie's slender fingers, oh, look how elegant they are on the piano, she should be a pianist.'

I could imagine Gracie with slender white hands. Since I'd seen the photograph, I could see her young and lithe and smiling, ready for anything the excitement of life could throw at her. But the idea that change could happen so quickly, that it could come as a shock to older people, was new to me.

'Pale, they were. Flawless.'

I could see there were tears in her eyes which she tried to blink away. I knelt down and took one of her brown-blotched hands in mine. It had never occurred to me that these changes would matter to her. I loved her just as she was, didn't I? But as the tears spilled over down her cheeks and she could not look at me in her shame of it, I saw that it was the waste of it all that mattered. The slender white hands that had barely had a chance to be held. My throat felt sick with sorrow, but I wasn't certain how much was for Gracie, and how much was for me, because I had always believed I was enough for her. While Gracie cried for her lost youth I was sickened by my own self-pity.

Since my invitation outside The Daffodil I had been plotting ways of going to the party without Gracie needing to know, but Celia turning up like that had forced my hand. Perhaps, after all these years, it was no longer an issue. Or at least, perhaps I could make Gracie see that it wasn't. There would be no need for me to see her old sweetheart, Mr Buckleigh, at all, and she surely wouldn't stop me from going to my first proper party. I sat down opposite her and produced the cakes we had bought.

'Oh, Joy. You needn't have done that, you silly. How much did that lot cost?' My silence told her who had bought them. 'I won't stop you going, you know.' We smiled at each other. 'In fact, I've been thinking about a dress for you. That new silk've come in, and I reckon we've just time to run you up something from the catalogue.'

She brought out the pattern book from beside her chair – a heavy book we usually kept in the shop. The corners of several pages had already been folded down, and they were beautiful dresses: the very latest fashions.

I went to stand behind her chair, bent down and hugged her. I could feel a tear sandwiched between our two cheeks.

'You're going to be the belle of the ball.'

I went to sit at her feet and stroked her hands as she leafed through the pages. 'I thought you'd be dead against it.'

'Me? All I want is for you to be happy, my love. I don't want you stopping at home and wasting your life like I did. You get on out there and find yourself a husband—' I opened my mouth to protest but she put her finger on it – 'then I shall have some grandchildren to entertain me in my dotage!'

'Your dotage!'

We giggled, and I hugged her lap.

'There's only one thing you must promise me, mind.'

'What's that?'

'There's a lad – Celia's brother . . .'

'James?'

'Is that him? Well, don't go messing with him, will you?'

'What d'you mean, messing?'

'Leave well alone. Go for any of the young men you like, but he's no good for you.'

I frowned, and sat back on my heels. 'What do you mean?'

Gracie had that hunted look I'd seen only a few times before, and the last time had been in the dress shop when Celia flounced in. She swallowed, and I saw that her eyes were glistening with tears. 'He's no good, Joy – just stay away from him. Promise me you'll stay away from him.'

There seemed nothing else to do. Nothing would stop me going to the party on Saturday night, and nothing would stop me seeing James Buckleigh. If Gracie was right about him, I was perfectly capable of finding out for myself. And I had begun to enjoy the feeling of Gracie being on my side, plotting to dazzle them all: the country girl in the most sizzling dress of the season.

'I promise.'

She squeezed my hand, then turned the catalogue round for me to see. 'This one would cause a stir: shaped seams under a lightly gathered bust – diamond-shaped bodice; softly pleated skirt; matching clutch bag – I could do that for you – it's just a little fold-over affair . . .'

23

The days until Saturday were like hunger. An empty stomach before a long-awaited meal. Everything around me became a threat to Saturday: opening a tin might chip my nail, walking in the woods might cover me in gnat bites, a sleight of the hand at work might snag the silk and ruin the emerging dress.

At night with my eyes closed for sleep, I would cover every possibility. I practised my entrances and exits, my hellos, my demure smiles, my modest replies to flattery. In my dreams I could flirt, make people laugh, win people over without even trying. And sometimes it would occur to me that I hadn't even seen James, except as a dull smudge in a photograph and as a dark profile in a car. But I had seen his sketches, been in his room, stood in the heart of his chaos, and I had smelt his shoes. Years of fantasy could not be wiped out so easily, and nothing could convince me he was not the man for me.

On Saturday afternoon I bathed by the fire and washed my hair over the sink. Gracie put grips in my damp fringe to give it a wave around my face. At four o'clock I tried on my cream-coloured outfit. At seven o'clock I put it on again and paced the parlour, breathing deeply. Gracie placed a dark green shawl around my shoulders to match my glass beads, the little velvet clutch bag she had made, and the shoes she had dyed for me.

I set off at around ten past seven, calculating that it would be better to be early than late – although, looking back, I cannot imagine why. The evening sun was still warm, and bathing everything in its mellow glow.

When I arrived it was barely twenty past, even though I had trodden slowly up the hill to protect my shoes. I stood at the gates and wondered how I should get in: there was no bell. The car was in front of the house, and I could hear faintly the sound of movement inside: a door shutting or opening, a woman's voice rising and dipping. I took a few paces back and stood by the wall at the side of the gate. Glancing at my little bracelet watch, I was suddenly embarrassed to be early. I didn't want to be found staring through the bars of the gate like some waif. I stood still by the wall, hoping no one I knew would walk past and see me.

Eventually the voices erupted from the house, and began to get louder.

'Oh please, James, please!'

'You're an arch troublemaker! I don't see why I should go out with some grubby little village girl just to please *you*!'

'James, you've *got* to – she'll be here soon—'

'I know what you're up to, Celia – don't think I don't know the little games you play.'

His voice was getting louder, and I realized he was coming to open the gates. I took off my shoes and ran as nimbly as I could down the road, but I could hear the iron clang as he opened the gates. I replaced my shoes and, just in time, started to walk as slowly and elegantly as my emotions would allow back towards the house.

'Hello!' he said, on seeing me. 'You must be . . .'

'Joy.' I couldn't bring myself to smile.

'Joy!' He stood and looked at me for a moment. I hardly

dared to look at him, but swallowed hard, and when I did look, I was distraught to find that he wasn't the ghoul I now wished he was.

'Well . . .' He indicated his own immaculate evening suit. 'You put me to shame.'

I bit my lip. I tried to remember all my well-practised greetings, the casual little laughs, that urbane, confident, popular Joy who had been so ready to meet the world. All I wanted to do was cry. I wanted to cry so badly that I had to hold my lips between my teeth.

'Won't you come in?'

'I . . . I don't really feel like a party. If you don't mind, I think I might . . .'

He came towards me and took my arm. 'Thank heavens for that! I don't feel like a wretched party either . . . Why don't we sneak off somewhere else?'

As he drew me through the gates, I could see that Celia, not realizing I was there, had gone inside. He led me silently to the car and, opening the passenger side, beckoned me in with a wink. I felt so wretched that all power had gone out of me and I did as I was told. And I was terrified of Celia coming out. The only thing worse than sneaking off with someone who thought I was a grubby little village girl, would be to spend an evening with a whole crowd of people who thought I was a grubby little village girl. As soon as we were out of the gates, I would ask him to take me home.

We drove up the road, and continued for a minute or two until he turned down a lane and stopped the car on the crest of the hill. The sun was gathering pink clouds around itself, and we could see way across the western valley.

He sat staring at it for a moment. 'Where would you like to go, then?'

'Home.'

He turned to look at me, and his eyes were the darkest green, his lashes long and black under thick brows. I took in his beauty and dismissed it. I loathed him and I loathed his sister. Everything they stood for made me sick, and I felt these things as a stranglehold around my throat.

'Oh, please don't say that.'

'I want to go home.'

He put his hand up to his forehead and raked his dark hair desperately. 'Heavens! You think I brought you here to . . . you think . . . look, I only wanted to avoid passing Celia's cronies on the road. And it's so nice here. I wasn't trying to . . .' He looked at me so helplessly, I put him out of his misery.

'No, honestly. I really do just want to go home.' I said it in such a bumpkinish way. I didn't care any more.

'Oh hang! You did want to go to the party, didn't you? Look, I can take you if you like. There's bound to be someone there far better than me – someone who can show you a good time.'

I fiddled with my clutch bag. Gracie had stayed up late embroidering the front with gold thread, and it broke my heart. 'Please. I know you don't want to be here with me, but you don't have to make it so obvious.'

He let out a huge sigh, 'Look, I'm sorry. It's Celia – she's such a manipulator – she plays these games with people.'

I stared at the luxurious chrome and green glove compartment. 'I'm beginning to see that now.'

The leather seat was so comfortable, the sunset so glowing – everything was so perfect – I had to stop blinking to prevent anything from spilling over on to my carefully powdered face.

'Come on,' he said, turning on the engine. 'I'm taking you somewhere.'

We went into Cheltenham and left the car at the top of the Promenade. He took me to the Gaumont cinema, but the showing was full. We trouped over to the Coliseum, but that was full too. I felt almost sorry for him, trying to do right by a grubby village girl. But he wouldn't give up. He suggested The Daffodil, which meant a long walk back through town. My shoes were already hurting: some grit had got in them from my shoeless scamper outside his house, and it had remained trapped against my stocking. By the time we came to the Promenade, I couldn't conceal a limp.

'You know, I ought to pick you up and carry you.'

I smiled weakly, and carried on disguising the pain as best I could. We walked on in a crushing silence, each second seeming to underline the failure of the evening.

All of a sudden he put his arm around me and grabbed me behind the knees, sweeping me up into his arms. He marched along the pavement, face fixed, as if nothing untoward had happened, and didn't put me down until we were outside the cinema.

We went in to see King Kong. I didn't tell him I'd seen it before, because I assumed he knew. But oddly, if he was to be believed, it was the first time he'd seen it.

We had missed the supporting film, and arrived just as the lights were dimming after the interval. The attendant showed us to two empty seats between two other couples on the back row. Even this offended me. Did we really look like a couple who wanted a back seat, dressed up to the nines as we were, so that we could slobber over each other in the dark?

I was relieved when the darkness came, though. That first dimness, so imperceptible that you feel you've imagined it, followed by the reassuring extinguishing of light. Now at last I could wallow in my misery without being seen, and I realized that the iron hold on my throat was so tight I was ready to burst. I would have to wait until the end of the film before there was any legitimate opportunity for a sob, so I bided my time, running through the things that had happened, from the insult at the gate to the strange arrival here in his arms. I slipped off my shoes in the dark and remembered doing so outside his house. I wanted to dwell on the insult, to run it over and over again, to be certain of it, to loathe it, to savour it. There could be no mistaking what he had said, and what he had meant by it. He saw me as so vulgar, so scummy, so pitiable, so coarse that he couldn't bear to be matched with me. (So Celia had lied, and that was something else which made me fume, but I would have to deal with that later.) And now he was trying to act the gentleman and overdoing it out of sheer charity. Well, he could keep his charity. I glanced at him once or twice, but he was staring solemnly at the film. I thought he looked at me once or twice, too, but I couldn't be sure. And I didn't care. The couple on my left were beginning to get amorous, and I felt uncomfortable. I could tell the couple on his right were rustling about a bit too. Both of us pretended not to notice. And what did he mean by 'grubby' anyway? I had been wearing a perfectly decent dress and cardigan last week. They had been clean. I wiggled my sore toes and pushed them under the seat. I was sure I didn't smell – did I smell? Lord above. I tried to lean away from him, but came across the couple who were now foraging in each other's clothes. And what did he think he was playing at, picking me up like that? If he thought he could make a laughing stock of me just because I worked in a shop, just because I didn't pour my tea like Celia and say wizard and frightful and go on exeats and stuff my face with buns every day . . . ooh! I had a good mind to stand up and walk out! I was just gearing up for this dramatic action, when there was a distinct little moan from the girl on my left, and James leant over to me and whispered, very close to my ear, 'Would you like to move somewhere else?'

'No, thank you,' I said coldly. 'I'm fine.' So I could hardly get up and walk off now.

Then there was the confusion of the armrest. I don't know at what point I noticed that both our elbows were on it, but as soon as I did all my nerves seemed to be in my elbow, at the exact point where he was touching it. And the light pressure of his arm through his dinner jacket seemed an insolence. But I would not remove my arm – could not, for it was quite comfortable there, and anyway, to remove it would suggest a giving way to him, and I would certainly not be doing that, thank you very much.

Then King Kong swept Fay Wray up in his arms. It gave me the oddest feeling, vastly overdressed for the cinema, our elbows lightly touching, watching a giant beast caressing a woman in his arms and sandwiched between two couples who were half eating each other.

When King Kong was finally killed, I managed to release my tears. I remembered a woman sobbing at this point when I had watched the film last week, and thinking that she was completely unhinged.

As the lights came on James did something that took me by surprise. He reached down and took my foot, then he gently stroked the sole to remove any grit, and placed it in my shoe. I know I should have become indignant at this, but it felt oddly natural. Before I could consider what little game he was playing now, I looked down and caught my breath in horror. There, on my unshod cream stocking was a swathe of darkness all around my toes and across my instep. In the shadows of cinema seats it took me a while to realize it was dark green dye. Almost certainly he would think it was grubbiness! I felt my eyes close. The humiliation was intolerable. Undeterred, he stroked the sole of my left foot and placed it in its dark green shoe. He sat up and considered me with a slightly anxious look. I didn't thank him. I sniffed and stood up, and wrapping my shawl tightly around me, I waited until the girl of the gentle moan had stood up too, her lipstick halfway across her face and most of her petticoat showing, before following her between the seats to the exit.

I said nothing as we made our way back to the car.

'I was sad that the ape died too,' he tried. I noticed he was holding his elbow out for me to take, but I ignored it. 'I felt especially sorry for him when he became a tourist attraction, didn't you?'

'Mmm.'

Nothing more was said at all, apart from 'Mind your dress,' as he closed the car door for me. I hadn't expected him to be quite such a match for my silence. It just proved that he didn't want to be with me either.

As we neared Buckleigh House, he asked, 'Where's home?'

'It's all right. I'll walk.'

'No, I shan't let you walk. Where do you live?'

'I'm all right.'

'At least let me take you to the end of your road.'

I shook my head, and he came to a halt in the road outside his house. I got out straight away, and he followed.

'There's a full moon,' I said, hoping he wouldn't try to walk me home.

'Nearly full.'

I took my shawl off and turned it inside out for luck. There had been enough evil forces tonight, and an old moon was a tricky one.

'You're limping,' he said. He was walking beside me, and showed no signs of going away.

We walked on, saying nothing, down past Mrs Emery's house, and the thick smell of budding lavender, through the tall beech trees towards the churchyard.

'Listen!' he whispered suddenly.

'A dog fox,' I said.

'Yes . . . yes, it is!'

We walked on into the village, my head pounding with things I should say, the indignation I should show, jumbled up with the phrases I'd practised for my fantasy evening. I stopped a few houses away from my own, and sighed.

'Goodnight,' I said.

'Is this where you live?'

'No, down there.'

'Well then, I'll walk you.'

'No.'

But as I turned to go home he followed me. I wheeled round.

'No. Please. Leave me alone.'

'I'm so sorry.' He came to an abrupt halt, and so did I. We looked at each other, and then at the ground. 'I don't think you enjoyed this evening, did you?' I said nothing. 'It was my fault. I'm not very . . . I'm not exactly . . . I'm sorry.'

I remained silent, but I didn't walk away either. I realized he might take this as some sort of expectation on my part of something more, but I was panicking in my head with the words I needed to say.

'You don't say much,' he said at last.

'That would be because I'm just a scummy old country bumpkin, I expect.'

I have to hand it to him, he looked bewildered, and he managed it quite well. But I wasn't going to let him off the hook that easily. 'And just so's you know, I've never been so humiliated in all my life – not by *anyone*. And you can keep your posh car and your big house and your flash fancy dress . . .' I didn't know what to say next and my voice was beginning to falter. 'I've never had such a *crap* evening in all my life – even for a grubby little village girl!' And then the sobs came, and I couldn't hold them back, and I ran full pelt to our front door and let myself in without looking back.

When I was sure he had gone, I took off the dress, slipped on my ordinary shoes and coat and crossed the road to the fountain. Then I opened the gate to the field and headed for the woods.

As soon as I felt the springy woodland floor under my feet I relaxed. When I was a child I thought the branches of trees were arms, and I climbed up now into a small beech, and lay full length on its low outstretched branch. The bark pressed into the flesh at my knees and thighs and ribs and breasts. If I spread my weight carefully it didn't hurt, but pricked my skin gently and made me feel alive. I lay there for hours, trying not to remember. The moon cast thick shadows in the undergrowth. Drifts of wild garlic shone white in its glow. I loved the smell of it. It was the reek of early summer, the promise of things to come.

I lay in the arms of the beech tree until the moon vanished, and the first band of peach gleamed through the dark leaves. Then I went home, printed in bark.

24

'I was twenty-four when I fell in love with Howard Buckleigh,' Gracie said. 'We were coming from opposite directions on Three Cross Lane and our bicycles collided.'

I had been lying on the bed for most of the morning, and now I turned my blotchy face to her.

'He hadn't done much cycling before – he wasn't very good. And he was very young . . . I think he was . . . nineteen . . . yes, nineteen . . .'

She had sat down beside me, but she wasn't looking at me. She was gazing at her knees, and out of the window, and at her knees again. 'He hadn't quite got the hang of the bike, you see.' She smiled at the rug by the bed. 'Told me he had never been in love before he met me, and that he would never be again – not with anyone else.'

'And was he?'

Slowly and carefully, she brushed some imaginary dust from her pinny. 'He married Rosamund Buckleigh.'

I got up on my elbow. 'I know that. He broke his promise, then?'

Gracie raised her eyebrows speculatively at the dressing table. 'I suppose . . . I . . .'

I sat up and reached my hand to hers. 'Did he court you then?

Did he take you home? Were there parties? Oh, Gracie – you never said – why didn't you ever say?'

She let out a long sigh. 'We walked out a good few times. This first time Mum and Dad were pleased as punch – told everyone, they did. And he did take me home – just the once – and I don't think I was approved of. They wanted someone with money, see, so's they wouldn't have to sell off any more land. But Howard, he didn't care tuppence what they thought, he was going to wait till he was twenty-one and marry me anyway.'

'So Celia's mother came along and spoilt it all?'

'No. That was much later. No . . . my father took it into his head that Howard was up to no good. You couldn't go walking out with someone above your station in those days without a proposal in the offing. It looked bad. It looked like he was just after his wicked way and that. 'Specially as he couldn't take me anywhere where we'd see his family or his family's friends, so it all got more and more secret. First his father banned him from seeing me, and my father said that was that, I should stop thinking about him because it wasn't going to happen, and I wasn't getting any younger, and if I waited for him to come of age I'd be an old spinster of twenty-seven, and who'd want me then if old Buckleigh still said no, and I said he couldn't stop us then, and he said he could, just you wait and see, and we did.'

'What . . .?'

'We waited. We met in secret for two and a half years. We used to go for long walks in the hills over towards Sheepscombe. We had picnics down by Damsel's Cross – no one to bother us but a few cows, and the trickling of that lovely stream . . . Oh . . . and in the winter we used to go to a cottage – one that belonged to the Buckleighs years ago but the retainer had died. It was all musty and damp. But we'd light a fire – we didn't mind – we were young . . . we loved each other, see, we couldn't feel the cold!' She chuckled.

116

'It's so romantic – *Gracie!* Go on then . . .'

'I can't. I need a cup of tea, and so do you.'

She wouldn't say another word until we were both by the range with the kettle on, and her with her knitting safely on her lap.

'Well, he turned twenty-one at last, and went to his father for his inheritance, so's he could buy the ring and all. Well, his father says no, you shan't have a penny, not if you're going to marry some trumped-up village girl. So Howard said he would marry me anyway, money or no, and his father said he would cut him out of his will. Well, Howard, he loved that house, you know. He loved all the land around as well—'

'So he gave in?'

'No. No. He said to me, Gracie my darling, I shall have to go and earn some money of my own. And off he went to Africa for two years. He asked me to go with him, but I said I couldn't leave Mother and Father, and how could I? I was all they had, and they didn't know I was still seeing him, and what would I do in Africa? So he went, and promised he'd be back.'

'And he came back with her?'

'No. No, he came back six years later. Only it seemed to me at the time he never came back. After two years I lost all hope. But then, see, it was the Great War, and I heard much later he'd joined up, and then I heard nothing, till I got some letters from Africa so old they could be misleading, and one long letter from the Dardanelles saying he knew I may not get the letter but congratulations anyway. Well, I just thought someone's told him I'm married so I wrote to him, but I never heard another thing, and I just thought he's dead, I thought, he's died like all the rest of them, sent headlong into it, a number chalked up and rubbed out. I was sure of it. Until the end of the war, when he was twenty-seven and I was thirty-three and his father was dead. I heard he was up there, at the house, a broken man after the war. And I heard he was engaged to Rosamund Longly-Howes, some posh girl his mother had brought down from London with a nice fortune. He'd been home two months and no one told me.'

She came to the end of a row and swapped needles. I sat thoughtfully for a moment, watching the teapot and waiting for it to brew. 'What did he think when he saw you after?'

'He keeps himself to himself. I only saw him properly the once. I was outside the post office and he was walking past with his dog – he had a big dog then, not that little yappy one. And he just stopped, and he stared at me as if he'd seen a ghost. And I said hello, and he said Gracie, Gracie, where are you living now, and I told him, and he touched my arm and then a car-horn went and it was his wife further down the street, and he said he was sorry, and I often wonder, sorry for what?'

'Well! That's obvious, isn't it?'

'Is it? Perhaps he was just sorry he had to dash.'

'Oh, Gracie!' The tea was stewed. 'I'm sorry . . . oh, Gracie!' She poured the tea.

'And there was the couple of times he came round here.'

'It *was* him, then!'

We sat quietly some time after that, Gracie's needles clicking, waiting for the kettle to rumble again. Digger, the cat, who had been listening from the rug, came and sat on my lap.

'Howard the Coward, then,' I said at last.

She slipped a stitch over and knitted two together. 'No one who fought in that war for four years was a coward.'

'No . . . A coward in love, then.'

She finished counting the stitches on her row, and raised her eyebrows as if to say 'Maybe.'

'His mother had been told I was already married.'

'Who by?'

She didn't look up. 'My father.'

118

Then she put her knitting down and looked up at the empty space on the mantel where the shepherdess had once stood. 'I only heard when you were eleven, the second time he came round.'

25

You might say that there were no secrets in Woodside. Everyone knew the tiniest details of each other's lives – stumbling over them rather than digging them out. In our close-packed village life it was hard not to. And the secrets that remained were colossal ones, life-changing, awful secrets so deeply buried by necessity. To come across one of these was a dangerous event.

My failed date with James Buckleigh could not qualify as a major secret, and by the following morning the entire Mustoe family were sympathizing. Robert showed a particular concern, so much so that he asked me if I should like to go with him to the pictures at the weekend. I wasn't used to being asked out, so I didn't know how to say no. I said it was kind of him, and then felt cornered, because I knew by the way he was looking at my breasts it was not kind of him at all, but I wanted to think it was.

There then followed a series of dates, dotted throughout the autumn, at times when my resolve was weak and crumpled by his determination. I think other girls in the village were quite envious, for he had grown into a very handsome young man, and I was even quite proud to be seen out with him, but I couldn't help a desire to repel him any time he came too close. I wondered if I was incapable of loving a man, if something had made me like this. I tried to make myself dream of being taken by Robert, of being made love to somewhere dark and wild in the hills, but I always had to transform him into someone who wasn't quite Robert for me to feel the lust that was beginning to overwhelm my private thoughts from time to time.

I let him kiss me because I didn't know how to stop him without making him feel ridiculous. And when he came close his smell was strong and sweet but so utterly pitiless I felt stifled by it. It was perfume for someone but not for me. As he approached I would try to breathe in and appreciate its deep musty undertones of pine from the wood yard, but by the time his arms went around me, my breathing would be scuppered and I would go under like the Titanic, submerged in the ruthlessness of his scent.

One day, as I was trying to fend him off for good, he said something interesting. We were sitting on a bench outside the pub; he was sipping a pint and I had a lemonade. He said he bet James wasn't as good a kisser as he was, and I said James hadn't kissed me. Fuelled by this news, he went on to insult both James and Celia, and called them both bastards.

'That's a bit strong,' I said.

'But they are – didn't you know?'

'What?'

'Bastards. Or at least, not exactly, but neither of 'em's legal – Howard Buckleigh didn't father either of 'em.'

He could see I was interested, so he went on, perhaps further than he intended, no doubt hoping the information would get him inside my petticoat. 'Ever wondered about yourself, then?'

I frowned. 'I'm not illegitimate.'

He gave the slightest of smiles. 'Who *are* your parents, then?'

With complete ease, I reeled off the story Gracie had concocted on our behalf, about being her second cousin's orphaned child.

That little smile again. I hated him for it. I felt I was teetering on the edge of something, and held on to the bench for support.

'But you know Gracie had a long affair with Howard Buckleigh. His wife goes off and has affairs with other men. Saddled with a wife he doesn't love; he still loves Gracie. What would *you* do?'

'What d'you mean?'

'Well . . .' He put his hand over mine on my knee. 'Isn't it obvious? I reckon you're the rightful heir to the Buckleigh estate, old girl.'

I pulled my hand away and stood up. 'That's wicked! It's rubbish. Who else thinks this? Who else've you told this load of tripe to?'

I marched off home on my own, with him following for a bit, but I was saved by Mr Bearpark walking down the road with his bike, and wanting to tell me about its new tyres. Robert scratched his head and went back to the pub for another pint.

I can't say I didn't consider what he'd said. I started thinking back to when I'd first arrived, and I remembered Howard, the gentleman who'd come to see Gracie, and seemed to think I was his to look after. But then I thought back further, beyond Nipper and beyond the woods, and the things I saw were so alien to either Gracie's home or the Buckleigh home, that I was certain it could not be true. And as soon as these images came to me I dropped them, and they pinged away from me as if on elastic, and away from me was where I wanted them to stay.

I grew to be so resilient to Robert's approaches that, short of committing a crime, he was forced to give up. Throughout

1938 and 1939 I saw little of him in a romantic sense, and I heard that he'd gone all the way with Spit and although Spit denied it, they were pretty much an item. I still saw him, of course, because he lived next door, and whenever he looked at me his face seemed to say that, one way or another, he would have me one day.

26

By the time war broke out I was nineteen and ready for a change. My dogged desire for stasis underwent a little tweak, and then another. At the pictures every week we saw girls being sung to, driven in open-topped cars, or pushed up against trees and kissed. They sipped wine, wore jewellery, screamed and cried, and slapped men's faces. They were worldly, confident and romantic, and wonderful things happened to them. It all seemed to be part of that glorious, terrifying and breathtaking thing that looms when you are young: the future. And Mo and I couldn't help but want a taste of it.

We both signed up for the WAAF, did our six weeks' training, and were stationed at a nearby airbase. I was immediately homesick for Gracie, but the presence of Mo and the excitement of the noise of the planes, the young men in their bomber jackets, the unknown outcome of each day, acted like a magnet to draw me in. I told myself I could go at any time, go home to Gracie and resume work on the sewing machine, and that helped me to endure the freezing huts we had to live in like prisoners of war, and the food which was tasteless and always cold.

The hardest thing of all was the sleeping arrangements. Not only was there no warm mass to cup me in her lap, but there were two rows of iron-framed camp beds: cold, institutional, they made me want to run away on my first day.

But on Saturday nights we had 'socials', and these made it clear we weren't imprisoned. For soon Mo and I and the rest of the girls could hardly move for flirtatious men. We sipped beer, sometimes, like the women in the movies (although not wine), we danced (although not in sequins), and we drove (only we were at the wheel, and they were trucks). It was a huge transformation from the country shop and girls of Woodside, and what we put up with in regulations and hardships was more than made up for in the long-awaited spreading of our wings.

In 1939 we were pretty much all home for Christmas. The usual Boxing Day hunt took place, and lots of us gathered outside the pub for the mummers' play. Mr Mustoe played St George, and Mr Rollins played the dragon, like every year since I could remember. Robert had taken to playing a concertina which his father had forsaken a week after purchasing it, and even George (who was thirteen by now) had a small part. Along with several other villagers they were blackened up with boot polish and wore clothes covered in tiny tags of coloured cloth.

Mo and I had travelled down together, and were a little disappointed to see so many people in full uniform: only our hats, navy knickers and skirts had arrived and the skirts had had to be sent back because of poor stitching. When we got to the pub in Woodside we weren't able to show off our new status in the world, because we were in mufti except for our hats.

Robert spotted us immediately. He came over and I knew he was going to kiss us both and leave a black smudge on our cheeks. 'S'good luck!' he said as he did just that, and he said as much every year. 'You needn't think I'm going to salute you, just 'cause you're wearing them caps.'

I laughed, and Mo nudged me and nodded towards a posse of hunters. There, in full RAF officer uniform, was James Buckleigh; on his arm was a young woman with a fur collar. I felt a sharp heat in my face and glanced away, back at Robert, who had followed my eyes.

'Bloody show-off. You wait till I join up after Christmas. You won't see me parading around in my uniform on leave. 'S if he hasn't got anything else to wear . . .' He was talking loudly, and I felt uncomfortable. I knew you had to wear uniform on leave. I didn't care who James Buckleigh was with, but I certainly didn't want him to think he was the object of our conversation. 'I'll get you two soldiers a drink then, shall I?' said Robert, and disappeared into the pub doorway. I was relieved he had gone, but it was too late. James had spotted us. He left his group and came over.

'Joy, isn't it?'

'Yes . . . hello.'

He smiled. He wafted over me: woodsmoke and woollen serge and leather, and a hint of that smell from his enchanted room all those years ago. 'Did you have a good Christmas?'

'Yes . . . thank you.' There was an awkward silence.

'Not hunting yourself, then?' I asked.

'No. I don't hunt.'

I couldn't look him in the eye, but I was conscious he was looking at me.

'And this must be . . .' He was smiling at Mo, and she was smiling back.

'Oh! Mo – this is my friend Mo,' and then (because I was flustered and angry and showing off to Mo) I added, 'another grubby little village girl.'

Mo's face crumpled, and she turned such a frown on me I instantly wished the phrase unsaid. But just as I was wondering how to redress things and catching a glimpse of James Buckleigh's disconcerted eyes, Robert came up with two steaming mugs of punch.

'There you go – ooh! I see you're being chatted up by the lord of the manor – or should I say, the "pretender"?' He was loud, he was awful, he had been drinking since the pub opened.

James Buckleigh looked aghast. 'What do you mean?'

Robert was a loose cannon. 'You know what I mean.' He tapped the side of his nose. 'I know there's something dodgy about your parentage.'

I saw James Buckleigh's cheeks harden as he clenched his jaw. He opened his nostrils like an animal smelling danger. His eyes narrowed, he turned his head very, very slowly, but just a fraction, to face Robert full on.

'I ought to knock your block off, you bastard!'

'Bastard, eh? I think we know who the bastard is around here, don't we? What's the matter? *Ashamed* of your real father, are you?'

I could feel Buckleigh's anger come off him like a heat. He gave me a quick punishing glance and I shuddered. He spoke slowly.

'I am very, very proud of my father.'

People from the hunting crowd looked over, and the young fur-collared woman came over and held on to his arm. 'Come on, James, you don't need to get involved with this lot.'

'This lot?' said Robert, heading for he didn't know where. 'I'll 'ave you know I'll be fighting for you, lady, after Christmas, I'll be—'

'Well, you'll have to salute James, then. He's an officer, you know. Or perhaps you hadn't noticed.' She brought with her a sickly cloud of sweet violet. 'You'll jolly well have to salute him then.'

As she steered Buckleigh away, he turned and said, through gritted teeth, 'I'll look forward to it.' Then he caught my eye, and scowled. 'And your face is grubby.'

I couldn't breathe. It felt as though all the oxygen in all the world had been turned off. There was a rush in my head and my ears started to pound. All the noises started to swim together. Robert was very close saying something about fuckers with beery breath and I pushed him away. Mo was saying to me, 'Well . . . you asked for that one!' in a false cheery voice. Some music started up. I drank my hot drink hurriedly and scurried home.

It was quite some time later, when I undressed for bed, that I saw myself in the dressing-table mirror. Right along my left cheek was a dark black smudge of boot polish.

27

The following day I rose early and rinsed some clothes in the copper, for I was leaving in the afternoon on the four o'clock train. There was a ferocious wind which would dry them quickly, and if I boiled my rags there would be plenty of time to dry them over the range. All the colour seemed to have drained from Woodside and I felt numb. When I pegged things out I saw what a state the back garden had grown into, and promised Gracie I would sort it out before I went back.

'Don't waste time on that, sweetheart – I'd rather spend time with you.'

'I'll only be a moment!'

'But it's so precious this time.'

'I'll be five minutes.'

'You'll get filthy – spoil your nice shoes an' all.'

I stuck on some old hobnail boots of her father's and his old coat from under the stairs, and I clumped out the back to sort things out.

The sheep on the hillside were ragged and grey. Heads down against the wind, round-bellied and slow-moving, they dreamed of being penned in for lambing in the months ahead.

I breathed smoke. My bare legs were bloodless with cold. The leaves we hadn't raked up in the autumn had formed a brown mulch between the vegetable patches, and most of the cabbages had been eaten to shreds. I squelched along the rows, collecting dead vegetables and throwing them on the compost heap. Some had great gooey brown roots that slopped against my clothes and legs. The wind flattened my hair on to my face. I thought about the day before and replayed the scene outside the pub in as many different ways as I could. But even if Robert hadn't kissed me, even if no rude words had been exchanged, even if I hadn't been anywhere near the incident, even then, even then James Buckleigh would still have been with that fur woman. Not that I cared in the slightest, except that it completely denied the slim hope I had entertained that he might just be different from that whole blinkered, self-absorbed, self-perpetuating (I threw cabbages with each adjective, as if they were rolling heads) set of posh, selfish, patronizing . . . not that it was a hope even – he had claimed to be different. And if he hadn't pretended to be different I would've gone to the party that time and I would've seen what they were all like and I would've forgotten him completely instead of having to remember being carried through the streets on a summer's night with no words spoken and his wretched, wretched, wretched –

'Joy! Joy! Someone to see you . . .'

Gracie's face at the back door spelt alarm. I clumped inside, wiped my hobnails on the mat, and went into the parlour, my skirt full of root vegetables and a sulphurous-smelling cabbage and exposing my cold pink legs to the thighs, my hair over my eyes and sticking out like a ragdoll, my fingernails clotted with mud. I don't know why I was surprised it was him: I was dressed for the part.

'Hello,' said James Buckleigh, with a slight smile. 'I apologize for the intrusion . . .' He held out his hand, and I let the vegetables down clumsily and held out a cold earthy hand. To his credit, he took it. 'I'm so sorry, I . . . I wanted to see Robert, actually. I have to see him urgently. Only I didn't know where he lived.'

'Robert? He's next door. I don't know if he'll want to see you, though.'

'I know. That's why I've brought Bee – Beatrice. She's in the car. To show him I'm not on an aggressive mission. You see—'

Gracie, who had been biting her nails, suddenly piped up: 'Oooh! You're not leaving your young lady up in the car, are you? Bring her in for goodness' sake – it's freezing out there.' And before either of us could say anything she was out of the front door cajoling the unwilling fur lady into our parlour.

'Come and warm yourself by the fire,' she was saying, and Beatrice took in our parlour with a strange look on her face.

'Isn't it . . . sweet!' she exclaimed. Then she looked around like a child who has seen snow for the first time at the exact moment that a dog relieves himself on it. Her eyes lifted up to the bar above the range, and my five muslin rags hanging over it. Despite boiling they still had faint menstrual stains on them. Seeing her look of repugnance I hurled myself at them and pulled them down, wiping my grimy hands on them.

'For gardening!' I panted. 'Thank heavens for my gardening rags!' Although I was angry because I would have no time to wash and dry them again before I left, I was also strangely relieved because it seemed there could be no worse depths to my humiliation, and it must at last be over. Perhaps, like Mr Mustoe with the rabbit, she would now fetch a large stone and club me over the head with it. I was unsavable.

'Would you like me to take you round to Robert?' I asked.

'I was hoping you might.'

I clumped past them both in my hobnails, pulled Granddad Burrows' coat more tightly around me, and stepped out of our front door into the chill wind.

Mr Mustoe was squawking away at the battered old cello he'd procured for Christmas. George and Eileen, their youngest, were playing marbles in front of the fire. Mrs Mustoe and Tilly were in the back kitchen cooking, Mo was ironing her blouse for the journey, and Robert, hungover, was reading a *Dandy*. They barely looked up when I went in, except Robert who admired the boots. Then there was pandemonium as they spotted the visitors behind me. The girls rushed about trying to tidy things (a vain hope in the Mustoe house), the children gaped, Robert sprang to his feet and Mr Mustoe practically saluted, standing proudly next to his instrument.

'I'm so sorry to intrude,' said James Buckleigh again, 'but I wanted to apologize for my behaviour yesterday—'

'Oh, that's no bother!' blurted Robert, entirely forgetting he had started it.

'—and I wondered if I might have a word with you – and perhaps Joy . . . in private, perhaps?'

Robert automatically led the way to the only other room in the house – the back kitchen – and he, James and I found ourselves alone and surrounded by steaming vegetables and an overpowering smell of onion and carbolic soap.

'The thing is . . . what you said yesterday . . . doesn't concern me in the slightest. It's just that Celia . . . well, Celia would be devastated if she thought people were talking like that. I wouldn't bother to mention it, it's just that she's not at all well at the moment, and this could just be the last straw.'

Robert nodded as if he were old mates with James Buckleigh, but I was shocked. 'Celia? What's wrong? I didn't know.'

'Well, it's confidential. She's . . . depressed. She's being treated for it. I trust that stays between us?'

'Of course.' I looked at Robert.

'Of course!' he said.

I had barely seen Celia since that fateful date. I knew I had avoided her but I assumed she had been avoiding me too.

'I wish I had time to visit her.'

'Perhaps next time you're home – she'd like that.'

And those few little words ('she'd like that') were a stay of execution. I could feel my cheeks boiling along with the carrots after the cold garden.

He looked at Robert. 'And you won't repeat what you said yesterday – to anyone?'

' 'Course not!' 'Course not! I was drunk as a lord.' He put his hand to his head. 'I shan't be doing that again in a hurry.'

'Thank you.'

James held out his hand to Robert, and shook it earnestly. Then he turned to me and held out his hand. I put my palm to his and felt his skin against mine. I could hardly believe he'd seized me up in his arms once, and I felt that all my clothes had dropped away, one by one, and that his had too, and that we were both naked as the day we were born, standing there, skin to skin. Then Robert slapped his arm around my shoulder and pulled me towards him.

'We won't breathe a word, will we, Joy? You can count on us!'

It was torture.

James simply nodded and made his way back to the parlour, leaving us standing there like a married couple. I wriggled free and followed him, intending to find out more about Celia, only to see that Beatrice had removed her gloves to warm her hands by the fire, and revealed in the process a ring as big as a threepenny bit. The Mustoe women were in thrall.

'Oooh!'

'Is it a diamond?'

'Oooh! Look at that!'

'Oooh!'

Beatrice tried to look imperious, but she couldn't help lapping it up. 'It's a twenty-two carat diamond set with emeralds.'

'When's the wedding?'

'July – with any luck the war will be over by then.'

'Where will it be, then?'

'In my local church – near Cirencester.'

'What's the dress like?'

'Well, it's all frightfully vague at the moment. But it'll be white shot silk, with a princess waist and gathered seams and a ten-yard veil of silk chiffon.'

'Oooh!'

'Lovely!'

'Oooh!'

Mrs Mustoe, Mo and Tilly didn't even stop their fawning when they saw me.

Then something even more dreadful happened.

James suddenly put out his hand and grabbed me by the elbow, pulling me back quite roughly. Then he moved in towards the fire, placing himself between me and Beatrice. Everyone saw it, everyone was aghast, and within a split second everyone decided to pretend it hadn't happened.

I was breathless with shock, and with the effort of trying not to show it. I could make no sense of it at all. It was as if he had tried to stop me getting close to Beatrice – as if I had been making my way towards her to punch her lights out. The enforced cheeriness of the others clawed at my heart. My pride, like the rabbit, was not worth saving. Beatrice turned her face to look at me and, at last, with a spectacular thlunk, the slab came down on my miserable skull.

28

After another period of training I became a Mechanized Transport Driver. The rest of my uniform turned up at last: a lovely barathea top – much smoother than the ATS one – with the albatross badge, grey-blue lisle stockings, pink suspenders (to go with the navy knickers), cotton bra, navy fabric shoulder bag and black shoes. Because I was in MT I also got a greatcoat, which was lucky, because that winter was freezing, and lots of the other trades didn't get them. I learned to drive trucks and small lorries. I transported crews to and from airfields, I chauffeured officers, I serviced vehicles and mended faults. Sometimes I would catch myself in a dark window and see a very competent woman carrying a spanner, and I was surprised to find that I admired her. She seemed vital and assured, and I would think of her when I opened a car door for an officer, changed gears proficiently or leaned a casual elbow on a wound-down window.

The girls who spoke like Celia baffled me. They thought nothing of undressing in front of everyone (no doubt because they had done so at boarding school) and didn't care how much was showing. The rest of us, the likes of Dot, Reeny, Betty and me, got used to this communal undressing eventually, but we remained modest in the where and when of it all. It wasn't that we were reluctant about our bodies and they were confident. It wasn't that at all. It was as if they *had* no bodies. As if they weren't remotely aware of their sexuality. They stomped about with bare buttocks, jiggling breasts, and the shock of their dark, secret triangles, as if there were no femininity attached to them. And the way they dragged on their stockings, joshing and strutting and speaking like newscasters, it was as if they had had the woman bred out of them. One of them, Gwendolen, said I was ashamed of my body. But I wasn't. I was *aware* of my body, and proud of it. I didn't want to be like them. But they were loud and compelling, and it continued to perplex me that I may have got it all wrong.

Still, I was no longer a girl with a question mark over my head, a waif who had walked out of a wood, a young woman dependent on a village spinster. I thought I knew who I was. I had friends who told me I was fun – Dot, Reeny and Betty – and dances to go to and a sense of belonging. And I had a nickname, 'Haps', which was short for happy, because I was and because I was called Joy. I felt more alive than I had ever done, and more than ever I felt I had a right to be alive. Even so, this new independence couldn't help recalling that old, shadowy self, wandering alone in the woods, and the coldness and severity of the camp brought on nightmares which skirted around other memories I had hoped were left behind.

I remembered nothing of my earliest years, and I remembered everything. I had successfully blocked it all out, and I was happy. I even had a nickname which said I was. You can see something, or you can choose not to see it. But I didn't realize then that, even if you squeeze your eyes tight shut for ever, it is still there.

For the time being, it was more immediate memories which concerned me. I still thought of James, and although I had never worked out his odd behaviour – or forgiven him for my humiliation – and although I had plenty of suitors to occupy myself with, it was always his face I conjured up in vulnerable moments of longing, when lights went out at ten thirty and all the daily events had been ruminated over and put aside. I would recall the labyrinthine smell of him, weaving from tart to sweet into balm and musk. I would see that solemn set to his jaw as he carried me through the streets, see his long hands on the steering wheel of the car as we watched the sun set, his eyes on me as he took my hand in the Mustoes' kitchen.

I remembered Celia, too. And although I wanted to go nowhere near Buckleigh House again, I resolved to check on her next time I was on leave. When I did, however, Mrs Bubb told me she had gone to Cirencester to stay with friends for a few months.

I had made my way up past the church. A stink of fox in the trees, and the dangerous Mrs Emery's. How tame Mrs Emery's house seemed now. In comparison, even the way Buckleigh House stood sideways to the road seemed tricky. It was as though it were indifferent, or turning away coyly, or sulking, or smirking at your expense. Anything but turn and face you. Even the house seemed to be playing games.

Just standing in the porch I felt entangled in the emotional chaos that house seemed to harbour. I was glad there was no sign of James or anyone else, and there was no sound except for Mr Rollins' mower and a lone sparrow twittering from the eaves. When I asked how Celia was Mrs Bubb said she was 'making progress'. Perhaps I should have been more concerned, but I felt I could do no more. I crunched my way back down the gravel path as if I were treading on hot coals, relieved to hear the familiar squeal of the iron gate as I shut it behind me.

29

Strands of pink on the eastern horizon were growing paler and brighter. I sat at the steering wheel of my truck, gauging the chill air with my breath as I waited at the barracks for my crew members to emerge. They piled in, nervous and cheerful, heads full of dreams.

'Morning, Haps!' said one of them, whose name was Ken. 'How are we fixed today, then?'

I told them my predictions for the day, which were almost always accurate: 'It's gonna be a corker.'

'You real, lovely Haps? Or am I still dreaming you?'

They always teased me, and I always let them. There had been one pain-in-the-neck who rattled me a bit, called Roy. He always tried to make me promise a dance or a kiss at the weekend as lewdly as possible, and then he would say things like, 'You couldn't deny a condemned man, could you, Haps?' And it broke my heart not to hear him now, because his Hurricane had gone down the week before.

It would be in the months to come – in the July and August of 1940 – that I would begin to feel I was driving them all to their death. But on this particular morning at the end of May there seemed little to panic about. The weather was set to warm up, the pilots were joking about the food and the bombers and

British tactics. We bumped along the Gloucestershire lanes, which had just burst into an incongruous summer. The trees formed great canopies of fragrant green and the sheep-speckled hills, rolling like soft green waves, seemed a gentle balm before the fear. I could always sense it in the back of the truck when we reached the airfield. There would be a silence as we turned off the lane, a terrified and provisional goodbye to the charms of nature.

I set them all down at the dispersal huts and was about to drive away, when an eerie noise came from nowhere.

Up ahead, a thunder gathered with an enormous black shape heading towards us. Looking up, I could see it was a stray Hurricane with thick black smoke trailing from the tail. It was trying to land on our airstrip, but it was too close already.

'What the . . .!'

Suddenly it dropped, hit the airstrip and burst into flames. It was a dual-control training plane, for two men wriggled out of their harnesses and fell on to the tarmac. The first disappeared behind the fuselage, shouting to the second. The other, having tumbled out, began to stagger around the ground near the front of the plane, clutching his chest.

'Jesus Christ!' said one of my crew. 'There'll be some fuel in there. She's gonna go!'

I started running. I could see the man still staggering by the front of the wreck and I ran towards him, the concrete pounding up through my rubber soles, the cries behind telling me to stop, to look out, for God's sake, for Christ's sake, to bloody well stop.

I reached out for him and pulled him towards me by his arm. He seemed to pull away, to try and crouch down in protest. 'My pilot!' he wailed. 'My trainee!'

'It's going to blow!' I shrieked, and yanked at him as hard as I could, but he resisted again. It was like a tug of war. I looked about for the other man, but I couldn't see him. 'Come on!' I screamed, and his obstinate feet suddenly started to walk.

We were halfway back to the truck when the plane went up. They let me drive him to the hospital myself, with medical help in the back.

30

As soon as I had my next time off I went to the little field hospital where I had taken the injured pilot. The hospital was merely a country house that had been requisitioned. There were steps up to an ivy-covered gothic porch; a patient was being pushed around the grounds, and in the early June sunshine the hospital looked a pleasant place to be.

Inside, the smell of polish and the echoing noises of efficiency made me feel queasy. I was told he was 'Flight Sergeant Bird' and directed to a ward upstairs.

It was a curious room, with thick cornicing and a wide ceiling rose, a vast intricately carved fireplace and one or two tall plants redolent of grand hotels. I looked at the two rows of beds. Nearly every head turned to face me, and those that didn't turned their eyes on me. I felt I had walked into a prison or a zoo, only instead of bars there were iron beds holding them down. And then in other ways it could have been someone's living room – clearly had been until recently – with an exclusive, quiet parlour game going on, which I had burst in upon unawares. I wanted to turn and run. A nurse padding around on the creaky floorboards was the only noise, and I realized that my every step upon the stair had heralded my arrival.

The nurse approached me, and I said who I wanted to see. Wordlessly, with a swift smile, she guided me down to the last bed.

He followed me with his eyes, but his head remained stiffly directed in front of him. His chest was heavily bandaged, and he wore a neck brace.

'Hello,' I tried.

He raised one hand slightly. I sat down tentatively on the bed.

'Bit of a close shave you had there,' I smiled.

He propelled some breath sharply through his nose, which could have been a laugh or a sneer.

'My name's Joy – but you can call me Haps, if you like . . .'

I was determinedly cheerful, but there was no response. 'What's yours?'

When there was still no reply, the man in the next bed, who was leaning on his elbow looking at me, said, 'He's a bit depressed, love. Won't get much sense out of him.'

I smiled. Then, as if in defiance of his neighbour, Flight Sergeant Bird spoke: 'Philip. Philip Bird.' Then he sighed deeply.

I repeated it gently. Then I folded my lips together, not knowing what else to say. I wondered if he remembered who I was.

'Do you remember me? I was the mad idiot who pulled you away from the plane.'

The man in the next bed got himself very comfortable now, as if waiting to hear the rest of the story. It felt suddenly very self-congratulatory of me to spell out my role in his rescue, and I shut up. In any case, Philip Bird did not seem in the slightest bit happy to have been rescued, and, after all the heroism I'd enjoyed amongst the men at the airbase, I now began to feel quite disconcerted and deflated.

'Well, it's good to see you in one piece, Philip. I hope you make a speedy recovery.'

I stood up to go, and he suddenly grasped my wrist. He held it very, very tightly, belying the weakness he seemed to present. I swallowed hard. Then he pulled hard at my wrist and drew me towards him, hissing in my ear: 'I'm a coward, you know!'

I shook my head furiously, and sat down again. 'No . . . no, you can't say that!' I spoke in a whisper too, so that the man on the next bed turned over and started reading a newspaper with his back to us. 'No one flying a Hurricane can be called a coward.'

'I left . . . He's dead, isn't he?'

I wasn't sure what to say, so I said, 'I'll find out for you.'

Then he asked me where I was stationed, how he could find me, where I lived. I assured him I would come and visit again, although privately I wasn't sure if the trainee pilot had escaped unharmed.

'So you're from around here? Woodside . . . where is that, then?'

In my relief to talk about something easy I started gabbling on. I told him all about Woodside, how I lived with Gracie near a bubbling spring, and how the sheep wandered into the streets sometimes, and how no one from Woodside thought there was anywhere else better on earth – although, now that the war had come, lots of them had been forced to find out.

By the time I left, his spirits seemed to have lifted. The nurse even made a point of asking me if I would kindly come again, as I had done him a 'power of good'. Nonetheless I was pleased to go, and skipped down the steps into the sunshine, planning to have some afternoon tea in the nearby village with Dot and Reeny.

31

The following day when I drove the men back to their barracks, there was a sombre mood amongst them. I didn't ask why, but I think there had been some near misses, and some bad news from another airfield.

When dawn came I made myself some sweet tea but couldn't drink it, and I went to sit in the truck until the first yawns of the squadron.

Before the others emerged, Ken got into the passenger seat. He looked as if he were trying to broach something important. I felt uneasy, because he was usually so chirpy, and now that he had stopped being chirpy, I became fully aware that we were a man and a woman sitting alone in a truck, young, lusty and full of longing.

'I was wondering if I could ask you a bit of a favour . . .'

'Try me.'

'I need some petrol urgently.'

'Oh?'

'Well . . . I've got some leave tomorrow and I need it for a honeymoon.'

'Honeymoon?'

He raised his eyebrows slightly, as if to study the effect this had on me.

'Yep. Sister's getting married in Southampton. Only the honeymoon's in Dorset. His father's got a car they can borrow. Just need the petrol, that's all.'

I sighed and got down from the truck, fetching my spare can from the back. 'She'd better be worth it.'

He got out of the truck too, and came to stand next to me. He took the can, and for a moment we were startlingly close. 'You know I'd do anything for you, Haps.' He was smiling now, and I knew he was teasing, back in chirpy mode again. Although something in his eyes, and the way he lingered over the petrol can, suggested he might have been serious. I felt very peculiar, because it made me wonder if Ken was the sort of man who, in other circumstances, could make me very happy. I suddenly wanted him for myself and – just for that brief moment – I knew that was possible.

'You were pretty impressive the other day, you know,' he said.

'So I'm told.'

'A man could feel safe with a girl like you.' He was smiling again now and I felt almost relieved.

'Safe?'

'Well . . .' he smirked, 'not *that* safe!'

The moment was over. He promised he'd return the can the day after next, and he owed me one. This debt he would repay in the form of a dance. I feigned immense gratitude, and he took the can into his barracks.

The truck filled up quickly. Ken tumbled back out of his barracks and into the truck, perching himself behind me. He said I smelt of fresh apples and looked like a peach. He asked – as he always did – if I would save every dance for him on Friday. There was always an RAF dance somewhere on a Friday. I surprised him by saying I would. I surprised myself. And once again an urgent desire for him took me by surprise. Now the sun was gleaming through each blade of grass, and a dew was steaming gently off gateposts and hedgerows. The sky was a picture book blue, and wrens and tits were twittering prettily in every direction. As we drove through the lanes, the cows – who always looked as if they'd never seen us before – gave little honking noises on cue, the fat lambs we had followed from birth were so chunky they were hardly distinguishable from the heavy sheep who gave deep brays now and then to keep them in order. The hedgerows were bursting with blue and pink and yellow and white. It was warming up. It would be hot. It was a day for love.

'See you Friday, then,' he said as he got down, holding my eyes while the others whistled.

'Okey-doke!'

He raised his eyebrows in astonishment, and went off humming 'Walking my baby back home'.

I leant by the truck for a while, watching them go and feeling the sun warm me. Love suddenly seemed easy. It was just a case of letting go. And at that moment, following Ken's happy rhythm as he foxtrotted into the dispersal hut, humming and smiling at me, I loved him.

32

I took a couple of days' leave as well. Although Woodside was only five miles away, I had to go by bus.

Gracie was overjoyed to see me. I felt like a film star when I opened the door. She had made a caved-in cake with 'Welcome Home Jog' in wobbly piped icing, and Mrs Mustoe popped round with a perfect fruit pie. Gracie and I chatted for hours, sitting in the garden on some dining chairs, lapping up the sun. Nothing had changed. I thought it would all be different, now that I had done so many unusual things, been to so many places, tricked death, saved lives. But to Gracie I was still her little Joy, and try as I might, I could not help but revert to her little Joy as soon as we were together. It was deeply frustrating, but I'd heard the other girls talk about it too. The changes I'd made were for me, not for her. She would always see me as the small girl who walked out of the woods, and nothing – not wars nor bravery nor maturity nor death – could change that.

I had a delicious lie-in the following morning, and was woken by Gracie sitting on my bed and saying there was the oddest man slumped by the fountain.

'You ought to come and see, Joy. There's something funny about him.'

I stretched, and seeing that it was gone nine thirty I followed her heavily into the front bedroom, where she held back the curtain for me to look out. There, on the opposite side of the road a few yards down, was our village spring. Like a sheet of ribbed glass it gushed from the side of the bank and bubbled into a stone enclosure. Sitting on the grass next to it, his arm draped over the stone edging, was a young man. His head lolled on his chest, and he was wearing a coat that was too small for him.

'He's wearing a woman's coat!' I said. 'And—'

'Oooh! I don't like the sound of that at all!'

'—pyjamas! I know who he is! It's the man I pulled away from the plane. I was going to visit him tomorrow. What on earth . . .?'

I ran down the stairs, then I ran back up and pulled on some clothes. I asked Gracie to come too, and between us we managed to pull him up and walk him back to the house. It wasn't difficult. He could walk well enough. But he was cold and weak.

'I was hoping I'd find you,' he said later, after a cup of tea and a giant wedge of my coming-home cake. 'I remembered you lived near the spring.'

'Did you walk all the way?'

He looked at me, his eyes drooping with sleep: 'Slowly.'

We put him to bed for a few hours, but I paced around, unable to settle to anything. Gracie was put out. She treasured this time with me, and I could see she felt it had been sabotaged by this uninvited guest, even though she was at pains to make him welcome.

'Won't he get picked up for desertion?' she asked. 'If he's just walked off like that?'

'I'll have to take him back.'

'Not now!'

'Later. We'll let him sleep.'

We tried to pretend he wasn't there. I did some weeding in the vegetable beds, and we made dinner together. The smell of steaming vegetables must have woken him, for when we took him a tray he was sitting up in bed, gazing in front of him.

It was hard to get him to speak, and he seemed to have become the silent man he had been when I first found him at the hospital.

'I'll take you back later,' I said gently.

He began to scratch at the coverlet nervously. 'Can't go back,' he mumbled. 'Can't . . . can't . . . no! NO!'

Gracie was really startled, and looked at me as if to say we might be in too deep.

'They'll be looking for you,' I said.

He scratched more rapidly and started to shake his head from side to side, making strange groaning sounds. Then he closed his eyes tight shut, as if to see anything was too painful.

'What is it you're afraid of? Why can't you go back?'

He opened his eyes and looked at me. 'Her – I don't want to see her!' He closed his eyes again and grimaced in pain.

'Who?'

More shaking of the head. Deep breaths. 'My mother. She'll come and visit. She made me do it. I never wanted to. She made me!'

I stroked his hand and said nothing. There was a long silence.

'I left him! He died. He died.'

'You mean the co-pilot?'

He nodded. 'I walked away.' His voice rose to a very high pitch. 'I walked away.' There were tears rolling down his closed eyes. I had never seen a man cry before, and I wasn't sure what to do. So I stroked his hand some more, and waited a little.

149

'You didn't walk away. I took you away. You were going to be blown up, otherwise.'

He swallowed, and whispered: 'Walked away. I did. He . . . he begged me to save him. He called for me. I could see him, crying out – waving. He was crying out to me from the tarmac – didn't you see him?'

'You mean the other man who got out?'

'Yes!'

I remembered the first man who had tumbled out of the plane, and then seemed to disappear. Ken told me he had survived, and gone on to hospital later when the ambulance came.

'He survived,' I said.

'No – I left him.'

'He survived.'

'Even if he did – I left him. He called out to me, and I left him lying there.'

He started to sob again. 'Please don't make me go back . . . I can't face them . . . I can't . . .' He cried bitterly for a full ten minutes, and the dinner went cold.

33

I took Philip back on the evening bus. Gracie was jittery about it, accepting that it was the right thing to do, but clearly inconsolable that this poor young man should cut short her time with me. Just before I left she gave me a pale blue cardigan she had knitted with a matching short-sleeved jersey – a delicate magnum opus on number 13 needles and four-ply. She also gave me a maroon silk dress with a beautifully shaped bodice; another long-term project of hers. She begged me to try it on, and I did. I could have wept. There wasn't time to pay the tribute it deserved. I could only turn about in front of the mirror and look at her gratefully, one eye on the clock and the last bus.

'I hope it's all right,' she kept saying, 'I hope it's not too short,' which was her desperate bid to prolong the process, to transform my reaction into the long delighted one she had been picturing for months. 'Well, I can always alter it for you.'

It is hard to say what attracted me to Philip Bird. Perhaps it was his wistful grey eyes, his handsome jaw, or just a deep sense of pity for him. He seemed so lost and at sea. But then again, maybe there was an intrigue about him. My curiosity never could resist a challenge. My injured airman was desperately unhappy about something, so unhappy he had wanted to put his life in danger and escape: and he had come to me.

When we reached the little hospital, Philip was surprisingly compliant. He allowed himself to be led away, head down without a fuss. The nurse at reception asked me if I wouldn't mind waiting a moment, for Dr Rowse would probably want to have a word. I looked at her white veil clipped back from her face. Her eyes were little dark beads and her beak stuck out like a falcon's. '. . . would like a word with you.' I felt suddenly nauseous. I could feel the pulse in my head speeding up and I thought I would faint. I wanted to run, but I sat down heavily on a wooden bench instead.

'Are you all right?' she was saying, her face horribly close to mine as she bent down. 'Would you like a lie-down – or some water?'

When I dared to look at her again, she had a gentle, plain face, and I could see she was barely older than I was and away from home. 'I'm sorry,' I said. 'I'll be fine. Thank you.'

Then the doctor emerged from one of the doors and came and shook my hand. He sat next to me for ten minutes and asked me a series of questions about Philip. What state had he been in when I found him? Had he fainted at all over the last twenty-four hours? Had he been nauseous? Had he been tearful?

I answered his questions as best I could, and then he asked if I would mind going to see Philip because he'd been asking for me. I was tired, but flattered, so I followed the doctor through a large oak door which he opened with a key.

'Have you locked him in?' I asked, startled.

'Oh no! His old bed's been taken up already, I'm afraid, what with the BEF returning home. So we've put him on his own. This just happens to be the drugs wing. Wouldn't want anyone getting in here. We're short on supplies as it is.'

Dr Rowse had a way of looking at me which made me uncomfortable. Not only was it patronizing, but it also managed to tell me that, although I was an experienced driver, exhausted by the day's events and desperate for a cup of tea, I was first and foremost a sexual being brimming with lust and tempting him with my breasts, my hips and my hopelessly feminine being. I made sure he was in front, and as we reached the last door he opened it and turned, placing his hand very low down on my back. 'This way . . . that's it.'

The space he left for me to go past him was so small, his face came right up to mine and I could smell the strong fetid scent of him. I was nauseous again. The white coat. The smell. The door. '. . . that's it . . .'

I swallowed hard, and was about to turn on my heels when I saw Philip before me, in a room on his own, propped up on some pillows.

'I'm glad you're here,' he said. The door closed behind us, and Dr Rowse disappeared with it.

'How are you now?'

He shrugged. I sat down on the bed and took his unplastered hand boldly in my own. 'You're going to get better. This is the best place for you.'

'I can't stand it here.'

'I know. But you'll be out soon.'

'And then what?'

I didn't know what to say. We sat together in silence for a while, and then the features on his face began to move. His mouth started to wobble, his nostrils flinched and his eyes closed tight. Large tears rolled down his face, and when he caught his breath great sobs came out: huge, unfettered sobs I knew he was ashamed of.

'It's okay,' I kept saying, stroking his hand over and over. Then I stroked his head, and for a moment he stopped and looked at me.

153

'It's not okay. I'm sorry! But it's not okay at all . . .' His voice rose in pitch, way out of control. 'I can't face anything. I can't . . . how can I go on after . . . what I've done?'

'The pilot is alive. The men in my squadron told me. I'm sure he doesn't think badly of you – I'm certain of it.'

'I walked away! I'm a coward!' More sobbing. 'I walked away . . .'

I let him cry some more, and then I had an idea. I would find the pilot and bring him to visit Philip. He was sure to put his mind at rest.

'What was his name?'

He sniffed and wiped his face. 'Jim.'

'Well, listen. I'm going to find Jim and bring him to see you.'

'Oh God!'

'He'll tell you it wasn't your fault.'

'It's all my fault!'

'Well, if it was, you can apologize, can't you? It's much better that way, than sitting here tearing yourself up about it.'

He squeezed my hand in agreement. I looked at my watch and decided I had to go. I had no idea how to get back to my barracks at this time. As I neared the door he said, 'You won't let my mother visit, will you? Tell them not to let my mother see me.'

I nodded, and made my way back to the reception, where, thankfully, another driver was about to leave and offered me a lift. Before we left I told the nurse at reception about Philip's mother, and asked about the pilot who'd been discharged a few days ago. 'He'd like to see him. I thought I might arrange it. His name was Jim – do you remember him?'

'Oh yes. Pilot Officer Buckleigh.' Then she raised her eyebrows and looked straight at me, with an impish smile. 'Very handsome!'

34

I was still on leave, officially, so when I turned up for duty the next day there wasn't much for me to do. I explained the situation to the CO and asked if I could take my truck over to Woodside and fetch Pilot Officer Buckleigh so that Flight Sergeant Bird could see him. She agreed with some reluctance, and I had the distinct feeling that although she paid me more respect, she had gone off me rather since the plane crash. It didn't do for the likes of me to be more heroic than the likes of her.

I paid far more attention to my appearance than I normally did. I dampened the front of my hair with water, and when I was out of sight of the barracks I pulled into the side of the road and sneaked on a bit of lipstick. Then I twirled bits of hair around my fingers to give myself kiss curls, and let them dry in the breeze as I hurtled along. Not that I was at all interested in James Buckleigh. Absolutely not. But I didn't want to look foolish in front of him either. The thought of him or Beatrice laughing at my plainness behind my back was unbearable.

My engine seemed noisy in the sleepiness of the lane. I pulled up just before the gates so that I could be hidden from the house. For a moment, standing on the pounded yellow gravel in front of the wrought ironwork, I was my seventeen-year-old self again, clad from head to toe in Gracie's masterpieces, and on the brink of something wonderful. And then, just as suddenly, it was snatched away from me as those words hurled themselves at my stomach again and knocked the wind out of me. *Some grubby little village girl.* I closed my eyes at the memory, but when I opened them, the gate was still there, and the gravel drive beyond, and I had to go in.

Nearer the front door I could hear strains of music. It wasn't like anything I had heard before on the wireless; it was deep and yearning and melancholic. I rang the bell and closed my eyes again, feeling more of an intruder than ever.

The door opened. A man in corduroy trousers and a Fair Isle tank top stood in front of me. His hair was greying, but his eyebrows were dark like his eyes, which looked kindly, it seemed, into mine.

'Can I help you?' he said, when I didn't speak.

'Oh . . . yes . . . Is James at home?'

The man smiled warmly and opened the door fully to let me in. 'Why yes, he is, actually. You with his lot, are you?'

I realized then that I was in uniform, and that it was an amazing leveller. 'Yes – sort of . . .'

'This way . . . he's out in the orangery . . .'

I followed him through hallways and rooms, and the leathery smell of the place clawed its way back into my head and unhinged me a little, just when I had felt in control.

This was indeed Howard Buckleigh then, and he was not quite what I had expected. He was a gentle, easy man – the gentleman caller – not the strange recluse I had imagined.

We followed the music, and it grew louder and more resonant until we reached the glasshouse. There sat James Buckleigh, his back to us, playing a cello. He had an open-necked shirt, and the back of his neck was quite tanned. His dark hair was shorter than I'd seen it before, and I took in the new experience of his silhouette against the green light of the garden. I concentrated on the tips of his ears, which seemed miraculous as the sunlight made them almost translucent, and they sat in perfect symmetry, wide-open pathways directly to his soul on each side of his head. It seemed a vulnerable place to have them.

'You should be resting that arm,' said the kindly gentleman, and when James turned awkwardly on his stool I saw that his left arm was in a sling, and partially plastered. His father supported the cello for him while he stood up. When I saw his surprise at seeing me, I felt my face colour. It would take a minute or two to explain why I had come, and until I did, he would imagine I had come to see him on some social visit. For the whole duration of the intervening seconds, he would see me as a foolish village girl who couldn't keep away. The time it took to explain stretched out in front of me like a long winding path, overgrown with brambles.

'Oh . . . er . . .' He offered me his free hand. 'Have you just arrived?'

He seemed a little embarrassed as well, and I wasn't sure if that made me feel better or not.

'I've come about Philip Bird.'

'Bird? How is he? How do you . . .?'

I explained as quickly as I could, and Howard Buckleigh patted me on the shoulder. 'We heard there was a jolly brave young lady involved – well done!' Then he went off saying he'd make some tea, because it was Mrs Bubb's day off.

Left alone with me, James looked almost confused. He invited me into a living room with print armchairs and a sofa, and urged me to take a seat.

'I don't understand. You say he thinks he deserted me.'

'Yes.'

'But that makes no sense.'

'I didn't think so either.'

'So . . .?'

'He says you were waving at him, begging him for help, and he left you. But I seem to remember – if it was you – (and it must've been) – that one minute you were there, and then you'd gone.'

'Well yes – I got the hell out of there. And that's why I was waving at him: to tell him to get away from the fuselage. He just kept right next to it. I knew it was going to go up. I was trying to tell him to move away. Surely anyone could see that.'

'That's what I thought too. Thing is, he's got it into his head . . . I've no idea why, but he's not quite . . . he's lost it a bit, I think. I mean, I've no idea what he was like before, but I can't imagine he could train pilots the way he is now. Won't you come and see him? I'll feel awful if I go back without you.'

His father came in with a tray of tea, grinning from ear to ear. James pulled out an occasional table, and a silver teapot with matching milk jug and sugar bowl were set down before me. Next to them on the tray were three flower-printed bone china cups with matching saucers, and a small plate of macaroons. 'Shall I be mother?' asked Mr Buckleigh. He seemed genuinely pleased to see me, and I began to relax. He was all fingers and thumbs: he spilt the tea in the saucers and dropped half of his macaroon in the milk. I liked him straight away. It was almost pleasant to be there, but very, very odd: sipping tea in the place I used to sneak around in, terrified Celia's mother or father – this very man – would come home and spot me. How different now! Here I was, sitting on their fine sofa with a macaroon: a legitimate guest.

Mr Buckleigh thought James should go with me soon. He was no stranger to shellshock himself, and those shadowy illnesses of the mind should not be taken lightly. James said he completely agreed, and looked slightly irritated that he hadn't said it first.

*   *   *

It was strange driving James. I couldn't help but recall the last time we had been in a car together, and I suspect he was thinking of it too. And of course the thought of it reminded me how little we really had in common, and how huge the gulf really was between us, and how foolish I was to have been lulled into a sense of well-being in their home.

'You're a remarkably good driver,' he said, perhaps to break the silence.

'For a woman, you mean?'

'No. What I meant was that you're a good driver.'

'Well, thank you. I ought to be.'

We made small talk for a while, but the picture of him shoving me away from Beatrice kept bobbing up in my head, and I wished he would stop being so pleasant and letting himself off the hook so easily.

'How's Beatrice?' I said, after a while.

'Fine, I think.'

There seemed nothing else to say. 'Good.'

Later I had another go: 'You must be quite excited?'

'Excited? Oh! About seeing Bird, you mean?'

'No! About the wedding!'

'Oh Lord, no! She's been going on about it for so long I think we're all heartily sick of it!'

I didn't care much for his tone. I felt almost sorry for Beatrice. 'When is it — I thought she said July?'

'Yes . . .' He waved a hand vaguely. '. . . Sometime in July, I think.'

'You think?'

He looked at me astonished. 'Well, who cares?'

'Well, you should, for a start. Aren't you planning on turning up?'

'Frankly, no.'

I swerved slightly to miss a rabbit, and almost drove us off the road, but managed to retrieve control swiftly. 'You bastard! Have you told her?'

'Steady on! It's not *that* important. God almighty!'

'Not *that* important? Your own wedding day! How can you be so callous?'

'My wedding day?' He was astounded now. 'It's not my wedding.' Then he chuckled. 'You didn't think . . . I was marrying . . . *Beatrice* . . .?'

I took a very deep breath and tried to think what to say. Once again I felt humiliated. Once again I looked an utter fool. 'So . . . who's she marrying then?'

'God knows. Some poor bugger with lots of money and no sense, I should think.' He could see I was shot to pieces, and tried to stop smiling. 'She's Celia's friend, not mine. That's why she was down here that Boxing Day – to take Celia back to Cirencester with her.'

I was glad I was driving: it was somewhere to look.

And then the unthinkable happened.

The truck began to slow down. I was suddenly not in control. I tried the accelerator but it didn't work. I pretended nothing was wrong, but soon it was so obvious that James mentioned it.

'It's okay – it's nothing,' I said, as the truck slowly ground to a halt. 'Nothing I can't fix.'

I got out and looked under the bonnet for a while. If there was one thing I was certain of it was my ability to fix trucks. I would get it going in no time, and my competence in a man's field would be a small victory, at least.

But there was nothing wrong with the engine, and I soon realized we were simply out of petrol. I kept my cool. I closed the bonnet efficiently and went to fetch the petrol can. He very sensibly said nothing, but watched me with what could well have been mistaken for genuine admiration.

I let out a moan.

'Is everything all right?' he asked, turning round in his seat.

'No. Oh, no!'

The petrol can was there all right. Ken had given it back, but it was empty. I cursed him under my breath and kicked the wheel. My dainty Oxford shoe rebounded off it and I had difficulty concealing the agony.

'Is that all it needs?' he smiled. 'A good kicking?'

I sighed; I closed my eyes; I sighed again. Then I explained that we would have to walk the rest of the way.

James Buckleigh was quite amenable to walking. He said he could do with the exercise, and if he was amused by my inadequacies with the truck I didn't see it, for I avoided looking at him as best I could.

After we'd been walking a few hundred yards along the road he stopped, and said if it was the same hospital he'd been at, then he knew a much quicker way across country. I also knew a quicker way, but hadn't dared to suggest it because it cut through a mile or so of beech trees, and I was afraid he'd think I was making some sort of pass at him. So I let him lead the way, and followed him – over a couple of fields – into the woods.

35

'How's Celia?'

'Celia! . . .' A blackbird somewhere above us started up his alarm call, 'Tak-tak-tak-tak-tak!' and we both looked up together. 'Celia has been spoilt. I mean, really ruined.'

'What's happened?'

He sighed deeply, and held back some brambles for me. 'Poor Celia. She hasn't had much of a life, really.'

This was so typical of people like James Buckleigh. They had no idea – absolutely no idea – of how the other half lived. I thought of Celia's wardrobe full of clothes, the house with a gardener, a housekeeper, greenhouses, a car, and rooms that Celia was unfamiliar with because she never visited them, outhouses she didn't know the contents of. I thought of her education all dressed in green with girls who washed in bathrooms and thought towns were for buying buns and clutch bags.

'Yes,' I said hastily. 'Life's been cruel to her.'

'No.' He slowed his pace and kicked a large rotten stick out of the path. 'I know what you're thinking. Of course you're right. It's all been very easy for her – she's had so much – so much given to her on a plate. But it's what she's had to do to get it . . . and what she hasn't had . . .'

'How's that then?'

The wood was giving off a potent stink of wild garlic, and as we made our way through the leathery shoots, I thought of the layer upon layer of leaves underneath us, hiding years of decay and insects and shoots and secret seeds yet to show themselves.

'When you have a mother who manipulates . . . When I think of it, nothing's been given freely. Celia's had to lie and spy and say the right things in the right places and shut up when she hasn't been needed. Every single thing has been conditional. There's probably not a brooch or a scarf that hasn't been lied for, wrung out of a mother who dangles everything in front of her like bait.'

This was bitter stuff. I wanted to hear more but, embarrassed by my earlier sarcasm, I hoped he would continue unprompted. He was silent.

'I see,' I said.

'Do you?'

The wood became suddenly very dense. A thick, polleny smell oozed out of everything, and the leafy undergrowth seemed like hidden pores, releasing the earth's sweat in quick reeking bursts as we waded through it.

I was overcome with curiosity.

'You mean . . . Mrs Buckleigh made Celia tell lies?'

'I shouldn't speak about her like this, I know. But she's made Celia so miserable. You see, Celia doesn't really have any friends – apart from Beatrice, I suppose, and she's hardly your sensitive type.' He pushed a branch away and held it until I'd gone past. 'You were probably the closest thing she had to a friend . . . at one time.'

'*Me?*'

'You sound surprised.'

'We hardly spent any time together. And you remember the way she got us to . . . she didn't seem much of a friend then.'

'I think she would've *liked* to have had you as her friend. But she couldn't. How can you be friends with someone you've been sent to spy on?'

Now it was my turn to be silent. It hurt. Even though I'd suspected something when I found Gracie's photograph in the wallet, even so, it felt like a new wound, and it hurt the more for being exposed so openly to James Buckleigh.

'I'm sorry – I shouldn't have—'

'No!' I said airily. 'It's fine.' My voice was high-pitched and offhand.

'It's not fine at all. I assumed you knew about all that years ago – I'm so sorry, I—'

'All what, exactly? What did she want with *me*?'

He rubbed his forehead anxiously. 'She thought your mother – Miss Burrows – had had an affair with—'

'—your father – Mr Buckleigh.'

'That's right.'

'She didn't.'

'I don't doubt it.'

'She would've liked to. They were in love, you know.'

He stopped and looked at me earnestly. 'What's that?'

I blushed. 'They were in love.'

'Hmm.'

'It's true. But before he met your mother.'

'I know. He told me so himself.'

'Did he? Then why . . .?' I swear he had only got me to repeat it to see my cheeks colour.

'But did you know that the woman he married was not quite so modest?' He was walking behind me now, talking quite loudly to make sure I was listening. 'Of course you do. That boyfriend of yours called us both bastards.'

'He's *not* my boyfriend.'

'Isn't he? Well, you see he was half right. She hasn't been remotely loyal to him. She only married him for his money. Always partying. Still does. Always flirting and taking things

164

too far. She's been in St. Tropez since before the war. He's quite quiet, you see. Doesn't go in for parties.'

'A bit like you, then.'

'Yes.'

It was uncomfortably hot, and my hair roots were prickling with sweat. 'So Mrs Buckleigh thought I was his love child.'

'In a nutshell.'

'But why would she care?'

'All to do with inheritance, I should think.'

'Yes but . . . Celia would have as much right as me.'

'If her father wasn't some gambling party-goer.'

'Oh.' We were deep in the heat of the woods. 'Yours wasn't, then?'

'No. Most certainly not. That's why Celia's always been hell-bent on belittling me if she can. A sort of defensive thing. Always trying to make me look stupid.'

'Like setting you up with village scum at an elegant party?'

He looked embarrassed. 'That sort of thing . . .'

We continued walking without speaking, and he led the way through a tricky bit of undergrowth. The silence, which I thought was awkward for him at first, soon became easy between us, and I realized he was as comfortable not speaking as I was. There was quite enough to listen to with the songbirds filling the air, their alarm calls as we approached, the soft sweep of our legs through the ferns, the cracking of twigs.

A bramble scratched my hand deeply and I drew in my breath. I was glad he was ahead of me, and I was watching the way he coped one-armed with the tall undergrowth when he turned suddenly to hold back a giant thorny stem away from my path. I passed ahead of him, but he grabbed my wrist. I had barely time to register the large thorn embedded at the end of the streak of blood on my hand, when he pulled it to his lips with his free hand and took the thorn from my skin between his teeth. He spat it out, wiped the blood with his cheek, and continued on his way ahead of me, leaving me as startled to realize that he *hadn't* suddenly kissed my hand as I would've been if he had.

36

'I hope it's not going to be much longer,' said the woman sitting next to me in the reception area. 'The buses only go on the hour from 'ere, don't they? And that's 'alf a mile down the road.'

She had hair the colour of old stone and deep-set blue eyes spliced by worry lines. I had been watching her hands for ten minutes, twisting a small white handkerchief around her long fingers. The skin on each hand was like a screwed-up brown paper bag that someone had tried to flatten out and use again. She seemed a bag of nerves.

'You come far?' I asked, just to be polite.

'Just outside Painswick.'

James, who had gone to call his father about a return lift, now held open the front door for a pretty pregnant woman who came in. James sat next to me. The new arrival sat opposite us and started crying gently, wiping a tear away with her sleeve and then opening her eyes very wide to try and stop any more.

'You all right, love?' said my woman, her worry lines caving into deep ravines.

'Oh – s'nothing. Just so relieved really. Geoff – my husband – he's only broke his leg in a few places – bailing out or something. I know I shouldn't say it, but I'm that relieved. He'll be out of action – for a while at least – and I'm so bloody glad, I am. Might even get to see his baby.'

'Oh there! Every cloud 'as a silver lining, see?' She turned to me. 'You got a young man in 'ere, then?'

I could sense James looking at me and I felt myself colour. 'Sort of. He's a sort of friend, really.'

'Go on!' She nudged me with a wicked wink. 'There's not many young men could see you as a friend, my love. You grab him while he's down, I should!'

We all laughed.

'Unless this is your young man . . .'

I shook my head vigorously and laughed. I didn't dare to look at James. There was a brief silence, then she continued, 'Still, you can't help but worry about 'em, can you? My son's in 'ere somewhere. I been worried sick about 'im, I 'ave. Worried sick. . . . Still, that's motherhood, for you. You 'ave 'em, you worry about 'em. Just can't help it.'

'You got many children?' asked the pregnant woman.

'Three sons.' She said it with enormous pride, as if it were a spectacular achievement, which, I suppose, in its own way, it was. 'Two's in the forces – army and RAF – and the other's a bit simple, like – 'e's doin' 'is bit on the land, look. Might be daft as a brush, but I wouldn't swap him for nothing – not if you paid me, I wouldn't.'

The pregnant woman gave a slightly strained smile, perhaps worrying whether her baby would be 'a bit simple'. 'What's it like, having sons?'

'Oooh!' The older lady took in a deep breath, all ready for this one. 'There's nothing like it, love. Tiz lovely. Oh! I love 'em to bits, I do. I really do. There's nothing I wouldn't do for any of them.'

'You must be very proud of them,' I said.

'Oooh! I am! Mind, I tried to stop 'em both from joining up. Worried me sick, it did. Still does. But they wouldn't listen to me, and that's always the way with young men when there's a sniff of action. Worries me something rotten!'

'It must be very hard.'

'Oooh! You wait! You tell that young man of yours to give you a good time before he goes giving you a litter o' kids. You 'ave your bit o' fun, my girl. Tiz all worry after that . . .'

Then, seeing the face of the expectant mother opposite, she repeated, for good measure: 'Not that it's not all worth it, mind. Love 'em to bits, I do. There's nothing like it.'

A nurse came in and shook a little bell. It was so loud and she smelt so nursey, it made me uneasy. She showed the pregnant woman, 'Mrs Audrey', to the stairs, and then went over to the little door of the drugs wing and unlocked it. To my dismay, the woman opposite us followed us to the door, and I realized straight away who she was.

We followed the nurse to Philip's room, and I wondered what I was going to do.

'Three visitors for you,' said the crisp cottoned nurse.

James immediately said he would wait and turned back.

Philip smiled at me, then saw his mother behind, and his face dropped. I shrugged helplessly, and held the door open for her.

'Phil!' she said, rushing over. 'Oh, my dear boy!' She tried to hug him, but he remained motionless.

'I'll go and wait,' I said.

'Don't go!' he called.

'I won't. I'll be in the reception. I'll . . . wait my turn.'

His mother turned round and looked at me, then at him. 'You didn't tell me you had a young lady! Well, I never . . .'

I didn't wait to hear any more. I felt so guilty for letting him down. I slunk off to the waiting area until she had finished.

I didn't have to wait long. She came out after ten minutes or so, blowing her nose in her wrung-out hankie. 'Doesn't want to see me! Tiz you he wants!' She blinked at me, sniffing. 'Not that I blame him, love. You're a lovely girl, I can tell. I'm glad he's got you, love . . . I know you'll look after him.' I felt my cheeks burning in front of James. 'P'raps you can tell me what's got into him. P'raps you can talk some sense into him.' She put her hand on my arm. It seemed tender rather than accusatory. She wiped her soggy hankie under her nose. 'I shall see you again, anyway, sweetheart. I'll be off an' catch my bus. You can go in.'

37

I didn't stay long with him. He wasn't angry with me, but he was in a dark place, tapping at his eiderdown repeatedly, over and over, nodding his head in rhythm. It was difficult to tell whether the room itself echoed his mood or infected it. The wallpaper was striped, and relentlessly cruel on the eye. The one long window faced north, and the heavy net curtains prevented any view upon the world outside.

'Food's good here,' he said, at one point, not looking at me. 'At least the food's not bad.'

'That's something.'

A great sigh. 'Yes!'

I began to question my being there at all. Maybe there was a bit of vanity in it, checking up on the results of my heroic rescue, little updates on my bravery. Or maybe I was flattered by his dependency on me. People's neediness was a mystery to me, and I wallowed in it a little. He was what Reeny would call 'a handsome chap', and I certainly found him attractive. But it was more to do with the way his face fitted together: something about the way his nose and his eyes and his mouth sat in his head seemed just right. He was – if I were a painter – the way I would paint a Man.

I found I was stroking his free arm, but he didn't seem to notice. I told him his friend Jim was safe and well and had come to see him. I gave his hand a squeeze and told him I'd visit again soon. I don't think he was even aware, as James went in, that I had closed the door and left.

Outside a tabby cat sprung across my path and into a flowerbed in front of the hospital's main bay window. It disappeared for a moment, and I stood making kissing noises at it to lure it out. Then its ears and eyes popped out above some lemon balm. It gave me a leaf-green stare. 'You're in up to your neck,' it said.

'I know.'

I reached my barracks at midday, having been escorted back to my truck by Howard Buckleigh. Exhausted, I lay down on the bed and fell asleep. I was woken by the sound of Hurricanes overhead, and Betty shaking my arm.

'Joy. It's five to four. They're back!'

I scrambled for my truck, and made it down to the dispersal hut in time to see the planes being checked over, and the pilots milling around.

When they were nearly all in Laurie Harper tapped me on the shoulder to say, 'Drive on.' I turned round.

'Where's Ken?'

There was no answer.

Then a usually chirpy Scot called Hamish said, 'Somewhere in the English Channel.'

As soon as he said it he looked at his boots. I looked around their faces, but they were all looking down. No one was laughing. I turned back to the wheel. Laurie tapped me on the shoulder again, and said, 'Sorry, Haps. Best get on.'

I didn't cry. Perhaps it was some instinct for self-preservation, but I don't think my body could have taken the weight of the grief. There was just too much adrenalin pumping round, and my head felt as heavy as a boulder as we bumped over the road. Tomorrow would be the Friday dance, and I had promised him. The fields were flooded in that evening glow that makes the grass and leaves translucent. The cows were huddled by their gate, heavy, expectant, longing for milking. As we sank into the village a child's wail drifted through an open window ('I *hate* cabbage!') and further on two women laughed by a washing line, a long chime of giggles that echoed down the valley. I clasped the steering wheel as if it were the last piece floating off a sunken wreck.

But that day of grief did not end there. There was more to come. There was a visit from James Buckleigh.

38

'There's a phone call for you, Burrows.'

I poked my head from the pit underneath my truck the next morning, and was surprised to see Sergeant Ince herself standing in the maintenance shed. 'Better look sharp – sounds important.'

I swung my legs up, dropped my spanner and cloth and followed her hurriedly, wiping my oily hands on my overalls.

In the office I picked up the receiver with a mixture of dread and excitement. I put it to my ear tentatively, my eyes swinging about the room as if something unexpected might follow this decision.

Sergeant Ince nodded at me to make some noise, so I said, 'Hello?'

'Is that you, Joy?'

It was James Buckleigh's voice. After the initial relief that it wasn't some hospital with bad news about Gracie, my thumping pulse began to thump even faster, as I imagined the possible causes of his personal call. I fancied him asking me on a date, right under Sergeant Ince's stuck-up nose – a date with a pilot officer – and me still in my overalls.

'Joy?'

I had never had a telephone call before, so I copied what I'd seen people do in films.

'Speaking.' I looked triumphantly at Sergeant Ince and twirled a curl around my finger.

'Joy! Listen, I'm so sorry to bother you, only I thought you'd want to know . . .'

'What is it? What's happened?'

'It's Philip. I phoned the hospital today to see how he was, and he's tried to . . . take his own life.'

'What?'

'Last night. He tried to commit suicide.'

'But . . . how . . .?'

'Overdose. He's in the drugs wing – stupid place to put him. They're keeping him in the same room for now, but—'

'Is he all right? How is he? I mean—'

'He'll survive. He's all right. They said he was sitting up in bed this morning.'

'Oh, Lord. Oh . . .'

'Listen, I'm going over there myself right now, and I was wondering . . . well, I wondered if you'd like me to call by and give you a lift.'

'Oh!' I was taken by surprise at the invitation: so close to my little fantasy, but not quite along the same lines. 'I'm not sure if I can get the time off. Almost certainly not. I'll see . . .'

Sergeant Ince gave me a curious nod, and James continued: 'Don't worry, I've asked your boss already. She says it's fine so long as you're back by four. I'm afraid I pulled rank a bit.' He laughed then, and I chuckled too – far too vigorously – in order to impress dear Sergeant Ince, who I suddenly pictured in a gymslip with an obscure tassel hanging from her waist and carrying a lacrosse racket.

I washed my hands and face as quickly as I could, and was just in time for the Buckleigh family car, which pulled up discreetly at the end of the lane.

When I saw his one hand on the wheel I wondered how on earth he had been changing gears. 'You shouldn't be driving,' I said.

'You sound like my father.'

Then he opened his car door and came round to the passenger side where I was standing. 'You wouldn't do a great favour, would you? Would you drive?'

I felt hugely complimented, not only because he was acknowledging my driving skills, but because he was entrusting me with the family car. After my truck it was like stepping into a work of art. The green door clunked neatly into place, the chrome sparkled, and the floor didn't smell of mud. I was swept back to the last time I had sat in this car, and was glad to be in the driving seat this time. So long as he didn't think I owed him anything for this favour. If he tried anything else on I would just stop the car and get out.

By the time I sat next to James Buckleigh I had had time to think about Philip. It seemed suddenly quite obvious that he would make an attempt on his life, and I was cross with myself for not having thought of it before. I should have warned the nursing staff not to keep him on his own. They should have been alert to his depression. I was also irritated that he should so easily try to take the life I had risked my own to save. And these concerns got all jumbled up with the soft pumf sound of the leather seat as we rumbled over the lanes and the smell of polished chrome, and the proximity of James Buckleigh's knees to my own, and my hand almost touching him as I changed gears.

Philip seemed pleased to see us for a moment or two, and then lapsed into a staring silence. James went to open the window, and after a lot of thumping about, managed to throw it up a little and let in the jabberings of a chaffinch outside.

I sat on the bed, holding his unplastered hand, and James sat on a camp chair beside him.

'Whatever is it, Bird? Whatever's made you feel . . .? Things aren't as bad as all that, you know . . .'

Philip Bird flopped his face to the wall, away from both of us.

'Philip,' I said, 'we're here for you . . . you can talk to us.'

He sighed, but said nothing. Then the door opened, bringing with it clonking sounds from the corridor and the hospital beyond. A nurse with a starched white headdress announced: 'Your mother's here, Flight Sergeant Bird. Shall I send her in?'

Philip flung his head back and forth and began to groan. 'Tell her to go away. She made me – she made me—'

James got up and went to the door. 'I'll go and see to things. Don't worry, Bird. She won't be in here unless you want her here. I'll see to it.'

I felt oddly relieved that James had gone. I don't know why, because Philip was no picnic party. He stopped rocking his head back and forth and started drumming his fingers on the counterpane. I think I imagined I could draw him out of himself. I thought I, Joy Burrows, could sort out all his problems with a little sensitivity and kindness. The thing was to get him talking.

'Is it too bright for you?'

He shook his head.

'Where were you born?'

No answer.

'Where's your home?'

He sneered.

'Has your mother travelled far?'

He turned to look directly at me. 'She hasn't come far, and she can go back easily. I want her to go back. She's seen me already. There's no need. I'll be all right, now.'

I nodded.

'Tell her that.'

'James is telling her now, don't worry.'

There was a silence.

'Buckleigh your boyfriend, is he?'

'No.'

'How d'you know him, then?'

'Um . . . we lived nearby . . . I suppose. I knew his sister.'

'Ah yes! The sister.'

'Do you know her?'

'No. Heard about her, though.' He sighed deeply again. The chaffinch chattered outside and filled the space we left. At first I felt awkward, but then it seemed perfectly natural to sit there, together, saying nothing.

'I like you,' he said, at last. 'I feel everything's all right when you're here.'

I wasn't sure if it was a compliment or a plea. He let his hand reach out slightly across the bed cover. I was afraid if I let him take mine it might mean something, so I took his and folded a second hand on top, like a friendly nurse.

'Can't you tell me what made you so unhappy?'

He gave a sharp puff of a breath through his nostrils. 'It's me. It's just who I am.'

His hand was cool and limp, and his eyes were the most pitifully unhappy ones I had ever seen.

'Well, tell me about you.'

'You joking?' He managed a smile. 'I'm trying to keep you here, not send you packing.' I smiled, and he managed one too. 'Rather hear about you.'

So I told him about the girls I worked with, what sort of work I did, how I knew the Buckleighs, how we used to play inside the house as children. He smiled from time to time, or nodded, but I had the impression that something else in his head kept stealing his attention.

I felt sorry for him, alone all day with his chaffinch for company.

Then, watching him, something swept through me: a wave of grief and nausea that stopped me speaking. His fine eyes were circled in red and fixed on an invisible point in the air. There was a permanent well of unblinked tears, and the occasional sigh. I had thought myself mad, but this was insanity. Everything about him asked why he had been brought back to the land of the living, why he hadn't been allowed to die. And seeing him there, so alive and yet so dead, made me think of Ken. I was angry with Philip for not cherishing his life, and I was angry with a world that had brought him to this, and furious that I would never have that dance with Ken, and grief-stricken that his glorious, flirtatious, vital smile had been wiped off the globe for ever.

I found I was sobbing.

Suddenly he squezed my hand hard. 'You feel it too, don't you?'

'What?'

He pinned my wrist to the bed and fixed impatient eyes on mine. 'The same way I feel about you.' He tried to pull me towards him.

'Please . . . you're hurting me.'

I wriggled free. I got up and started to run to the door. James was just opening it with three cups of tea on a tray, and it spilt into the saucers as I dived past. I ran into the reception, took one look at Philip Bird's mother – who raised her eyebrows at me expectantly, then frowned at my state – and ran past her, out through the double doors, down the steps, across the road and into the woods.

I didn't stop running until I was out of breath. Then I collapsed against a tree, exhausted, and screamed and screamed and screamed until I thought my head would burst and all the songbirds stopped their singing.

39

After a while I heard him, like a distant rook, calling my name. I looked about for somewhere to hide, but felt too hot and heavy to move. I wiped my cheeks with my sleeve, but my temples were wet with sweat, and my hair stuck to my head like mud. The woods were perspiring with me, oozing little pockets of dampness underneath their leaves, and my precious lisle stockings were stuck to my legs, wringing wet, as though years of poison were seeping out through my skin. My blouse and jacket seemed made of hedgehog, and hot sharp spikes prickled my chest and back at every movement.

A nightingale gave a soft alarm call, and I waited for its song: 'diu diu diu diu-doo-it', but it didn't come.

'Joy! Joy! . . . Where are you?'

I crawled over to some ferns, and crouched under them, sticking to the gritty earth like a spat-out toffee.

I could hear him rustling along the path, coming closer.

'Joy! . . . Talk to me.'

I was still as a stone. I'd had years of practice. I knew how to breathe so the leaves didn't move, how to hold a shape which wouldn't send a bird away batting its wings.

He was closing in. The rustling came closer. Twigs cracked.

'Joy! Come on . . . we can drive back . . .'

I could hear his boots close to my ears, hear him sigh. A hand on my shoulder reaching through the ferns. 'Joy! Whatever is the matter? I've been looking everywhere . . .'

I remained curled up and said nothing. He bent down and tried to find my face, but I couldn't let him see it. I pressed it hard into my knees and covered the sides with my arms. Then he started to stroke me, and said nothing. I coiled up harder into my knot, and he suddenly stopped.

I still hadn't looked at him. Everything fell silent again, except for the fluting of a blackbird above me, and the deep woodwind of two distant wood pigeons. I knew he was still there. I could feel his presence like his hand upon me. Then there was a breath drawn in, and every now and then the sound of his hand brushing the material of his uniform, the occasional creak of a boot.

I don't know how long we stayed like that. It seemed a long, long time, but I was so uncomfortable it may only have been ten minutes. Even so, when I looked up there were bluetits flipping leaves over for insects, the blackbird had gone but, sitting cross-legged two yards away from me, he was still there.

I sighed. James said nothing.

'I want to go home,' I said.

He got up and stretched his legs. 'You mean Woodside?'

'No – the barracks.'

'Why not come back to our house? You look as if you could do with a break – come and have tea or something.'

I had risen to my feet by now and every inch of me ached. I knew I was a mess. I leant my head against a tree and closed my eyes, like a child who thinks they can't be seen if they can't see out. 'No – please. No.'

Then suddenly his free arm was leaning on the tree too, arching above me. 'You can't go back in this state.'

'Oh God! Don't look at me!'

I turned my head away, aware what 'state' I must be in.

181

'I don't mean that . . . I mean, you can't go back while you're so . . .' I slapped my hands over my face. 'Okay, I'll close my eyes,' he said. 'I don't need to look at you . . .' He was right up against me now, and I could feel his thigh against mine. 'I love the smell of you!'

Diu diu diu diu diu diu-doo-it.

The shock of lust I felt when he said this terrified me. My emotions had been jolted too much and I began to run. I ran back to the hospital, calling at him over my shoulder to leave me alone.

I walked the three miles back to the barracks, and he didn't follow me.

40

Sergeant Ince gave me a bollocking.

'The agreement was Pilot Officer Buckleigh would bring you back by four.'

'I'm sorry, ma'am.'

'Where have you been, looking like something the cat's brought in?'

'With Pilot Officer Buckleigh at the hospital, ma'am.'

'Then why has he telephoned twice to see if you've got back safely?'

'I—'

'Your last leave was cut short, wasn't it? Getting this injured pilot back to hospital? Perhaps we should see if you can't have a bit more leave shortly.'

'Thank you, ma'am. But I'm all right.'

She looked me up and down, said it was not for me to decide, and dismissed me.

Dismissed, of course, is an interesting concept. To put something out of our mind. To pretend it isn't there. To give it none of your attention so that, to all intents and purposes, it seems not to exist. I had been dismissing things all my life, but now there seemed so many things to keep in my mind I hardly knew how to cope.

Betty tried to persuade me to go out to the dance anyway, said it might cheer me up. 'No point sticking around this dump on our own,' she said. 'S'not disrespectful or nothing. All Ken's mates are going, look.'

But I refused. I sat on my camp bed and listened until the last whoop and giggle were just shrill far-off birdsong. Then I pulled the suitcase out from under my bed and lifted out the dress Gracie had made me, the dress I would have worn for Ken. Slowly, I slipped it on over my head and buttoned up the side. There was no full-length mirror so I stood on tiptoes by the mirror over the basin. I stroked my hands over the silk. A pretty lozenge-shape formed the bodice, and it had been top-stitched to within a hair's breadth of the edge. The bust was gathered into the top two edges, descending from the point. The buttonholes were tiny and hand-stitched and as neat as factory-made ones. The collar was lined and top-stitched, the short sleeves ever so gently puffed and edged with a matching button, and inside the back of the collar my name was embroidered in dark red Sylko. My eyes welled as I thought how little I had thanked Gracie for this labour of love.

Exhausted, I was wondering where to go with this train of thought when Betty burst in.

'Quick, quick! Get your things, you've got to come now!'

'What . . .?'

'There's a man at the end of the lane asking for you – a real dish. My God, Joy, if you don't come now, you'll regret it. He's a Flying Officer or Pilot Officer or something.'

'Oh Christ! It's James Buckleigh.'

'James who? Jesus, you're a dark horse! How d'you know him?'

I waved a hand lethargically.

'Bloody hell, Joy! If you don't come right this second I'm having him myself!'

I don't know if it was Betty's obvious attraction to him – for I hadn't really seen him through anyone else's eyes – or the sudden memory of my last encounter but I decided to follow her. And I didn't want him going to Sergeant Ince and making some official meeting with me I couldn't back out of.

Because the girls were planning on going to the pub before the dance, it was still only quarter to seven, and the lane was dappled in sunshine. Betty walked her bicycle, and I walked myself, awkwardly folding my arms as if I weren't planning on going anywhere.

The top of the lane marked the boundary to our camp, and there he stood, half in the shadow of an old beech tree and mottled in sunlight. He had an anxious, questioning expression, as if he weren't sure how he'd find me.

I waited until Betty had ridden off – and she certainly took her time, smirking and winking and fiddling with her dress – before I looked him full in the face. I gave a half-smile and looked away at a leafy twig that was sprouting from the smooth trunk of the beech.

'I'm sorry.' He looked down. 'It was stupid of me to come this evening. I should've known you'd all be going out.'

'I'm not.'

'Aren't you?'

'No.'

'It's just . . . you're wearing a lovely . . . outfit.'

In a desperate bid to make it clear I hadn't put it on for his benefit, I said stupidly, 'I *was* going out, but my date had the bad manners to get himself killed.'

'Oh, I'm . . . oh! . . . That's terrible. I'm so sorry!'

I sighed deeply, perhaps giving the impression I didn't care, or perhaps that I cared so much he couldn't possibly understand. Then I instantly felt this was unfair. I watched his awkwardness from my occasional glances at him, and saw that I was being unkind. The truth was I'd felt more sorrow just now over Gracie's dress than I had over Ken. About Ken I felt

185

empty. It would be months, years even, before the true sadness of him hit me. And then it would be a sort of collective sorrow for the waste, so many hopeful young men humming 'Walking my baby back home', on the brink of tenderness that never happened. I suddenly felt sorry for James, standing there earnestly in his sling.

'It's all right about yesterday,' I said. 'I'm not angry or anything, if that's what you're worried about.'

'Well, I was, actually. It was unforgivable. I don't know what came over me. I'm really very sorry.'

'S'okay.'

'Look, there's something else. I wanted to . . . Shall we walk?'

He seemed to be thinking of the direction of the pub. But I started in the opposite direction, which took us along the road between fields. I didn't want Betty or any of that crowd eavesdropping on anything. I found a stile and started to cross it into a field which was so steeply sloping it had escaped the plough. He followed me, and we drifted for a while in a beautiful sunlit scrubland. The limestone had carpeted the ground with wild thyme and trefoil, eyebright and squinancy wort. He walked with a modest gap between us, and I began to imagine him saying what he had said the day before, and it seemed unthinkable. So ridiculous did it seem that James Buckleigh should have pinned me to a tree and told me that he loved the smell of me, that I almost willed it to happen again. And yet now he was chatting about this and that with such an anxious look on his face, it was not even a remote possibility. Perhaps I had imagined it. My nerves were unstable. A lot had happened in the last twenty-four hours.

'You've had a pretty rough time, haven't you?' He said it in a serious tone, as if he were about to broach something. I said nothing, and shrugged. 'You'll be pleased to hear that Philip is out of danger now. He's back at our house and being pampered by Dad and Mrs Bubb.'

I stopped and stared at him.

'It's just for a few days. They're giving him a desk job next week . . .' I continued walking, kicking at some knapweed as we came closer to the edge of the field.

'He'd like to see you . . . Do you think that's . . . a possibility?'

I kicked at the ground again, sending up bittersweet wafts from the grasses. I was so irritated and so utterly unable to tell him why that I tried to change the subject.

'Listen! Have you noticed there's hardly any birds singing? Not yet mid-July and already the birds have stopped their territorial stuff because their fledglings have grown.'

'Yes,' he said helplessly. 'I had noticed.'

'Only, listen! D'you hear that?' One bird kept up a lethargic little twitter, as if he could only just be bothered.

'Yellowhammer,' he said.

'Oh yes. I forgot your interest in birds. A yellowhammer and . . .' I put my head on one side, showing off, 'a corn bunting.'

'I know about you and Philip.'

'What?'

'I heard it all. I was there.'

'But—'

'I'm sorry, Joy. That's what I came to tell you. I meant to tell you yesterday, but . . . look, I didn't mean to overhear, it's just that I opened the door with the tea, and he'd just started speaking, and you know how we wanted to get him to talk, and then I knew if I went back out the door would squeak again, and I was afraid it might put him off, so I just stood there stock still and . . . I heard it all. I'm afraid I told him to back off and told Sergeant Ince you needed some leave.'

I must have looked horrified.

'I only told Sergeant Ince,' he said. 'I half explained it to her because I thought you needed some time off.'

'Oh God!'

'And Father because—'

'Oh, for God's . . .! And Uncle Tom Cobleigh and all! Oh, God Almighty! Who asked you to . . .? Can't you just . . .?'

We had come to a stile at the bottom of the field, which led into some woods. I leant on the old oak bar and held my head in my hands. I felt angry and exposed. He leant on the stile too, and apologized again. Then he said nothing, just waiting for me to unravel.

I was aware of his closeness and, like the day before, I sensed he would wait a long time for me. I was too wrung out for a repeat performance, so I lifted my head and narrowed my eyes at him.

'That's so . . . so typical of your sort, isn't it? You just barge in there, firing on all cylinders, and to hell with other people's feelings!'

'My sort?'

'You just . . . you just . . . play with people! It's all one big game to you – everything!' I couldn't tell if he looked fierce or hurt, there was such a sombre frown on him. 'How dare you interfere in my private life! How dare you! How dare you!'

'I'm sorry.' Now he looked so forlorn and contrite I wanted to slap him. Even this seemed like a game. Why didn't he fight back?

'You and Celia, you're just the same! You dangle people on bits of string and laugh at them!'

'No!'

'Is that what they teach you at your posh schools? Or is it bred into you? I've seen it! I see it every day – Sergeant Ince, all the officers – all jolly this and jolly that and just naturally leading the rest of us, because that's what you lot do, isn't it? Do they give you lessons in belittling? Do they beat you so hard and with so much enjoyment that you just have to do the same to everyone else? . . . Tell me!'

I was ferocious. I was well out of order. I could feel a trickle of sweat run down between my breasts, and I knew it would flower into a dark patch on the silk wherever it came to rest.

'Actually, I left my "posh" school and went to grammar school. I kept running away, so Father took me out of it.'

I was still breathing heavily from my rant, and I couldn't back down. 'Well then, it must be *bred* into you!'

'What must?'

I had lost my way a bit, so I lashed out with what really annoyed me about him. 'You know very well what I'm talking about. You think you can just *toy* with the likes of me, don't you? People like me, we're just playthings for the likes of you and Celia. You can build us up to make us feel special and then you can just *push* us away, just humiliate us in front of everyone with one little . . . *push!*'

'Oh . . .' He looked mortified.

'Yes . . . "Oh!" . . .'

I stopped because I was practically snorting with rage. He had listened and said little, nodding from time to time, holding me with his eyes and the strangest, most tender of looks.

I climbed the stile, because I could feel tears coming again. He followed behind, watching my bare leg closely as I swung it over. Once again an urgent lust took me by surprise. I wanted to lead him further into the woods. I wanted to clear the ground of emotion, and found myself longing for him to show that secret side to himself that had shocked me so much before.

We rustled through patches of milkwort and white bedstraw. There was the occasional whiff of badger as the sun began to fade. We came across a stretch of wild strawberries, and I plucked off the little red droplets and put them in my mouth. I willed him to put one in mine, but he did not.

We didn't speak, but the shuffling of leaves, the cracking of twigs, and the low steady croon of a turtle dove all spoke to us in the heavy, scent-filled air. He seemed quite comfortable with the stillness, and I remembered how he had once carried me across town without so much as a word.

The gap between us grew less, and soon we were walking so close that our clothes brushed. It could have been accidental. Then we came to a log over a stream, and he held my hand to help me over. There was no need. He knew it, of course. I had grown up in woods. I should have been helping him.

He held back branches for me, and I noticed that now he was leading. When we reached another stile he stopped, and said, 'Will you help me off with my jacket?'

'Are you warm?' I folded his jacket back and peeled it gently away from his good arm.

'No, I think you're getting chilly.'

He put his jacket around my shoulders. It was a small gesture, but it had an electric effect on me. That part of his clothing that covered his whole upper body – his arms, his chest, his heart – was wrapping itself around me, and it was still warm. As I pulled it close, a little waft of him came out of the fabric like a spell. I was transported back to the room in Celia's house, the mysterious room of wagtails and coins and feathers, the smell of leather and wood and the insides of his shoes, the deep disturbing smell of him.

I put my foot on the stile and he stopped it with a hand on my knee. Every part of me tingled.

'I'm sorry about the trap,' he said.

I looked around, confused, a little pang of fear starting inside me. 'What trap?'

Then, he slid his hand down inside my naked leg, and said, 'This one.'

I looked down at his hand, and I could see my naked knee was shaking. He leant in very close to my face, and repeated gently, 'This one. The one I found you in.'

He was stroking the scar at my ankle. A hawk moth fluttered between us and landed on the bark of an ash. My voice did not work, and I found only a whisper:

'You!'

He lifted my knee down and came to join me on my side of the stile. His hand went up to the small of my back and he pushed himself hard against me, sandwiching me between himself and the stile. 'I'm sorry, but I *do* love the smell of you. I love everything about you, Joy Burrows . . . and I always have . . .'

41

The light was already beginning to fade and, to my disappointment, he suggested we head back.

'Why didn't you tell me before?' I asked. 'How could you keep something like that a secret from me?'

'I only just found out myself. There can't be many girls who look like you . . . and then your ankle, this evening . . . that was when I knew for certain.'

'But how did you get to be with the Buckleighs? And what happened to Alice?'

He was holding my hand now and it felt good. A symmetry at last: him on one side, me on the other, and two palms touching.

'I was already with the Buckleighs.'

I was confused.

'After you disappeared, Alice looked everywhere for you. She was ill – can you remember? – that dreadful cough. She just seemed to get worse and worse. But she was on her own. The others were in some sort of trouble with the police, and she got separated. So it was just her. She was coughing up blood and everything . . .' His hand began to grip mine more tightly, and I could see him frowning through the dusk. '. . . so she went to see her gentleman. You remember a "kind gentleman" who let her take his apples? So . . . that's how it happened. Dad took Alice in and looked after her. Well . . . Mrs Bubb did most of it, I suppose. Only Alice didn't last too long after that. Died just before Christmas, and she begged him to keep looking for her little girl who'd gone missing in the woods – that's you, of course.'

'So he brought you up as his own?'

'No, no. I am his own. Well, I'm his best friend's, anyway. My real father died in the trenches and my mother died of Spanish flu a couple of years later. But yes, by then I think he already knew about Celia – about her not being his child – so he was quite happy to take me in and bring me up as his own.'

'Is that why Celia resented you so much?'

He shrugged. 'Celia had enough problems of her own.'

'Mrs Buckleigh?'

'I never did find it easy to call her "Mother". And she never once tried to be one. It wasn't the fairy story it might sound, you know. It wasn't like that at all.'

'So what about the woods? How did you know Alice?'

'I didn't come here until I was five – I lived with my grandparents before that. Then I just went a bit wild, I suppose. Used to play in the woods all the time. And I got to know the gypsies, of course. I practically lived with them in the daytime for years. Then as soon as she got wind of it—'

'Celia's mother?'

He nodded. 'She paid me so little attention, she hadn't noticed what I was up to. Then when she did . . . I was packed off to prep school pretty smartish. Didn't even get a chance to say goodbye.' I frowned, trying to take it all in.

'The last time I saw Alice,' he said, coming to a halt and looking directly at me, 'was round about the first time I saw you.' He looked suddenly sad. 'I fully expected to go back and find you again after those first few days, but my bags were all packed and waiting for me. She didn't even give me any warning.'

He told me how he had repeatedly run away from the school he was sent to, and how eventually he had won a scholarship to the nearest grammar school.

'I hated that too, to be honest. But at least I was set free at the end of the day. And I joined the Air Defence Cadet Corps later. I always loved the idea of flying. To know what it must be like to be a bird . . . it's the nearest you can get to it . . . I love it.'

We reached the place where he had parked the car.

'What time do you have to be back by?'

'Not for a good couple of hours yet.'

He opened the boot and took out two thick rugs. Then we headed back, deep into the heart of the woods.

He made me tell him everything I could remember after the police raid: how I had found Gracie, how she and I had told no one. We kept remembering times we had glimpsed each other: awkward, incomprehensible times which made sense to us now. I laughed and groaned at how deeply I had taken offence at the grubby little village girl phrase, which was clearly just a repetition of Celia's. He marvelled at how he had never noticed my scar before, but reflected that I had always been wearing stockings until tonight.

'Not when you saw me come in from the garden with all those vegetables.'

'No. You're quite right. Your legs were completely bare and pink with cold. But I can assure you I wasn't looking at your ankles!'

We laughed at all the incongruous moments we'd had, which now fell into place. But I was still angry about the shove in front of Beatrice and the entire Mustoe family.

'Ah . . .' He looked up at the sky, and then shook one of the

194

rugs out on the ground. He sat down and patted the rug beside him, but I stood my ground, waiting for the explanation. 'I've never been that superstitious, not compared to Alice . . . but you know how she always said a man shouldn't let a woman cross between himself and a fire?'

'I can't remember that.'

'Well, it's old Romani stuff. A woman's power . . . I wouldn't normally . . .' I sat down to hear the explanation, which was sounding a little weak. 'It's just that there was something about you that day. You really got to me. It was as if you were full of magic – I mean really full of magic . . . I can't explain it . . . It felt like you had so much power, and then there you were crossing in front of me with the fire behind you and it seemed that if I didn't stop you . . . I don't know . . . something awful would happen.'

I laughed out loud.

'You see,' he said, 'something awful has happened. You have complete control over me!'

We lay back together and looked at the clear night sky. A few stars were dotted around, and then, as we continued looking, they seemed to have back-up. Thousands more arrived as our eyes adjusted, and then more, and more again . . . This is how it always used to be when we lay out all summer nights. You waited . . . it happened. And he waited for me now, listening for me to throw out little dots of light. He teased it out of me with patience.

I bared my soul to him beneath the stars, and he listened. And then, with a few whispered words of encouragement, he laid all of me bare to the softly risen moon.

42

James's interference paid off after all: I was told to take a few days' leave. He was still off with his arm injury, so we booked into a local inn, called The Mill.

It was an idyllic time: more vivid and detailed in my memory than any other. He lent me a gold ring of Alice's for when we booked in as Mr and Mrs Buckleigh, and our playing at husband and wife – child-like and giggly though it was – must have sparked off the same train of thoughts in both of us. Everything about our pretend marriage was wonderful. We called each other 'darling' and even invented an array of pets and two children who were staying with an aged aunt. The children were called Daphne and Cecil, and we became so carried away with our imaginary life together that we found ourselves lying to the landlady and her daughter during mealtimes, and trying not to look at each other in case we laughed.

The landlady was a stout woman from the Midlands who had moved to the Cotswolds with her husband nearly twenty years before. Their daughter, Lil, was not unattractive in a puppyish sort of way, but I couldn't help thinking of a gorilla in a dress. She had a heavy, wide back, short neck, and a brown pageboy hairstyle with a thick sausage of hair rolled back above her forehead. She must have been barely seventeen, and had a little girl toddler. At first the landlady implied that she was her other daughter, but Lil enjoyed putting us straight over our evening meal.

'We wuz all set to get married we wuz, but he went missing first day of the war. Missing presumed dead.'

'Dead, my arse,' muttered her mother from the bar. 'Missing presumed gallivanting more like.'

Lil looked piqued, so I admired her little girl. She was a glorious tousle-headed pixie with wide blue eyes, cherub lips and a tiny pointed chin at the base of a round face. She toddled over to our table and said endearing things like 'Da!' whilst hammering the cutlery up and down, all of which made Lil blush with pride and the landlady throw her hands up in apology. It was clear that Lil adored her little girl.

James's warm reaction to the child sent a shiver of excitement through me. But I was rescued from broodiness by him saying things like, 'Doesn't she remind you of Daphne at that age?' and I would reply, 'The spitting image! Though Daphne couldn't talk for years.'

'No, can't you remember that time she first spoke, darling? Her first words were . . . What were they, darling?'

'Stop it!'

'That's it! You were trying to force her into some pyjamas you'd just knitted her. "Stop it," she said, clear as day.'

And so on, until Lil asked us if we'd had our children young as well, and my clenched giggles began to hiss from the sides of my mouth and James had to claim I'd been drinking already.

The night was wonderful. There was a bathroom at the end of our corridor, and I took a long warm soak in it, even if the water was only a few inches deep.

James had opened the windows in our room on to the sunset, and we sat on the windowsill together, our toes touching, looking out on the still, dusky hills and the cloud of gnats jittering about in the shade of the garden. He took me like a gypsy takes an animal: sure of its approval, but slowly, stealthily, mesmerizing it with ever decreasing circles into complete surrender.

We trod water in the cool expanse of cotton sheets. Then we swam. The lightest of touches was heaven. If it was clumsy, I don't remember it that way. I remember the vastness of the bed, a huge blank canvas for us, the cotton like an extra skin stroking ours, and the utter, unchallengeable joy of it all.

We didn't sight land until the curtains turned pale with sunlight, and the scufflings of a bird clattered in the eaves.

I sat at breakfast waiting for James to finish shaving in the bathroom. I felt so transformed by our night together, I wondered if it showed in some way. I wondered if the landlady could see that I had crossed into a new phase of my life: did it show in my face? Did she have the slightest idea that I had been happier than I'd ever been in my life in her 'pink room' with the rose wallpaper and the tiny patch of mould above the curtains?

Breakfast was in one of the rooms off the main pub, but with the same wooden pub tables and chairs. Lil appeared with a large pot of tea and asked if I'd like to wait for my husband. When I nodded she hung around and tried to get chatting.

'You here for a special occasion, then?'

'Just . . . my husband has some leave.'

'Oh!' She gave me a look which spelt a wink. 'Must be nice to get away.'

'Yes.'

Her child planted herself in the doorway and smiled. She was looking directly at me, and I felt such a violent pang of emotion that I flinched. 'Oh . . . she's so . . . you must love her so much.'

'Susan?' She looked over at her daughter, and grinned. ''Course I do, dun' I' poppet?'

Susan was tapping a small wooden pig around the door-jambs, shooting us coy smiles from under her curls.

'What's it like being married then?' she asked me suddenly.

'Oh . . . It's wonderful. Like . . . nothing changes, only everything's more . . . certain, more secure . . . it makes you feel . . .' I drew a sharp breath, for suddenly James was in the doorway, carrying a tray of huge slabs of bread and home-made strawberry jam.

'It makes you feel like a big breakfast,' he said grinning.

I didn't know how long he'd been there – whether or not he'd heard my exultant views on marriage – but he seemed genuinely radiant.

Lil got up to go and potter in the kitchen somewhere off the corridor, and we two tucked into our breakfast, locking eyes and entwining fingers. Suddenly there was a whimper, and we looked over to the far table to see Susan – who had been crawling underneath it – stand up and look around in panic. I watched her dear little face as it crumpled, as the bottom lip grew swollen and trembled, as tears brimmed in her eyes and furrows tried to find a place in her spongy brow. It had slowly dawned on her that Lil had left. She didn't know why, and in that silly moment she didn't know if it was for ever or for five minutes, if it was to fetch tea or to abandon her. I could see, with an empty, sick feeling in my stomach, that all the little girl had registered was this: her mother had left her.

I felt the full horror of it seeping over me, a blot of blood spreading from a hopeless wound. I was leaking despair. If I empathized with little Susan, I did not reach out and comfort her. Instead I found my face had succumbed to my thoughts, and James was reaching over to me anxiously: 'Joy?'

Lil came in with a fresh pot of tea, and then gathered Susan up in her arms. To all the world Susan looked merely relieved.

But I knew where she had been these past few moments, and how much more it had been than a simple wail.

The moment soon passed, and James and I went walking. I had never seen him as relaxed and good-humoured as he was during our time at The Mill. And I wondered if my own persistent elation at being with him was heightened by a sense of impending doom. I wished James were a farm labourer or a munitions worker or a train driver – anything but a pilot. There was too much in the balance.

On day three, as we were driving back, I took the ring off my finger. He told me to keep it, and we returned to Woodside engaged.

I asked him to drop me in the village, while he went to see his father and Philip. If I'm honest, I just wanted to show off my uniform and although I couldn't tell anyone before Gracie, I wanted the world to see me in this new state: I wanted to walk through Woodside in love.

It was hot and quiet, and the odd clink of cutlery suggested that most people were indoors having their dinners, or outdoors with their sandwiches in the shade. I saw Spit Palmer with a new baby, pushing it in a pram across the road to the post office. She didn't see me. She didn't take her eyes off the baby, cooing and smiling so much she could easily have been knocked down by a bus. I saw Mr Bearpark in the distance, walking his bike uphill, and the elder Miss Wallock – now utterly doolally – with her pram of lambs. She had two, and they were really lambs no more: quite hefty things, with fat woolly faces and the smug look of pre-schoolers who really ought to be walking. They had that permanent smile that sheep have, and the pair of them looked about from their vehicle like two kings in a carriage. 'We'll just pop in the post office for a stamp, shall we?' she was crooning to them as she passed. 'Close your eyes by the butcher's.'

What drove a woman to such hideous lengths? What desperate needs had been flouted that she should pretend these fat lambs were her children? Was it a sense of incompleteness? A driving force? A need to be loved? A need to give love? There was a lightness to my step at the pleasure of this last thought: a love so great and bubbling it needed to be let out. The sun was on everything – even the road was warm through my shoes. Perhaps it was no more than completing the circle: a need to pass on the love that was given by your own mother. Then I thought about Celia's mothering: Celia's smothering. How simple it was to abuse that easily earned power. And I tried not to think about that other mother: the one whose mothering I could not conjure up.

The world seemed full of mothers. Even Digger, when I reached home, was slumped in a box by the front door, sunning herself in sheer contentment with four kittens at her teats. I crouched down to admire her brood. 'How do you know how to do it?' I whispered. She just wriggled on to her back and stretched out lethargically, while her kittens scrambled to get into a new sucking position.

She opened one eye and looked at me, and then closed it again, as if it were a daft question.

Gracie knew I was coming, because I'd written two days earlier, and of course the house smelt of baking. She greeted me in her apron, covered in flour, and squeezed me tight.

'Joy, my sweetheart! It's so good to see you! I'm sorry about the cakes – I did them for twenty minutes, but I think the oven's playing up . . .'

She took me into the kitchen to indicate some very brown fairy cakes, and looked so apologetic I had to hug her all over again. I hardly had my coat off before I told her: 'Gracie, you'll never guess! I'm engaged!'

'Lord above! Whatever next?' But she was smiling from ear to ear, and clapped her hands together as if she were already designing my dress in her head and planning the booties for the grandchildren.

'Oh! I hope he doesn't live up north or something. Don't let him take you to the other end of the country—' She could hardly get her breath.

'He's local.'

'*Local?*' She was radiant.

'Yes. He lives in Woodside. You'll never guess who . . .'

'Go on, then . . .'

'James Buckleigh!'

The blood drained from her face. She gripped the back of a chair and stared at me cheerlessly for a few moments, then she looked away into the middle distance, and slumped into the chair.

'What is it? Gracie . . . whatever's the matter?'

She swallowed, and cast me such a chill glance that I sat down too. 'You can't marry James Buckleigh. There's something you ought to know.'

43

I still had my coat on, and little pins and needles of sweat were spiking me under the thick wool of it.

'James Buckleigh isn't Howard's real son.'

'I know.'

'But he's a gypsy.'

'He's *adopted*. James told me about it.'

'He's told you? Then . . . Why are you marrying him?'

I pulled a face. 'Surely you don't think I should refuse him because of that? Gracie . . . you can't possibly hold that against him.'

'Of course not. I was just thinking . . . When you first came to me – you might remember this – Howard came to see me. He said this gypsy woman he'd looked after, she'd asked him to keep a lookout for her girl. And I swear, Joy, it sounded just like you – just like you – in fact, I'm certain it *was* you. Only, of course I denied it. I knew they could look after you much better up at the house and I wouldn't have a leg to stand on so I said . . . well, you know what I said.'

'It *was* me. I *was* the girl Alice meant.'

She looked at me, newly aghast. 'But Howard adopted a gypsy boy – I reckon he was hers too. That makes you James's sister!'

I let out a relieved burst of breath and rescued her quickly, and she was so grateful for the deliverance that she ate one of her own cakes. When I mentioned Mrs Buckleigh's estrangement from her husband she ate another one.

'James wants me to go up to the house later,' I said.

'I could come with you . . . if you like,' suggested Gracie, 'if that would help . . .'

There was something of an appeal in her suggestion, and I caught an unguarded girlishness in her as she touched her hair.

So, after much preparation, we decided to go to Buckleigh House. Just before we left I grabbed one of her cakes.

'You'll have to clean your teeth now,' she said, nervously putting on lipstick in the hall mirror. 'But they're so burned – I'm sorry they're dreadful.'

'They're lovely.' I glanced at her disbelieving face as she adjusted her hat for the umpteenth time. 'They may not be perfect, but they're warm. That's what matters.'

She smiled, and glanced in the mirror again. 'Oh, what do I look like?' And she changed her hat twice more before we set off.

As long as I live I shall remember that moment when Gracie and Howard locked eyes in the entrance hall of Buckleigh House. He popped his head out coyly from behind a pillar. James and I exchanged eager smiles, because it had been almost four hours since we'd touched, and there was a magic all over again. Because we were diagonally opposite, as were Howard and Gracie, our looks formed a cross, a giant kiss in the air between us in the hallway.

Gracie had turned completely pink, and giggled like a child when the grandfather clock chimed loudly next to her. Howard, who looked like a man in a desert who'd seen water, seized on the opportunity to laugh as well. He promptly forgot how to

speak English. 'Well . . . er . . . this is a surp . . . let me . . . um
. . .' He backed into a large room. 'Do come this way . . . I . . .'
and he tripped over a huge potted plant stationed by the door.
He fell, got up again, and dusted himself down. There was
something flamingo-like about him as he stood with one long
leg bent and his head hung low. 'Potted plants . . . seem to
move around all over the place!'

James whisked me away to another part of the house, and I
felt so excited for them both that I wasn't prepared to be left
alone with Philip.

'I was just off to see the vicar,' said James. 'The banns have to
be read a few weeks before we get married.'

It was thrilling to see him so resolute about marrying me, but
I couldn't for the life of me see what the hurry was all about.
'Do you have to do it right now?'

'Yes, I do. I know I shouldn't have been so irresponsible with
you, Joy, but the thing is . . . the thing is . . . you could be . . .
you know . . . with child.'

'I suppose . . .'

'And if you are, I don't want you or any child of mine being
left without a penny.'

'But you can marry me any time, can't you?'

James had a way of putting his elbow up over his forehead
and scratching the back of his neck. I noticed he tended to do
this when he was nervous, or didn't know what to say. He did it
now, and the penny suddenly dropped. Until then I had simply
seen it as a mild neurosis on my own part: a woman thing.
These foolish women who will worry so about their men,
when they simply should remain stoical and cheer them on in
battle. But wait: he was worried too. So worried he thought he
might not survive the next few weeks. He finished scratching,
and I threw myself at him pathetically. He held me very close
and said, 'I want you to be Mrs Buckleigh, sooner rather than
later, that's all.'

He showed me into a sunny room at the back of the house where Philip was reading a newspaper, and then he disappeared to make his visit to the vicar. Philip looked up and smiled: the first genuine smile I had seen on him. He was very different. He was able to stand up – which he did, to greet me – and walk around. There was a half-finished game of backgammon on a small table, which I guessed he'd been playing with Howard.

'I'm really glad you've come.' It seemed he could hardly stop smiling, and I sank down in a chair opposite him with some relief.

'You seem much better,' I said. 'Really – so much better.'

'Yes. They're putting me on a desk job next week. I'm quite looking forward to it actually. Although . . .'

'What?'

He chewed the inside of his cheek and indicated the newspaper he'd cast aside. 'It seems like a terrible cop-out, somehow. All these pilots going down.'

'Which pilots?'

He looked at me questioningly. 'Haven't you . . .?'

'I've been on leave for a few days – what's happened?'

'Just . . . all starting to happen. I ought to be up there with them.'

I didn't want him to start feeling guilty again, so I said, 'Flying isn't the only way to help win the war. They could do with people like you on the ground – who know what it's like up there.'

He smiled again. 'I hear congratulations are in order.'

44

The wedding was a low key affair and took place on the first Thursday of August. Mr Mustoe gave me away. I wore the same silk dress I had worn on my first date, and Howard had paid for some cream shoes to go with it. There were no official guests, apart from Gracie and Mrs Mustoe, but in the event Mo got some leave to attend, and George came with Emily (the baby Mustoe grown up), Spit Palmer thought it would be too romantic to miss, Miss Wallock offered to play the organ, Mrs Rollins thought she might just pop in and see the dress and Mrs Bubb was a sucker for weddings. Mrs Emery said you couldn't miss a toff's wedding, and Mrs Tribbit said she would keep her company, and Miss Prosser thought it would be discourteous not to go, and soon there was a ragbag of assorted Woodsiders filling every available pew.

The only photograph which remains shows us looking surprised more than anything. There I am in my lovingly made silk dress, and he in his uniform. We might almost have just walked home from the cinema that evening long ago, only to find that we were, to our astonishment, man and wife.

*   *   *

August and September were a living hell at the airfield. Planes went missing almost every day, friends died, people's lives shattered overnight, and in late summer German planes started attacking the air bases. Up until then I'd always believed that life was like a path, and you were either happy, or sad, or on an even keel. I didn't imagine you could be so very happy in love, whilst another strand of your life was such a nightmare. I didn't think you could feel sick and tearful and shocked all through the day, but filled with delight and anticipation all through the night. And also, up until then, I had always thought of happiness as some sort of joyous rapture, whereas in fact, for most of the time, happiness was just preserving what you had; it was stasis, a solid base, security. Happiness was no change.

The truck of men I drove in late August didn't contain a single pilot I'd driven in June. Some were on leave, but most had simply flown south or east and not come back. In a direct hit to our airfield in September we lost four Hurricanes, the laundry and Betty (who was collecting our newly washed shirts).

The confident women in my barracks that I had found so alien began to cry like mere mortals, and I found I loved them just as I loved Dot and Reeny. Ken, whose death had seemed a monumental tragedy in the early summer, was now just a speck in an ocean of brave men and women with their lives unlived.

I hadn't realized until then how close we were all becoming. I never in my life felt such a strong sense of belonging. It was terrible and it was wonderful. There were things in that war I never want to witness again, but I wouldn't have missed it for the world.

In late September Dot lost her little sister, Pat, in an air raid on the Midlands. She broke down saying Pat was fourteen and she'd only just started her periods. There were eight of us red-eyed around Dot, and no one had any supper that night although we were all as hungry as dogs.

I felt very sick: sicker than usual. I actually threw up in the lav. Not long after that I was discharged under paragraph eleven for being three months pregnant. I was devastated.

I resented being pushed out of the war. That may seem ungrateful, when so many people were being killed, but the alternative, waiting and knitting, felt so utterly pointless.

I was cajoled into joining the WVS, and bottled jam and knitted and rescued old clothes. I sent packages of jumpers with heavily darned elbows, worn shoes and grey underwear to people who had lost their entire families under rubble. Sometimes we sent them jam. I often wondered what it felt like to be torn about by grief, and to open a parcel containing Woodside WVS damson preserve and a couple of old off-white vests and pants.

In my frustration – though heavily pregnant – I decided to set up a farm. The house had an orchard and a field (which the Ministry of Agriculture already had its eye on). I bought farming manuals, enlisted the help of Mr Rollins and, later, a couple of officers who were billeted with us, and soon we had twenty chickens, a cow shed with one cow and half a field turned into a huge Victory Garden. We bought a horse for the other half: Howard resurrected an old cart and soon we had it up and running to save on petrol. If it hadn't been so cold and damp it might've been quite romantic.

In the meantime I had a baby boy in the April of 1941, and a girl in 1943. Both events filled me with what I can only describe as wild, unassailable joy. Holding each of them for the first time I felt an *explosion* of joy. I was a volcano firing off in all directions, an eruption of euphoria, and passion, and tenderness.

Andrew and Jill spent their early years without their father, but the house was anything but empty. Like many in wartime, we were a cock-eyed sort of household. Mrs Bubb had her little grandson, Johnny, from Coventry staying, and later we had two evacuees from London: a brother and sister, Donald and Maggie. There were often a couple of soldiers billeted with us. Howard encouraged Gracie to hold the WI meetings there sometimes; the Mustoes were frequent visitors, and Mr Mustoe brought what was left of the brass band to play after church every other Sunday; Mo and Tilly visited whenever they were home on leave, and they knew me so well it was like being back with the girls on the airfield.

I knew I was happy, and yet I felt a growing uneasiness. I used to think it was James being away. He had been posted further afield to the South of England, to 'relieve' pilots on constant missions. I knew this meant to 'replace', because the newspapers were full of pilots who hadn't come back. Later, after Jill was conceived, he was posted to India, doing flight tests and flying reassembled planes to the front line in Burma. All our young men had gone to risk their lives in places with silly names: Sidi Birani, the Kithera Straits, Oesterbeck, Nijmegen. I used to find myself singing, '. . . before we send him to the Dardanelles', one of my favourites as a child. The odds were stacked against us. I used to imagine what it would be like to be a widow, in order to prepare myself. I pictured the children growing up in that old house, the evacuees gone, Mrs Bubb retired and Gracie and Howard married perhaps, and living in her house, or passed away. I thought of our night in the woods under the stars, and though I thanked God we had had this, James and I, I wondered if that was all there was: our allocation of happiness.

45

Despite the hardships, things went pretty smoothly for a while. Picturing the worst from time to time did nothing to prepare me for what would happen in the spring of 1944. I could not possibly have imagined such a turn of events.

Jill was barely a year old and at her most difficult. She could walk a few paces, but wanted to crawl everywhere. She could reach all sorts of dangers she hadn't been able to reach before, and which hadn't been around when Andrew was a toddler. Cigarette lighters, for instance, left constantly around on table-tops by our two latest billeted officers, Anthony and Douglas.

Douglas was a quiet young man, given to mooching around the grounds and gazing at sunsets, reading and rereading letters from his fiancée. When he wasn't outside he was in the room at the top of the house he shared with Anthony. Anthony was always teasing me about being Farmer One-Cow, and often his teasing was so persistent it was tantamount to flirting. With my arms full of Jill or my wellingtons ankle-deep in dung, I found it hard to believe anyone would want to flirt with me. It was perhaps for this reason that he got away with it for so long. It was weeks after his arrival that Mrs Bubb warned me to 'watch out for that one'. Still, I couldn't imagine any harm coming from Anthony. They were involved in some intelligence work somewhere in Gloucestershire, and couldn't tell us what they did after they left in the morning and before they came home at teatime.

In any case, whatever Mrs Bubb said, Anthony was attentive to Andrew and Jill and the evacuees. Even if he left his lighter all over the place, he did make the children laugh, and often played games with Jill on his knee in which he told her very solemnly to sit still and then opened his legs so that she fell through. He was an extra pair of hands about the place, and he and Douglas mucked in at haymaking or whenever there were tasks that required a bit of muscle.

Having established his niche in our household, Anthony began to take small liberties. He would make me cups of tea and prop my feet up by the fire, or he would adjust my headscarf to contain a stray piece of hair. Sometimes he would be up before Mrs Bubb and I would come down to breakfast to find a little wild flower beside my plate in an old meat-paste jar.

'You're going to have to speak to him,' Mrs Bubb told me one day. I could tell from her tone that she might well have done so herself. 'He'll've left a few mementos in this war, I shouldn't wonder. Seen his sort before. Give him an inch and he'll take a yard, you mark my words. Oh yes!' She closed her eyes as if remembering. 'I've seen his sort!' Mrs Bubb had always been an ally and I was afraid of her disapproval. She had often told me how good it was to have me around, how much happier the house felt with me and the children in it, how much easier I was to work for than either Celia or her mother. And she had always been respectful towards me. So this advice felt like a spike in my side. I was behaving improperly, or at least, I was not responding appropriately to improper behaviour. Whatever would she think of me when James came back? If I acted now, it would not be too late. Even so, I wished she had acknowledged the one thing that had prevented me from acting until now: it had been a long, long war, and my youth was floating past in pig-shit and raking and child-rearing and waiting and waiting. It was so exciting to be flirted with, so thrilling to be the focus of someone's attention for reasons other than feeding.

Reminding him that I was married seemed almost like a flirtation in itself, but anyway I did it one morning after a particularly daring attempt of his to touch my waist.

'I know,' he said, cocking his head at an angle, 'but what does "married" mean these days?'

I was astonished. I went to pull on my wellingtons in the back porch. I was so indignant at his easy dismissal of my marriage vows that it took me a moment to gather myself. 'I love my husband. That's what it means.'

He folded his arms and leant against the porch wall, surrounded by ancient outdoor coats on hooks and the fusty smell of discarded boots.

'He's in India, isn't he?'

I straightened myself and gave a level, determined look by way of reply.

He raised his eyebrows. 'And you must know what happens out there!'

I took my woollen work coat off its hook and started stuffing my arms into it.

'Come on, Joy. Don't be naïve. You know they provide women by the score. And I'll tell you what,' he lowered his voice as if he were offering top military intelligence, 'what those girls can't do, no one can!' He chuckled, and it seemed like a sneer.

I was foolishly hurt by what he said. I felt wounded and raw, and his enjoyment of my discomfort left me feeling stupid. 'I don't quite know why you're telling me this.'

He took my shoulder as I turned to go out, and said in a low but confident voice, so close I could smell the tea on his breath: 'Oh, I think you do.'

I pushed past him and into the bright morning. I wanted this man out of our house. I felt cheapened by him. But I had no power to move him, and I knew then he would be there every morning and every night, confident of wearing me down, of getting what he wanted, one way or another.

46

In the days that followed Anthony stepped up his attentiveness towards the children, as if by making himself indispensable to their happiness he could force my hand through some sort of gratitude or sense of obligation. When that failed, he began to mention his family house in Sussex, his inheritance, the car he had bought just before the war. I suppose he imagined that, because I had married James and lived in this house, I must be the sort of girl attracted to wealth. He may have taken my indifference for coyness, because he developed this tack with offers of meals in restaurants, visits to important friends' houses, a share in the privileged life of an officer.

Sometimes I was almost charmed by his chirpiness with the children, but very occasionally I would see a glimpse of something more sinister: a sudden flaring of the nostrils when all did not go his way, a movement in the muscles of his cheek as he concealed a clenching of the teeth, a thin, determined set to the lips.

And then again, just as I imagined he was off my trail, I would sense him watching me as I came out of the bathroom, see him skulking in an alcove and fixing his eyes on me with an intensely knowing look.

This is when I should have said something to Howard, but I

didn't. I did ask if we were obliged to have the officers, and he explained that we were. When he asked if there were any problems, I said that there weren't. I felt suddenly very foolish. What could I possibly have said? Nothing had happened. It would have seemed unpatriotic to want one of them to leave because I thought he was making eyes at me.

In the early days of June 1944 – around four o'clock – something unexpected happened.

I was collecting sheets from the beds ready for washing. I went to the officers' room as I always did for their laundry, and felt suddenly curious. They were away all day and there was no risk of being caught – for another hour or so at least – so I began to look through their things. Douglas had very little: a photograph of his family, one of his girlfriend, and a small travelling alarm clock. He also kept a diary which I didn't read – not because I was morally good, but because I wasn't curious about him. Anthony had a small leather writing folder inside his underwear drawer. I unzipped it and inside were three photographs: one of his family, one of a girl, and one of himself standing beside a car. The girl was fairly plain, but clearly well-to-do. She wore a jewelled necklace, off the shoulder evening wear, and her nose was tilted in that slightly imperious way Celia had with her nose. On the back was written 'Stella, Jan 1943'. I zipped everything up again and placed the folder back in the drawer. Further back, buried in the socks, was a magazine of naked women, and another of pornographic cartoons. I looked at this for some time, because I had never seen anything like it. Some of the things the men were doing to the women were unthinkable, and the obvious aggression in the pictures made me shudder.

Returning to the landing with my arms full of sheets, I spotted someone through the window. There, on the gravel drive in front of the house, stood a young man in uniform. I hurried down the stairs to the front door.

He stood quite still, his eyes looking around him earnestly, and when he saw me he smiled.

'Can I help you?' I asked.

He continued smiling.

'George! George – I didn't recognize you! It is you, isn't it?'

He stepped forward coyly and let me embrace him. I invited him in and offered him tea, but he insisted he didn't want to stop me doing whatever I was doing.

'I was having a cup of tea,' I said. 'And then I'll take the potato peelings out for the pigs.'

I tossed the sheets into the scullery and then joined him in the kitchen. He hardly stopped smiling, and I found I was delighted to have him there. I told him he looked so grown-up in his uniform, but that was a lie. In fact I thought he looked painfully young and vulnerable, and I wanted him not to have to fight in this war at all.

After we'd exchanged news, he accompanied me to the pigsty and chuckled at the pigs. I offered to show him round the little farm we'd created, and he agreed keenly. He smiled a lot, at everything, but all the while I felt he was hiding something.

We went right the way round the grounds: through the Victory Garden, the field, the orchard and back across the lawn to the stable, near the yew trees which ran up to the wall and the entrance gate.

'Is everything all right, George? Is there something worrying you?'

He took a deep breath and let out a faint sigh. It was clear there was something, so I waited. He ran his hand down the nose of our horse, Ivan, and continued looking at him as he said, 'The thing is, Joy, I only joined up because everyone else was. I didn't really want to at all!'

'There's no shame in that. It makes no odds, does it?'

He turned to look at me. 'The thing is, I know I'm going to die. And I'm scared. That's the truth of it: I'm scared.'

217

He looked at me so anxiously that I put my arm on his sleeve. He puffed out a sigh again as if this confession had been a monumental effort.

'I think everyone's scared. I know James is. You wouldn't be human if you weren't afraid. It's not anything to be ashamed of.'

'I don't know if I am ashamed of it. I'm not scared of dying, see. It's not *that* I'm scared of. I know I'm going to die. I just know it. If you'd seen what I've seen . . . The thing is, I'm scared of . . .' He trailed off and sighed again.

'What is it, George?'

He began to run his hand across the wood grain of the stable wall. 'I'm scared . . . of not . . . of dying before I've even . . . lived.' He looked at me desperately. 'Joy, I haven't kissed anyone. I haven't made love to a woman. I'm eighteen and I haven't even kissed anyone!' His voice was beginning to shake a little, and I put my arms around him. He held on to me so tightly I felt tears prickling my nose and eyes.

'Last time we were at Buckleigh House together you weed on me,' I reminded him.

He held me back from him so that he could see my face. 'I promise I won't wee on you this time.'

Then before I could disentangle myself his lips were on mine, pressing into mine with such warmth I felt a flood of emotion. His left hand cupped the nape of my neck and I couldn't believe the tenderness of it, or the relentless hunger of it, which matched my own for James – matched my own except this wasn't James. But he was so much a part of my childhood, and so much a part of everything good and wonderful I remembered, that for a moment I was Buster Keaton and he was a sheepdog doctor. And suddenly his hand was on my breast, and the sparks shooting off hotly in all directions were so like the ones I felt with James, and it felt so good to be with James again, that suddenly he *was* James.

218

No sooner had these thoughts begun to rush in than I caught him. I pulled his hand away and then I pulled back.

'No! I'm sorry—'

'I'm sorry, Joy. Forgive me.' He was breathing heavily now, his lips wet and swollen with kissing. 'I'm sorry, I shouldn't have.'

His contrition, his heavy sorrowful face in the midst of his lust somehow ennobled him. I wished I could have given in to him, shown him everything he wanted to know.

'It's okay,' I said, straightening my blouse. 'Please don't worry, George.' I held his hands to show him that I wasn't offended. 'But I don't think you're going to die. Not yet, anyway. I don't think you're going to miss out on any of it.'

I led him out of the stable, and there was a new shock awaiting me. There, slouching against the stable door, with his eyebrows mockingly raised, was Anthony.

47

The sly curve of Anthony's smile could not have been better calculated to make me feel my shame. He could not have better judged his appearance, lolling there as an obvious spectator, to renew my awareness of what I always knew myself to be: bad. Rotten through and through. It was as if Gracie had spent a lifetime trying to convert me, trying to instil some goodness into me, but it had, after all, been nothing more than a clever cover-up. With his sneaky voyeurism he had caught me out being what he knew me to be: wicked and irredeemable. I had seen it mirrored in his eyes as he watched me try to pretend he hadn't seen me. And when George had saluted him, he had saluted back, smirking. Such clever malevolence I had only seen in one other person in my entire life. He had been sent to punish me. Sent to remind me of my own wretchedness. I was wild, I was mad, I was evil, and no one had guessed. All these years and I had fooled everyone. But he knew. Anthony had known from the start.

By this time Gracie had moved into Buckleigh House permanently. Sadly, the move had not heralded a union between herself and Howard, an idea I had cherished for so long. She didn't seem unhappy though. Most days she helped with small chores and kept me company over a cup of tea. What she did on the other days I didn't know, but if she visited her old house I had little time to visit it now. However, she often appeared only briefly at weekends for a quick cup of tea, looking as though she'd been out walking or digging her garden.

On one such day, we sat in the orangery knitting. The beech trees on the far side of the road leading up from the village to the Buckleigh House gate were host to scores of rooks who were making a dreadful racket. I was distracted, because I wanted to tell Gracie about Anthony, and ask her advice, but I was afraid now either that she would tell Howard or that she or both of them would approach him and find out about the incident with George. I couldn't bear the thought that it might get back to James. I lived in dread that I had ruined the most beautiful thing that had ever happened to me and, more horrifyingly still, it seemed obvious to me now that I had always been unworthy of happiness, and that its withdrawal from me was almost inevitable.

I must have looked flustered because Gracie asked me if everything was all right.

'Those rooks,' I said, trying to rethread a darning needle with wool that had become too fluffy with handling. 'A grim time of year for birds.'

'June? Lovely time I should've thought. Wake me up with such a chorus in the morning – oh, I love it best of all in June.'

'Not so good for fledglings.'

'Oh? I suppose not. But still, we all have to leave the nest.' She clicked away with her needles and then looked up almost guiltily. 'Well, all save me, I suppose. I'm still sitting four square in my folks' nest, aren't I?' Then she gave an apologetic little chuckle. 'Wouldn't have minded being shoved out myself, though.'

As if in indignation that Gracie had escaped the natural order of things, the rooks began to croak in unison: loud 'krohs' and 'krahs' that flooded in through the open orangery windows.

'You don't know the half of it with rooks,' I said. 'Once they've booted them out, they build a little circle of thorns around their nests so that the fledglings can't come back.'

'Never! Fancy doing that to your own children. Well, I never!' She shook her head in disbelief. 'How come you know so much about birds? Did James tell you that?'

The darning needle was becoming sweaty in my fingers.

'You always did know a lot about birds. Even when you were small. I expect it comes from your time in the woods . . .'

There it was again, a little flash of something, something darting away from the edge of my memory – almost, *almost* I had it by the tail, but it had gone.

Maybe Gracie took my frown and my silence to indicate a discomfort with this line of questioning, for she quickly abandoned it.

'Fancy that, then. One thing encouraging your children to leave the nest, but what sort of parent stops them from coming back ever?'

I began to feel sick and thirsty. 'I'll open another window and create a through draught, shall I? It's so hot in here.'

48

My agitation about Anthony's discovery of me and George together did nothing but grow. And I was quite right to be worried about it, for the following day my worst fears were realized.

It had promised to be a perfectly normal weekday. For the whole of the previous evening, however, both Douglas and Anthony had been detained at work, and had returned very late indeed, so that Mrs Bubb had had to give them a cold supper well after midnight. This had been the night of 5th June 1944, and it wasn't until later that we would learn the nature of the secret planning they were engaged in.

At breakfast, Howard asked if Mrs Bubb or I would like a lift to Gloucester in the cart. I certainly could have done with a day out, but Mrs Bubb looked exhausted, and I had heard her complaining earlier that the village shop was right out of Oxo and never had any decent soap, so I insisted she take the opportunity for a day's shopping. Although, if I'm honest, I also felt a vague uneasiness about spending a long trip sitting beside Howard – whose company I usually enjoyed – so soon after the George incident. I had no reason to think he knew about it, and if I had been wiser I would have told him about it – and about Anthony – right from the start. But as it was I wished Mrs Bubb and Howard a pleasant trip, and they set off shortly after the officers' MC truck puttered off down the lane.

I stretched my legs out on the chair in the kitchen and yawned. The evacuee children had already set off for school, Andrew was playing with Jill outside on a rug, and would no doubt stay out all day playing in his imaginary worlds, with occasional forays into the kitchen for a drink or a sticking plaster or an additional prop for his game: a wooden spoon, a newspaper, a piece of string, a jam jar or a crayon.

Yesterday's wind had died down, and I looked forward to a pleasant day. After the chores I would potter: just me and the children, for the first time in ages.

It was in this mellow frame of mind that I unhooked my socks from the line above the range and proceeded to put them on. I was surprised therefore, to hear footsteps on the stairs, and was just rising to go and look in the entrance hall when the kitchen doorknob began to turn. I watched it with a growing sense of nausea.

Anthony stood beaming in the doorway. 'Did I miss breakfast?' He yawned emphatically then came in and slumped down on the chair by the range and splayed his legs in a relaxed and proprietorial way, as if he might almost be about to summon breakfast. 'Bit of a lie-in today, I'm afraid.'

I could feel my heart beating indignantly. 'But you've missed the transport. The truck went ages ago. What are you going to do?'

He scratched his head nonchalantly and said, 'Oh dear! Looks like it's just you and me, then. Dearie me.'

He lay back and closed his eyes with a smile. I loathed that smile. It was knowing and mischievous, hardly even pretending to be benign, and there was something abusive in the power it knew it wielded over me.

'You haven't heard, then?' he sighed.

'What?'

'You haven't had the wireless on?'

He looked at his watch.

'The communiqué from Supreme HQ will be out by now, and at midday Churchill will make an announcement to the House of Commons.' He patted his hands on the arm of the chair. 'Yep. Today's the big day, young Joy.'

I made my way hurriedly towards the back door. Once in the porch, I could slip my wellingtons on and be out of the house before anything could happen. He wouldn't dare do anything in front of the children. I prayed they would stay close to the house now. I could hear Jill making 'deh' noises not far off, and I willed her to stay put. But before I could exit the door to the porch, Anthony strode over and shut the door behind me. I stood in the kitchen, sandwiched between him and the door, and I could smell his sleepy breath as he towered over me.

'Oh, don't be unsociable, Joy. It's D-Day! There's no escaping it. This is it!'

'What do you mean?'

That smile again. 'This is the day we've all been waiting for. This is what me and Dougie have been planning all these months, you see. All this top intelligence work and this is the culmination of it. Allied troops have landed in France – the biggest sea-borne invasion ever. Bet you didn't think I was doing such important work, did you?'

I looked away from him.

'Did you?' He persisted, with a slight edge of aggression this time.

'I had no idea, no.' I swallowed hard, and my mouth was becoming very dry. 'Good. Well, I think I'd better . . . I have to check on Jill—'

'Joy, Joy, Joy!' He shifted his weight a little and I thought he was going to step back, but instead he put his arm around me. 'I think this calls for a celebration, don't you?' I tried to wriggle free but the tightening of his grip was so sudden and brutal that

225

I knew struggling would be pointless. 'I think a man deserves a little "entertainment" when he's worked so hard for his country, don't you?'

Up until this point I had tried to deny my worst fears about his intentions, but there could be no doubting them now. If I clouted him it would be excusable, surely? Why didn't I, then? Why didn't I?

'No! Please, don't! You've got me wrong. I'm not like that—'

'Oh, I think we both know you are, Joy.' And just in case I hadn't understood the allusion, he said it again, deep into my ear. 'I think we both know exactly what you're like.'

He had pushed his groin right up against me and I thought I could feel everything through the serge trousers. He took advantage of my shock to grab at my breast and knead it roughly before dragging open the neck of my blouse and pushing his fingers on to the nipple and pinching hard.

The worst of it all, as I suddenly seemed to stand outside myself and watch the disaster like a bystander, was that I had this terrible, shadowy sense that I deserved it. I *was* wretched, and it was clear he knew that I was. 'You're a bad girl, Joy, and you know it!' he panted, as if to verify my sense of worthlessness. He took my buttock in his hand and lifted me hard up against him. 'You're a bad, bad girl and you love it, don't you?'

I tried to push him but he squeezed harder on my nipple with each shove, pressed his lips on mine and gave threatening little bites. Even so, it was not any physical handicap, but my utter sense of worthlessness that more than anything prevented me from freeing myself.

He had worked his fingers inside my corduroys when a sudden pounding on the outside back door made him start. He released one hand and stood back from me, opening the kitchen door behind me slightly with his right hand. It was glass-panelled, and opened on to the porch where, as I turned, I saw the back door let the sunlight flood in as a young woman in MTC uniform gingerly opened it.

'Sir! You're needed after all, sir. HQ need you straight away!'

He recoiled from me as though he had no idea who I was or what I was doing there, ran his hands through his hair and tilted his head back slightly.

'I'll be right there, Cribbs. Wait in the truck.'

'Sir!'

I took advantage of his disentanglement to dart past him into the sunshine, holding my blouse together at the neck and striding shoeless into the sunlight, where I waited until the truck took him away.

When Howard and Mrs Bubb returned later I had gathered myself. Although people had been celebrating throughout the day, we listened to the wireless together and heard the good news officially for ourselves. The best news of all – brought to us by Douglas – was that he and Anthony were to leave for good the next day, their mission over, and were being posted elsewhere. Once I heard this I really did feel like celebrating, and D-Day has remained for ever in my memory as my own Deliverance Day.

49

I would never have guessed it, but it seemed it was Howard's idea to celebrate the advance into France with a party in the grounds of Buckleigh House. He let the Women's Volunteer Service do most of the organizing, and it was to be held towards the end of June.

Although I liked the idea, I found myself becoming quite anxious about it as the day approached. I wasn't cut out for this lady of Buckleigh House lark. Having to speak to people before I was spoken to wasn't my thing at all. I felt increasingly uncomfortable about myself. I seemed to lack all social graces and even, at times, simple courtesy. I was clumsy and oafish whenever I was in the village. When I bumped into Miss Wallock I asked after her elder sister, only to find she had been dead two months; and I cooed with delight at Spit Palmer's tummy, asking about the due date, when she had merely put on a bit of weight after her last baby. Celia would never have been so clumsy. Or if she had, she would have known how to wriggle out of it, or turn it to her advantage. It would all have weighed so lightly on her. Of course they wouldn't have liked her any more for it, but they would have talked about her a lot less.

Maybe Howard saw my concern, for he said to me on the

morning of the party, 'Do all the organizing you like, but this afternoon I don't want you to lift a finger. Just stand at the front of the house and relax.'

The rain started, and it didn't let off until three o'clock. Mrs Bubb ran around like a woman possessed, making last minute notices reading 'Please Remove Your Shoes' in case they all came in the house by mistake for the lavatory (which she had clearly labelled in the back porch).

People started to arrive, tiptoeing over the gravel and the sodden grass in their Sunday best. Mrs Emery was the first to appear, and I shook hands with her. She was surprisingly short for a woman who had inspired constant terror, and her husband, whose sleep we had so persistently disturbed, was a quiet red-faced man who wouldn't say boo to a goose. He came fully equipped with his Punch and Judy show. Normally terrified of his wife, as the animator of Punch he seemed quite happy to beat the living daylights out of her.

The brass band showed up next, and as soon as they started to play, the sun seemed tempted out of the clouds and everyone walked with a little spring in their step.

Everything was going well until I walked past the tea stands, which ran down the side of the lawn. One woman said, 'Go and fetch a cloth, would you, love? Only this tea's spilt all over and the cloth's sodden.'

I was about to turn and go in search of one, when Mrs Tribbit, the grocer's wife, piped up, 'Go on, it's no good pretending you're too good to wipe a table, Joy Burrows.'

The other women nudged her as if she might have gone too far, but Mrs Tribbit pursed her lips defiantly. 'Don't think I can't remember the filth that came out of *your* mouth, my girl. Once a gypsy, always—'

'Is there a problem?' It was Howard.

Mrs Tribbit flushed and looked down at the table. 'I was just saying . . . We need a cloth.'

'I see. Well, if you'd like to follow me into the kitchen, I'm sure Mrs Bubb will provide you with one.' There was not an edge of frostiness in his voice. He smiled warmly, and for Mrs Tribbit there was nothing to do but attempt a smile also, and follow him to the kitchen. I was left with the other woman, who looked away and busied herself pouring tea. I walked awkwardly over to the 'children's area' where Mr Emery was still setting up and Mr Mustoe was pretending to be a clown, squirting himself in the eye and sitting on hooters. The smaller children laughed outrageously, the older children stuffed their faces with sandwiches, and the very young looked utterly bewildered. I stayed there, smiling and clapping, until a suitable time had elapsed for me to pick my way back to the house and hide.

It was easier to make a quick exit towards the Victory Garden. No one was there, and I decided to make my way to the paddock at the end and find some solace sitting against the stone wall, hidden from view.

Just as I reached the raspberry bushes I heard a loud rustle behind the runner beans. I stopped in my tracks and listened. Another rustle. This time the bean poles swayed dangerously from side to side as if someone were uprooting them.

'Who's there?'

No answer.

'Who is it?'

The movement stopped. The party and its noise were way behind me now, and I felt uneasy. Slowly I tiptoed forward, as noiselessly as possible. I peeped around the edge of the runner beans and there, looking very shifty, was a large ewe.

'What are you doing here?' I asked.

She shot me one of those 'I know absolutely nothing I'm only a sheep' looks and bolted past me with perfect timing, knocking me right off my feet. I followed her through the fruit orchard and up to the five-bar gate at the edge of it.

'You lost?' I asked.

She looked at me shiftily again and, having worked out she probably couldn't leap it, she began trying to dig under the gate. I tried to stop her, but she kept on scuffling with her hooves and her nose, butting the gate manically until her face was streaked in blood.

I sat down beside her and talked to her as gently as I could. I could smell the iron-blood and the oily sweetness of her wool. I rested my face on her side and remembered the coarse softness of a sheep pillow. I had slept with sheep during my escape. I had spent nights under the black sky with them, sandwiched between them for warmth, quietly accepted as a human lamb.

'That's my bloody ewe, that is!'

Turning round I saw Farmer Witchall.

'Sorry! I was just having a shufti round your land – see what you're growing, and that. But that's my bloody sheep!' He walked right up to us and put his hands on his hips when I explained how I'd found her. 'You know what, don't you? She's come five fields to get 'ere. Broken three fences most like, and two walls she's probably damaged – 'less she jumped 'em. And she's still got three fields to go!'

'Go where?'

'After them bloody lambs, ent she?' He jabbed a finger at a hill on the horizon. 'See them? That's her lambs up there.'

I looked up at the hill. Hundreds of fat lambs were dotted in the distance, all weaned from their mothers that very week. 'She'll find 'em an' all, if you let her.' He had the ewe by the scruff. 'Don't worry. I'll have her in the cart in no time. I was on my way back soon anyway.'

He took her off to the road, and I watched the weary ewe waddle away defeated.

At six o'clock the wretched party was still going on, and Howard came to find me in my room.

'I'd like you to do something for me,' he said. He stood

awkwardly in the doorway, not sure what to do with his long arms. 'Would you come with me and do me a huge favour?'

I followed him out to the front of the house, where he spoke in a very low voice to a man in a suit.

'Ladies and gentlemen!' boomed the man. 'Ladies and gentlemen!' he said again, waiting for silence. 'Let us give a very warm thank you to our host and hostess!'

Then Howard did something he had never done before. He took my hand, led me on to the middle of the lawn, and in front of the entire neighbourhood, in front of Mrs Tribbit and Mrs Emery and Miss Wallock and the Women's Volunteer Service and the Home Guard and my old teachers and the evacuees, he danced with me.

Somewhere off to the side a group of musicians were playing a slow, Celtic waltz, and looking over I could see Miss Wallock with a fiddle under her chin, smiling in our direction.

There was an ancient melancholy in the music that conjured up generations of couples swaying gently together at the end of the day: on quaysides, in pubs, in barns, under the stars. He was no mean dancer, leading me with astonishing prowess about the muddied lawn, but when I looked up at Howard's face I could see the price it had cost him to appear confident and break his own mould. Droplets of sweat on his brow, and his cheeks rigid with smiling, he was unable to look anywhere but down. I felt his hand on my back and all the tender warmth of him and what he had done. It was the music of lovers, a cunning concoction of joy and lament, and I wanted to cry for him and Gracie and for lovers everywhere kept from loving each other. I wanted to cry for all the love that could have been, for this tall, gangly man who'd loved all through the trenches, and for all the wasted years.

People were clapping: distant popping in our ears. 'Dance with Gracie!' I whispered.

He smiled, and walked me back to the house. The lawn filled with couples dancing.

'Dance with her,' I said again.

He gave a breath of a laugh and went into the kitchen to find his pipe.

The following morning I helped the children stack up the remaining chairs on the front lawn, ready to be taken back to the village hall. I was just returning to the house when Donald, one of the evacuees, dropped his stack and gave a little yelp.

'Who's that?' he shouted. 'There's someone there!'

Running towards him and following his line of sight, I saw someone darting through the orchard. I ran over to the far end of the orchard and the five-bar gate and waited. The ewe stopped a few feet away, looking hangdog and cheated.

Already, her face was coated in fresh blood, and her fleece was matted with bits of twig and leaves and dust.

We stood studying each other for some time.

'You love them that much?' I said.

I unhooked the rope from the top of the gate, and watched her great grey woolly behind as she bolted past me and trundled across the next field. 'Yes,' she said. 'Of course I do.'

50

All seemed well after that, or as well as it could be with James away and in unknown danger. July passed peacefully and with the happy little landmarks that children's growing provides. So long as James came back safely, I couldn't imagine anything rocking our boat again. But I hadn't bargained on another visitor late in August: one who would pose a far greater threat to my happiness.

It was just beginning to get dark when I heard the slowly beating wings of a wood pigeon as it wheeled away, heralding the crunch of footsteps on the gravel outside. I looked up from my darning, head cocked, waiting. People continued to speak jauntily on the wireless as if nothing had happened. Howard must have let him in, because I heard voices in the hall and no sound of a bell.

'Look who's come to see you!' said Howard, as he showed the visitor into our living room.

A foolish hope that it might be James – home for some unexpected reason – fluttered and then sank back into my chest. There was a burst of canned laughter from the wireless as I saw Philip Bird standing anxiously before me, and Howard went to turn it off.

'Oh,' I managed.

'I'm sorry to intrude so late.' He was flushed and troubled, and brought with him a waft of energy and manhood that the living room seemed unable to accommodate. I stood up to fetch him something: biscuits? Ovaltine? He declined all refreshment, but eventually took a small brandy handed to him unbidden by Howard.

'How are you?' I said at last, when he was settled on the sofa next to my armchair.

'Oh, not too bad.' He twirled his glass and frowned into it. 'Well, actually, my mother's very ill. That's why I'm back this way.'

'Oh.'

'I'm so sorry to hear that,' said Howard, playing the host far better than me. 'Is it serious?'

'Her heart. She's had a couple of small attacks before, but this one was more serious. It doesn't look as though she'll . . . I don't think—'

'You poor chap. Is there anything we can do? Is she in hospital?'

'No. The doctor's been. Says she just has to rest.'

Howard was attentive, but I was aware that I was merely sitting there, unable to comprehend the reason for the visit, and wishing that he had not come unannounced. I would've liked to have heard the rest of the wireless programme.

He caught my eye, and apologized again for intruding. Then he glanced at Howard as if Howard were intruding. Then, scratching his head, he addressed me awkwardly:

'You know I haven't always . . . I'm not a very good son.' He rubbed his hand over his face, as if he might wipe off the old one and reveal a new one. But he didn't. 'The fact is, I can't stand being there. I just had to get away.' There was the faintest hint of a sob in his last word. 'I'm sorry. I shouldn't have come.'

At this first show of emotion Howard was instantly courteous, but managed to find a reason to absent himself, secure in the knowledge that emotion was a woman's business, and nothing for him to concern himself with.

As soon as he had gone I wished he hadn't, for it was easy to see why I had once been so attracted to Philip. Despite the fat tears that now rolled down his cheeks, and the memory of his depression, he was to me an extraordinarily handsome man. I reached out a hand over the arms of our chairs, and he took it.

'Is there someone with her?' I asked.

'Oh, yes. A neighbour. She's being well looked after. It's just . . . I can't stand being there. I know it's awful, but I was wondering . . . I don't know, if there was the slightest possibility I might stay the night? Just one night—'

'Of course.' I said it without thinking. He was clearly too distraught to go back tonight. And since he'd come by bus he would have to return on foot, or else Howard would have to get the cart out, and I knew he didn't like using it in the dark. It was obvious he should stay now he was here.

'How's James? I still feel bad about the accident. Did he get over his injuries?'

'Oh, that. Yes. He flew on the south coast for a bit, then got himself injured again. He's test flying planes in India right now. Anyway, I'm sure that accident with you wasn't anyone's fault.'

'I suppose not. There was some confusion over who had the control: him or me.'

The words hung in the air like a kestrel, absorbing more weight with each second of silence.

I could feel his hand stroking mine now. I pulled my feet up underneath me in the armchair and leaned towards him. 'Tell me about it. You never really explained why you don't get on with your mother.'

'Ah! Families! Bloody families!'

I waited for him to elaborate, but he didn't. So I tried, 'What's your family like, then?'

'My family? What's my family like? Well, there's a question . . .' He shuffled himself towards me too, and I made sure not to look too interested in his reply, in case it stopped the flow. 'My father died when I was eight. TB, he had. Survived the trenches, survived the flu, and died of a bloody cough!' He paused, but still I said nothing, waiting for him to continue, hoping he would lead himself somewhere. 'That left us all up the creek. Mum had no work and four children. She'd had five, but my little sister died when she was two – diphtheria, it was. Beautiful little girl . . .' He rocked his head back and looked up at the corner of the ceiling, and I could almost see the little girl's face he looked so wistful.

'I'm sorry,' I said.

'Broke everyone's heart. Mum . . . she never got over it. Never. We were none of us any good after that. Especially Daisy . . .'

He broke off completely, and I seemed to have lost him.

'Daisy?'

He swung his eyes round to look at me, as if I were a stranger who had just walked in the room. 'Yes – Daisy. She got it worst.' He rubbed his temples slowly, and I waited. 'See, she came after Ivy. And no one could replace Ivy. Perhaps if she'd been a boy . . . But our Dad doted on Daisy – he loved her, and that seemed to make things worse. There was something not right about her, Mum said. Something not right about her, and that made Dad look after her more. But she wasn't having any of it. She already had a son who was simple – Sidney, my older brother – and she couldn't handle another one. And when Dad died that was it. She made Daisy go into a home. Just because she had one daft son already and because the poor little mite had the bad luck to come after Ivy, and because she could never be Ivy, and because Dad wasn't there to stop her. Only . . .'

I began to feel queasy. I wasn't sure I wanted to hear the ugly story of his family's unhappiness.

'. . . she didn't take Daisy to the home.'

A huge wave of relief passed over me. I didn't want poor Daisy in a home because of that foolish woman's grief. I didn't want the woman I'd met to be responsible for such a crime. Suddenly his head was bent forward and he was crying again.

'I did,' he whispered.

My mouth was suddenly full of saliva, and I couldn't stop it coming. I felt I was going to be sick. I didn't want to see him crying. I put my hand to my lips, but really I wanted to put it over his, too.

'You did?'

'She made me. Mum made me take her. She said I was to tell her I was taking her to a nice place for tea, and then I was to leave her. And I was eight. What could I do? She said we were poor and with Dad gone and us all too young to work we'd all starve, and Sid was fit for nothing, and another one like Sid would be the death of her. What could I do? I believed her. Though we all knew Daisy wasn't like Sid. She wasn't anything like Sid. But what could I do?' He seemed to be asking me, but I could say nothing. 'So I took her. I took her to Good Shepherd House and I left her there. And she screamed when I went. And the nuns said don't turn back, so I didn't, but I could hear her screaming, screaming . . .' He closed his eyes. 'I did what the nuns said, I did what my mum said, only they're not the ones who can still hear her screaming. My own little sister, my dear, dear little sister, and I just walked . . . away . . .' His voice by now was almost inaudible between sobs.

My agitated foot caught the base of a plant tub, and I stared down at it.

'Perhaps . . . perhaps she didn't know what had happened to

238

her. Perhaps she thought you hadn't heard her, that there'd just been a terrible mistake, that you'd intended to come back and get her later. But that something had happened to you – something terrible – that prevented you from coming.'

He snivelled. 'Maybe.'

'Perhaps when you didn't come, as the weeks went by, she thought that it hadn't been a mistake after all. Perhaps she was terrified that her mother, her brothers – the people she relied upon to love her – had simply cast her out. And when she couldn't understand why, she began to invent reasons for herself. She must be very bad, very, very bad and unlovable to have made this happen. And if she still didn't quite believe it, the nuns made sure she did. They told her she was a wicked, wicked child and God was punishing her for not behaving, and nobody would ever love her if she didn't brush her hair properly, clean the toilets properly, stop coughing, do what she was told.' He stopped sobbing and looked at me. He swallowed hard.

'And then one day, maybe she worked out that the bunch of keys which were always hanging behind the desk near the back door would magically open doors, and the two on a separate little ring would open the back door and the back gate, and that the scum who guarded them sometimes left them hanging there if called away to some trivial urgent incident like a child wetting the bed and needing six hard slaps. So perhaps in the time it took for six hard slaps, your little sister got the keys and tried them, and God was on her side because the second one fitted. Only she wasn't quite as mad as they thought she was because she only took the two keys and closed the door quietly behind her, and so it wasn't until morning that they noticed the child had gone. Perhaps she ran off into the woods and kept running . . . running . . .'

I had been getting louder and I had let go of his hand. I stood up now and ran from the room, knocking my darning off the arm of the chair. I slipped on some shoes by the front door and grabbed my coat, and I ran from that house as I'd run all those years before. I headed for the road and the woods beyond, my breath heavy with panic, and I just kept on running.

51

By now the evening had closed in and the woods were dark. I ran until my coat was sticking to me and I felt my anger steaming out of it. The evergreens were no good: only deciduous trees were understanding. In search of their calm and empathy I ran into the beech wood, but there was no respite. They were all tall and sleek as poles, straining upwards, their natural wideness stunted by their competition for the light. They had no arms to save me, and I ran on, the sweat seeping through my clothes like sap, knowing now exactly where I was heading.

Back on the road I passed Mrs Emery's and headed for the village green. There was only half an old moon, hidden by clouds, and I could barely make her out but there were the arms, outstretched wide and low, waiting to embrace me.

I climbed on to her stoutest branch and stretched out, letting her bark press gently into me like a kiss.

After some time of stillness, apart from the pounding of my heart, I felt the chill of the damp clothes. I took them off, one by one – even the stockings – and replaced them all inside out. I remember Alice Snow telling me to do this for good luck if ever

I was lost. It would fool evil spirits who might be looking for me in the woods. Whatever my motives in carrying out the task, I was certainly lost.

Lying back on the branch, it occurred to me now that if everything had changed for me, then it had changed for Philip, too. One moment he was racked with an inescapable guilt which threatened his very existence, and now . . . what? Was everything all right again? Did it make everything better to see that I'd turned out okay? Or was it worse, to be told that your worst fears were true, that yes, I *had* felt betrayed? I *had* cried for a year and a half, I *had* been left to rot in that godforsaken hell-hole and I *did* remember him leaving me, turning his back, not looking round? I remembered everything.

And what of my mother? Not Gracie, but the real one, that fretful woman in the waiting room. The very things that had warmed me to her now repulsed me. How she worried about her children, how proud she was of them, how she'd do anything for them, even simple Sidney, she wouldn't swap him for the world. Everything she had said became hateful. Did I want to see her? No, I did not. I pictured revealing myself to her, seeing her face when she realized what I had become. Would she be thrilled, that I had turned out so well? Not a mad child, after all? And would I then have to accept her as my mother, pretend that none of the intervening twenty years had happened? Would I be thought of as ungrateful or cold if I couldn't let bygones be bygones? And what would become of Gracie? I couldn't hurt Gracie.

Or would it be altogether different? Would the woman of the furrowed brow and felt hat be heartbroken to learn that I was sane, and that I knew everything? Would she be tormented with unbearable guilt, forced to confront what she thought she had buried for ever, hoping it would just go away? I tried to imagine each possibility, but neither of them appealed. It occurred to me with a wry smile that if I never saw her again, then the only time I had ever seen her since she'd sent me away she had stood up and spoken these words: she had asked me how her son was.

It occurred to me also that I did not have to make myself known to her at all. There was no reason why Philip should tell her he'd met me, and if I asked him not to mention me, well . . . he owed me that at least . . . didn't he?

And yet, there was something reassuring and easy about telling the truth. The truth had a solid quality about it which defied mutation. Unlike lies, which could go on for ever, the truth was as finite as the moon's surface, whole and contained in the simplicity of its sphere. And I was tempted by it. Once the truth was out, there could be no more doubts. Whatever happened would happen, and that would be an end to it.

But was the alternative deceit? Was withholding the truth – just deciding not to use it – a lie? Maybe I could simply carry on as before, unburdened by what I might provoke, but taking on the burden of what I knew.

Whichever way I looked at it, my deep past had been uncorked. My lifelong tactic for self-preservation had been blown, and I would have to find another. But this was the new thing I had learnt: it doesn't matter how deeply you bury something, or how well it's hidden, it is still there. And I had spent my life pretending, because it was easier that way. I hadn't remembered ever having a choice about it, but there had been two: when I met Alice Snow, and when I met Gracie. On neither occasion did I choose to reveal what had happened. Now I had a brother who barely wanted to live, and a mother who had never wanted me alive. And yet I must have always known this, so why did it hurt so much more now? I must have known it, because that was why I was running away – running – from the moment I fled Good Shepherd House with its nuns and nurses, I did not run home, I ran *away*, because I already knew. I must have already known.

Just as there are days in your life you never forget, so there are nights that stick in your memory for ever. The night of 25th August was like that. I did not sleep; my stomach was full of bile and my head full of worms from an upturned stone. Each minute dragged its feet through the night, and I kept seeing her face again, sitting in the waiting room with a furrowed brow, worrying over her sons – her *sons*! There was nothing she wouldn't do for them. Even Sidney, simple Sidney, she 'wouldn't swap him for the world'. A daughter, maybe. But not the world. Oh God! And Philip – a brother – my brother. The one who walked away. I always knew I'd had a brother, one I was close to. I could no longer see the back of his head as he walked away, resolute, doing what he was told. I couldn't get in that close. But I could feel it. I recall the feeling of rejection, the helpless, hopeless calling out to a trusted loved one, the betrayal, the disbelief, the horror, the closeness of the nuns with their beaky noses like the nurse at the hospital, their cruel little snipes, the meanness with which they used my terror to their own petty ends, to ensure I did chores, to achieve trivial little heights of obedience, because it was no wonder nobody loved me, no wonder nobody wanted me, no wonder no one had ever come back for me . . . They hissed at me in the darkness, spat out the cruelty of the years I had spent there, and I wriggled in their bitterness into the small hours.

I looked up at the moon, concealing half of itself in the blackness of the night, the other half glittering to the invisible sun, and I thought: I know there's more to you than meets the eye.

The tree bark pressed into my shoulder blades, and I sensed the sap rising inside it. Up there in the tree-tops, with all the dark shivering leaves, I conjured up mothers: kind, self-giving mothers like Gracie, childless women bursting at the seams with mother-love like Miss Wallock, jealous mothers, efficient mothers, strict, ambitious mothers, mothers who controlled, chaotic mothers, bereaved mothers, possessive mothers, anxious mothers, inexperienced mothers, mothers worn-out and depressed, mothers overwhelmed with love, mothers who never wanted to be mothers, women longing for children and mothers-to-be. The moon sent down all these women and tossed them into the gently writhing branches. Each one of them with the power to change lives, and each one unaware of it. Because it wasn't written in stone, what they did; it wasn't even written in blood. It was printed in memories, little indelible keepsakes that would never rub off.

52

'You fuck off out of here! Go on, fuck off!'

The voice told me I must have dozed at least once, for the green was bathed in orange light and the last birds of summer were chirruping softly above me. Vile It walked away after her warning, like a nesting bird: secure that she had delivered it but wanting no real battle.

When I opened my eyes again there was more commotion. I looked up at the glorious leaves, still mostly green against the pale morning blue, and smelt the cluster of colognes from close beneath me. The voices were lowered.

'She always was . . . you know, a bit . . .'

'Barking mad!'

'Completely lost it this time . . .'

'My sister always reckoned . . .'

'Barking!'

I allowed myself a swift glance downwards, and saw the little herd of village women craning up to my perch, their morning shopping enhanced by a bit of insanity. I looked back up at the branches and closed my eyes.

The next thing I heard was a familiar voice but one which I did not at first recognize.

'Haven't you got homes to go to? She's not mad, you daft

bats. That's just how she is. Now shoo!' Then it was close to my ear, and it was clear that the owner had climbed the tree to sit beside me on the branch. 'I was hoping to see you while I was home,' said Mo, finding a neighbouring branch to lean into. Then she sat there, chatting to me about the games we used to play, remembering the oddest details, laughing and making me smile, until Howard and Gracie came to take me home.

Gracie stroked my face. To my astonishment, Howard took me in his arms, kissed me gently on the forehead, and carried me across the green through a crowd of onlookers, up the road and home.

He carried me tenderly up the stairs like his own errant child: a treasure lost and found. Gracie bathed me like she had when I was small, only in the grand bathroom rather than a tin tub. She squeezed warm water over me from the sponge and bid me not to try and speak. Then she wrapped me in a huge white towel and hugged me dry.

It was clear they both knew. What I hadn't expected, though, was that Philip would still be there.

'I think you should see him,' said Gracie after breakfast. Her tone was gentle and encouraging. 'He needs to go to his mother who may be dying, but he can't go until he's seen you.'

I closed my eyes tight shut. She put her arms around me as if I might fall down. 'It's not easy for him either. There must be things you want to know. It might help. Just a quick word.'

I went into the living room where he was waiting awkwardly by the fire. There *were* things I wanted to know. But then I wanted him to go, and not come back.

'Daisy—'

'Joy.'

'Joy. I'm sorry. It's really hard to know how to put this . . .' He frowned at the brass coal scuttle, '. . . but the thing is . . . I want you to know. . . . I'm so, so sorry. I . . . there's not a day's gone by I haven't—'

'Tell me about my family.'

'Well . . . Dad died – as you know—'

'TB?'

'That's right. He used to dote on you.' He said this eagerly, as if to say there was at least *one* scrap of good news in my family album. 'Thought the world of you, he did . . . And then – Mum – you know. Um . . . Then there's Sidney – he's not quite the full shilling, then Eddie – he's a bit of a lad. You know – bit of a success with the girls, that sort of thing. Um . . . Then there was Ivy, of course, and you.'

'How old was I when . . . Dad died?'

'Four and a half.'

It was clipped, exact, like words he had repeated in his head for years.

'And . . . how do you know . . . what makes you say he doted on me?' I knew I was begging for crumbs of affection, but I had to know.

'He was a gamekeeper – up at the big house near us – and he used to take you off with him, whole days at a time. Did the same with us when we were little, but he reckoned you were different. Said you had patience with birds. He never accepted that you were daft. Not ever.' Then his face lit up as he pictured something else. 'And you used to help him in the garden – followed him everywhere, you did.'

'Was there lavender?'

'Lavender? Oh, tons of the stuff. Herbs, vegetables, he had green fingers. All went a bit to pieces after him. And you.'

I felt my throat swell up inside. 'And what about the rest of you? Did you get along with me?'

He chuckled. 'I used to have to look after you. That was my job. I dressed you in the mornings, made sure you ate all your food, took you to school—'

'So, did I sleep with you? I remember sharing a bed with someone.'

248

'No. You slept with Sidney.'

'Sidney?'

I felt suddenly nettled. Who was this wretched Sidney who was so much more important than me that he stayed in the bosom of the family whilst I – the entire shilling, all twelve pennies of it – was cast off to rot in a home full of sadistic nurses and embittered nuns?

'Yes. You slept with him as soon as you'd been weaned, I think. He's very affectionate, Sid. Always after someone to cuddle.'

There was an uncomfortable silence while I thought about this, and while he, no doubt, wondered what I was thinking about.

'What's he like?'

'Sid? Like I said, he's affectionate, a bit simple. But he can peel vegetables, clean his own shoes, feed the hens – you know, practical stuff. Used to sing you to sleep, though.'

'Sang to me?'

'You know . . .'

'What did he sing?'

He looked up at the cornicing for help. 'Um . . . "Now the day is over" and . . . "For the –"'

' "–moon shines bright on Charlie Chaplin"?'

'Yes!'

We both smiled, and our eyes grew watery.

'What exactly's wrong with him, then?'

'No one really knows.' Then, as if reading my thoughts, he added: 'Mum found him very difficult to bring up – he was a real handful. I think she was afraid you'd be like him.'

I stood up, because I was in such torment now I couldn't sit still. I paced to the window and sighed. 'So why didn't she send him off?'

When I paced back I saw that Philip had his eyes closed. 'I don't know. I really don't know what she was thinking. You need to ask her that.'

'No!'

He looked up at me, startled.

'I don't want to see her. This has been hard enough for me – can't you see that? I don't want to have to see her. Please, *please* don't tell her about me—'

'But—'

'No! Never!'

He stood up and put his arms around me. We remained closed for some time, like two halves of a metal-sprung peg. I sensed the tears in his eyes, from the tenseness of his torso and the occasional quick intake of breath. But I did not cry. I felt like an observer of human behaviour, still as stone and just as unimpressionable.

I pulled back suddenly.

'What did you think had happened to me?'

Sensing my coldness, he let his arms drop to the sides. A cuckoo clock in the alcove by the fire chose this moment to cuckoo ten times. Each time his little door nearly closed, and the bird hovered before delivering his two cheerful notes again. We both glared at him, but he carried on doggedly chirping his full quota to the bitter end.

'I thought about you all the time. I never stopped thinking about you. It was terrible.' The silence was blaring after the cuckoo. 'I went back to find you.'

'You did?'

'Yes. When I was fourteen. I started work then, you see. I knew if I went back before then, I wouldn't be able to take you away and look after you.'

'And they told you I'd run away.'

'No. They told me you were dead.'

Something fell away inside me. 'Dead?'

'Said you'd been moved to a hospital somewhere far away and died of diphtheria.'

I tried to take this in. All the years I had assumed they were

250

looking for me, a grand search with police or other dour men in black scouring the fields and woodlands. But in fact I had been natural wastage. They had eradicated me.

'Who did you speak to?'

'A nun. Sister Conceptua. I remember her.' He clenched his jaw for a moment. 'She didn't know where you were buried. I couldn't even visit your grave.'

His eyes were welling up again and I should have seen how much he needed me to embrace him, but I was filling up with my own new horror, and could only stand like a limp puppet as he threw his arms around me and begged me to forgive him.

I was glad when Howard came in and said the horse was ready.

53

The following day there was a phone call informing us that Philip's mother – my mother – had died the previous evening, and inviting me to the funeral. Luckily, Howard had answered the telephone, and I had not had to make my excuses on the spot. Neither Gracie nor Howard commented on my indifference, but as the morning wore on, Gracie tried to broach the subject.

'I could go with you, if you like. It's only a thirty-minute bus ride.'

I didn't want to keep on brushing it away, so I said, 'She was happy to let me fester in a home all these years – as she saw it – so why should I let my world be turned upside down by a chance meeting?'

Gracie shook her head. 'That poor boy who came here was suffering. His mother shouldn't have put him through that. It's not his fault. You can see that, surely. You ought to go and make your peace with him at least. You ought to, by rights.'

I knew she was right, but I was so angry with this wretched family that had hidden itself from me all these years I needed it, and now popped up when I didn't want it. I tried to explain how I wanted everything to stay the same, but how the truth had appeared like an interloper. I tried to explain how I hadn't known what truth to tell, and what to hold back, how I had never known about my past, but yet had always known.

We set off in good time because there was a change of bus involved. The little village was barely fifteen miles away in a north-easterly direction, and I couldn't help wondering at how close I had been all these years.

We were invited to see the body in the front room of the house, but Gracie and I went directly to the church. As we walked, little memories began to flicker. Old gateposts, elder-flower bushes and long-forgotten hedgerows ambushed me along the way. The church I remembered slightly, but not like this. The last time I'd been there the graves were a forest of standing stones, as tall as me.

The oak pews were cool after the bright September sun, and a monotonous organ tune whined away, meandering around each of the new arrivals like a wasp discovering a new bun.

Evidently Mrs Bird did not have many friends or relatives, for despite a valiant twenty minutes of organ playing, the organist turned round to see just a handful in the congregation. Having utterly exhausted his tune, and invented variants thereof, he rested his hands on his lap.

As the vicar spoke, I kept my gaze on the five men in the front row. There was a doddering old man with brilliant white hair, who had been helped to his place very slowly by the two middle-aged men now seated on each side of him. I didn't recognize them, and assumed they must be uncles – brothers of my mother, perhaps, and the old man: could he be my grandfather? But the two who really held my interest were seated next to this trio: a young man in army uniform with a very straight back, and a young man with an extraordinarily small head.

'. . . shall remember Elizabeth as a devoted mother of Sidney, Philip and Edward. But of course, we must not forget how hard she struggled to bring up these fine children alone, after the early death of her husband Edwin. She has given them what the very best mothers give their children: support, encouragement, and, of course, love. How easy it is, these days, to . . .'

I dropped my hymn book on the tiled floor with a very loud thlunk. It echoed around the high, wood-beamed ceiling, from Christ on the cross to Christ the Shepherd. No one turned round, except the man with the very small head, and I could see from his reddened eyes that he had been crying a good deal. He stretched his neck up tall (which was a strain, for he had virtually no neck to speak of) to see what was going on, like a child who doesn't want to miss anything. Eventually he turned back round, when the young man with the straight back got up to the lectern. I dreaded him paying homage to her. Gracie put her hand over mine, and I realized I was digging my nails into my handbag. There followed just a simple reading from the Bible, of no particular relevance to anyone's life, as far as I could see. But I got a better look at Eddie, who was not especially tall, but who had impressive confidence and teeth.

Standing by the grave, Sidney did not stop sobbing. He cocked his little head to one side and blubbered like a toddler. I felt my stomach lurch. I wanted him to stop. A part of me responded in exactly the same way as I had to Lil's daughter, when she had wailed in her mother's absence. Another part of me wanted to march over to him and shake him very hard. And this other part made me a very unpleasant person, and I wanted to be away from there as quickly as possible, because I wanted to be someone likeable.

Gracie insisted we went back to the house afterwards, whispering that I might always regret it if I didn't. I was afraid of being recognized, even though there was simply no one there who possibly could after all these years.

The house made me tremble. All the way from our first

sighting of it – when the bottom halves of the funeral guests disappeared into bushes of fading lavender – to the interior: the front room with its yellowed walls and smell of polish; the kitchen with its brown oily linoleum and reek of paraffin.

Gracie took my arm and placed her hand on top to steady me. We heard a woman next to us saying to her friend, 'Well, she's lucky she got a place in the churchyard, is all I can say.'

'She is that,' replied her friend. Then they moved towards the sandwiches and we lost the rest of it.

'What does she mean by that?' I asked.

Gracie, who looked a little troubled, adopted a sudden carefree tone: 'Oh, I don't know. I expect the graveyard's getting full. They do, you know, in these village churches.'

And that was it. I couldn't believe she hadn't considered – like me – the possibility of suicide. Was it not possible that someone – maybe even Philip – had revealed the truth to my mother, and it had been too much to bear? But then, I thought, she would've wanted to meet me, surely? Wouldn't it be easier to confront your own guilt and gain deliverance? Or perhaps not. Perhaps she was too afraid of what she might find – of what I might say . . . Hadn't Gracie considered any of this?

We found ourselves standing next to a piano, and I couldn't take my eyes off the photographs perched along its top. Gracie followed my darting eyes: family groups, portraits, brothers together. There was no sign of me. What had I expected? But it stung me, even so. And then Gracie nodded to the mantelpiece opposite. We edged our way over, moving through a group of chattering neighbours.

'So how do you know my mother, then?'

I turned, and there was Eddie, showing us all of his very fine teeth.

'Um . . . I met her at the hospital. I'm a friend of Philip's.'

'Oh!' He said it in a tone of wicked innuendo. 'Well, he's a bit of a dark horse!'

'No – a friend. We're friends.'

'That's what they all say!' He gave me a good-humoured wink, and carried on beaming. 'I must say, I never thought old Phil would make a catch like you.' And then, with the smoothness of a chat-up line, he asked: 'Where exactly are you based?'

I lied, and said I was at the same base as Philip. Gracie started to correct me, but thought better of it. The small-headed man came up with two paste sandwiches, and put them both in his mouth together.

'Oh, this is Sidney, by the way: Phil's brother – and mine! Say hello, Sid. This is Phil's girlfriend.'

'No—'

Sidney smiled at me with white dough-filled teeth.

'Sidney! Offer the ladies some sandwiches!'

Sidney turned round to the food-bedecked table behind him and, taking two sandwiches from the plates, gave us one each.

'I'm sorry,' said Eddie, not even bothering to lower his voice, 'he's a bit simple, I'm afraid.'

'That's so kind of you,' Gracie said to Sidney (rather defiantly, I thought).

My eyes moved over to the mantelpiece, and the real object of my interest. There it was, in the most elaborate frame yet: a picture of a little girl. Gracie nudged me. 'There you are!' she whispered. 'The spitting image!'

'Beautiful picture, isn't it?' said Eddie, following our gaze. 'That's our sister.'

I noticed that Sidney had latched himself on to my other arm, and was stroking my sleeve.

'Sister?' I think I looked suitably surprised.

'Yes, we had a sister once. Beautiful little thing. Died of diphtheria.'

'I'm sorry.'

Eddie could do wistful as well: 'Yes . . . broke my mother's heart, did our Ivy. She was like a light going out in our family.'

Sidney had leant his head against my sleeve now, and was nuzzling up to me. He must have felt my pulse quicken. My instinct was to run, but Gracie was holding on to me on my right, and Sidney on my left. 'So there were four children, in fact?'

'Yes . . . four.' I was watching him. He didn't flinch.

'Daisy, Daisy, give me your answer, do . . .' sang Sidney in a faint voice. He, at least, remembered five.

'Come on, Sid, I think you're making a bit of a monkey of yourself . . .' He looked at me again. 'I'm sorry – he's very emotional at the moment. What with Mum dying and everything. And he's worried he might have to – you know—' Then he lowered his voice to a whisper and exaggerated his mouth movements, '—*go in a home.*'

I practically yanked Gracie away with me, and Sidney remained clinging to my arm all the way out to the lavender.

'I'm sorry, Gracie. I've got to get away from here. I'm sorry. I'm sorry . . .'

Gracie said it was all right, and she shouldn't have made me come. I said, no really, it was my fault, and so on. We were halfway down the road when we realized there was someone behind us. Little grunting noises – like someone trying to speak through closed lips – made us turn. There was Sidney with a bunch of lavender and a penknife. Gracie must have seen that he had clearly used the knife to cut the lavender, but I felt more uneasy. He held the greying lavender out to me, his tiny head on one shoulder: 'S'for you, that is,' he said. 'S'for you, that.'

'Thank you,' said Gracie, on my behalf.

'Thank you,' I was shamed into saying.

On the bus home, I gazed out of the window as the newly harvested fields drifted by. I thought of the hares and field mice cornered by the stubble and forced to flee. The brambles swept past, covered in blackberries, many already dried into little brown scabs. Luscious clusters of elderberries appeared and dark sloes hung against yellowing blackthorn leaves. Orange woody nightshade made festive chains along the hedgerows, and there was a ripeness to everything.

'Don't judge her too harshly, my love. Extreme poverty can make monsters of the best of us.'

I closed my eyes as if it could shut out what Gracie had said. When I opened them I was looking at my own kid-leather gloved hands and my shiny buckled handbag.

'Well, nothing – nothing – would make me do that to my own children . . . There's no excuse for her cruelty. None.'

Although they seemed to have been generated by a warmth for my own children, the moment the words left my mouth they sounded bitterly cold and judgemental, and I felt cheated of my own right to utter them.

I looked down and saw that my hand was on my belly, and Gracie had placed her hand on mine.

'You know,' she said, 'you'll have plenty of room up at the house.' I looked at her and smiled, not quite sure what she was saying. 'I could look after him if you wanted.'

'I'm not expecting!' I laughed.

She looked across me out of my window, and then at my face. 'I don't mean a child.'

'Who do you mean, then?'

'I was just thinking . . .'

'Who?'

'Well, if you wanted him to come with us rather than in some dreadful home, we could take Sidney in . . . couldn't we?'

'Sidney?' I scowled out of the window. 'Why on earth would I want to look after Sidney? They've never done anything for me, have they? Where were any of that lot when I needed them?'

'I only thought—'

'Well, don't think.' I could barely believe what Gracie had

just suggested. '*Sidney?*' I drew myself up stiffly on the seat. 'I've got my own family now. I don't want anything to do with that family.'

Gracie examined her gloved hand on the back of the seat in front and said thoughtfully, 'I wasn't thinking of them, I was thinking of you.'

I didn't answer, because I didn't want to discuss it any further, and she didn't pursue it. But over the next year I often wondered what she had meant by that: thinking of me.

54

It was a miracle to be a parent, and I was constantly taking my bearings. It was only then, as I watched my son turn four, that I could see the true horror of what my mother had done. Of course I had felt it – all my life I had felt it. But even when I made the decision not to acknowledge her – even at her funeral – a small part of me had been willing to accept that there may have been circumstances I hadn't understood. I had even felt guilty for my part in our estrangement. But now . . .

There was nothing, not poverty, not illness, not criticism, not wars or deluges, nothing could make me give up a child of four years old; and to condemn him to an institution, a madhouse . . . Everything was different now that I had children of my own: now I knew the full extent of her crime.

Despite its grandeur, Buckleigh House was a cold and draughty place outside the radar of the kitchen. I warmed the pyjamas by the range and wrapped the children in my arms under the stone-cold sheets of the beds. On winter nights I would join Jill in my double bed, enveloping her warm little figure. She was wrapped up to the neck in soft flannelette and as oblivious to the cold as a hibernating animal. At my back the freezing air would melt away, and I would wake cocooned in a warmth so perfect it seemed impossibly adjusted by some angelic thermostat. Then the noise which had woken me would fling itself into the room and into the bed beside me. I would snuggle down, a child in each arm, like a great lucky sheep who'd been allowed to keep her lambs way past June. Then we would tell dozy stories to each other under the covers until we heard Mrs Bubb's alarm clock upstairs. Moments of joy woven into the long hard winters of the war.

It isn't true that absence makes the heart grow fonder. That was not my experience, at any rate. Absence just seemed to make the heart forget. As the months rolled on into years, James became a series of postcards, a focus for romantic thoughts, a bright but blurred vision of the future. He became so remote that I had to look at his photograph to find him again, and even then I didn't always succeed. Sometimes it was hard to remember if I'd ever really known him at all. Half-forgotten nights under the stars, a few passionate kisses in the woods and at The Mill: did this constitute knowing a man? At times like this I felt fragile and guilty. It wasn't that I didn't long for James. I did. I just wasn't certain any more if he was real.

I tried to explain everything that had happened in my letters to James. I told him how I had met my own mother face to face. I explained how I didn't know what truth to tell, or what to hold back. I didn't know how much others would get hurt, how much I would hurt. We wrote to each other two or three times a week. It had become almost like writing a diary. For sometimes a week would pass before I received a letter from him, and at other times three would arrive together. And when we read each other's letters, they were in response to some letter written long before.

Nonetheless I looked forward to the letters, and came in from the animals each morning in the hope of finding one waiting on the door mat, or in the toast rack where Mrs Bubb put them if she came across them first.

One wet morning in September there was one for me in a different hand. I eyed it for several minutes before I found the courage to open it. I waited until I was alone, and went into the living room.

Dear Joy (Daisy!)

I hope you don't mind me writing. Naturally, I have been thinking of you a lot while I'm here. Not much goes on, and yet my world has turned upside down of late. I'm talking about discovering you again, of course. But I'm afraid there is more news, and not so good since then. Eddie died in Italy last week. I only just heard and thought you ought to know.

I wonder could you do me a great favour? Sidney has had to go into a home for the time being since Mum died, and I know he's very lonely. The nurses tell me he's also getting quite ill with the upset of it all. Do you think you could visit him? Eddie said he took quite a shine to you at the funeral. It would mean so much to me. You wouldn't have to tell him who you were or anything. Our neighbour, Mrs Farrell, has all the details. I know it's a lot to ask, but just in case you have time.

I want you to know that I love you – very much. There's not been a day gone by I haven't wondered about you. I hope you can find the happiness you deserve with Buckleigh. I'm sure you will.

Your very loving brother,
Philip

I dropped it into the fire and watched the flames curl round it, watched the paper take up the swiftly spreading scorch mark like blotting paper. And I did feel, as the little explosion of heat from it burned my cheeks, that I had blotted something out for good.

Some two weeks later another letter arrived in the same hand. I put it into the fire without opening it.

Eight, maybe nine days later, something odd happened.

It was mid-October, and the evacuees were practising for a harvest concert or play. We were all in the living room watching them when the telephone rang. Howard got up to answer it and the children plodded their way through 'We plough the fields and scatter' which, lovely though it was, seemed to go on for ever in their hands. They decided to use the tall velvet curtains as stage curtains – regardless of the few inches of stage it allowed them – and before long they were improvising an early nativity which went on so long it involved Jesus celebrating his first birthday and sheep singing 'The Farmer's in his Den'.

Howard had been gone some time, so I went to see if all was well. Closing the living-room door quietly behind me I heard him speaking with his back to me. Usually, Howard considered his own voice needed to travel the distance covered by the telephone line and barked insanely into the receiver, but even he had lowered his voice now: 'Just don't tell Joy. Whatever you do, don't tell her. She mustn't know. You must absolutely promise me.'

I froze for a moment behind one of the giant potted plants, but the conversation seemed to pass on to other things. I closed the door again behind me, more loudly, and made my way to the kitchen, smiling at him as I passed.

Not long after Apple Day I heard that Philip had been killed in a direct attack on his site office. My brother died, that's what I should say. All I could think was that it wasn't James. I was very sorry, of course, but there were people dying all around and there wasn't time to be ground down by it all. Nonetheless I was shocked at my lack of grief. I even affected dark looks in front of Gracie and Howard but I felt a fraud. If I'm honest the greatest grief I felt was that with him died a lot of unanswered questions. There. My selfish homage to my own brother. What sort of person had I become?

55

The following morning the evacuees came running into the kitchen shouting.

'There's someone in the orchard nicking apples! We seen him!' panted Donald. 'I shouted at him and told him to clear off!'

'No you didn't!' said his sister, looking at him incredulously. 'You ran away.'

'Well . . . I sort of . . .'

I was already heading for the orchard, running as fast as I could, potato peeler still in hand. The orchard was still swollen with leaves, every stubby tree puffed out in green and heavy with fruit. It made visibility difficult, but as I dodged between the low branches I heard a rustling up ahead at the far end near the fence.

'Wait!' I shouted. Tripping and skidding on windfalls, I soon spotted a small boy scrambling to his feet. 'Wait a moment! Please!'

He turned tail and belted off towards the gate, and I made ground as he stumbled over it. I could almost have reached out my arm and touched him as I said, 'Take whatever you need! It's all right.'

At this the boy stopped and turned for a moment. His

pullover was comically bulging in all directions with a dozen or so apples and he held it in at the waist with both hands. His hair was scruffy, his knees grubby and scabbed, and his face no better, but for the briefest of moments his eyes looked so directly into mine that I froze like a hare. What did he see? He seemed to be assessing me, a mixture of wariness, curiosity and control. They were Nipper's eyes. It was difficult to know which one of us was the more astonished.

'Okay?' I said, when I got my breath back. 'Whatever you need.'

It was the briefest of nods, and he was off, tearing over the field like a deer – like his father before him. I watched him, but couldn't see where he disappeared. They were back then, the gypsies, and still going strong. I allowed myself the faintest smile as I retraced my steps, but then had to deal with Mr Rollins and the children approaching with rakes and pitchforks.

Unaware of the weight of my own sense of guilt, I threw myself into the war effort and the household with even more gusto than before. That autumn I collected sackfuls of rose hips with the children (the Ministry of Health were offering two shillings for every fourteen pounds), stinging nettles and comfrey leaves.

Despite the damp and the cold and the dreariness, I used to love the surprises in my pockets. A bright red leaf maybe (placed there with the unreasonable expectation that it would remain flat), stones chosen for their smoothness or colour or some other special quality known only to my children, old conkers, teasels, whole dandelion heads, twigs in shapes which – for a few brief seconds – had seemed exceptional, all these spoils I would turn out at the end of the day. And although they were limp or torn or crushed or dried up and entirely forgotten by their hitherto earnest collectors, something of the first childish pleasure on finding them remained in them, and I held them in my palms like tangible moments of joy.

Gracie had already found a new lease of life bottling fruit and making jam. She had become so keen in the WVS that she could now turn out perfect pies for England. Between us, we made every kind of jam and chutney possible with English fruits, and we held enormous jam-making sessions at the house with over twenty women sitting around the great kitchen table.

Howard had never seen anything like it. He was astonished and delighted at the new uses his home was being put to, and at the unexpected visitors that appeared busily working around every corner. But although necessity changed all our habits, he was bewildered, as the weather turned bitterly cold, when I took all the children out collecting cowpats for fuel.

I had grown very fond of Howard but, to be honest, every time I saw him I had to fight off a little frustration. I couldn't understand why, after such a mutual explosion of attraction between himself and Gracie, he had managed to stay so aloof for so long. Although she never showed it, I knew it must hurt her deeply. I remembered the way she had patted her hair in front of the mirror that day we first came up to Buckleigh House together. What was he playing at? Was he so attached to tradition that he couldn't divorce his loathsome wife and marry Gracie? Could he not allow himself a little flirtation? A kiss? A wink? He was civil enough to her; they were relaxed in each other's company and smiled a lot. But I wondered how she could bear it.

That winter we had very little coal, and on Gracie's suggestion I went down to her old house with the boys, Johnny and Donald, armed with a sack. There was only an inch or two of coal left in the coal-shed. It looked more but I saw that the few coals had been propped up by something else, making it look deeper than it was. After a bit of scrabbling around Johnny fished out a filthy bag and opened it. 'Phwoar – some smelly old rags.' And I saw once again the cream silk dress and the green velvet one, along with the two others Celia had added.

They were mildewed of course. Gracie laughed when I told her the story behind them, but insisted we should wash them. I wanted to throw them out, to get rid of all traces of Celia, and a time when I had betrayed my friends. They were all beyond repair, but the silk one had a few patches of good material in it which I offered to Gracie for her embroidery. I think Gracie could see how much poison I saw in those dresses with their grey rashes of mildew. She knew instinctively how to stop them hurting me.

'You should make something out of it,' she said.

So I did. I made a pair of silk cami-knickers for Mo and sent them to her billet. Gracie always had good ideas.

But that wasn't the end of it. She unpicked a thread of gold – one I hadn't seen – running through the mildewed border of a dress, and she embroidered a cushion with it. The cushion was stuffed with the shredded silk and embellished with rosebuds: the emerald buttons salvaged from the velvet dress. Then she had found a fine thread of crimson from the tartan pattern of another mouldy dress and used it to embroider the tips of emerging rose petals.

'You have to look carefully for the good bits,' she said. Anyone else would have thrown them all away.

As the evenings grew lighter, there was talk everywhere of the war ending soon. On clear nights I took Andrew and Jill with me to the paddock and lay with them snuggled together under blankets. The stars were never out, and we would find pictures in clouds: ducks, sheep, Mr Rollins, dragons, swans, a sad lady, an eagle, a big boot. Once Andrew saw a woman holding a child's hand. It took a while for me to see it too, but it was observant of him, and I was proud. Then we watched as the breeze made the child's arm longer and longer, and Andrew chuckled until they both melted into other shapes, and the impossibly long arm disintegrated at last into thin air.

Mrs Bubb and Gracie said they would catch a death of cold, but I wanted my children to know the earth I knew, and I wanted them with me. I wanted them with me until the blackbird sang his last fluted note and we were enveloped in the loamy smell of dew.

56

In the following spring, the May of 1945, most people were preoccupied with the end of the war. But our household had a different drama to deal with, one which would make me reassess everything we'd been fighting for.

I awoke very early one morning – before any of the children – to the sound of voices in the kitchen. I dressed and opened the curtains to see a strange car pulled up on the drive outside. It was open-roofed and flashy, and the moment I saw it I felt uneasy.

As I approached the kitchen I could hear Howard's voice slightly raised and sounding agitated. The other voice was a woman's. I recognized it straight away.

'Celia . . .'

She was sitting in a chair at the huge table, with one arm hanging loosely over the back of it. She still had her hat on: an emerald green affair set forward on her head, so that she had to raise her chin slightly to see out. She wore a shapely suit in the same vibrant colour, except for a ginger fox fur which she fondled with her free hand.

'Joy!' The chin went up, and she seemed to be peering down her nose. 'Well, look at you! As radiant as ever!' She adjusted herself in the chair but did not get up, so I went over and sat at the table with her, aware how I must look in my working corduroys and no make-up.

'This is a surprise!' I said, feeling at a sudden disadvantage, as I always did when Celia was around.

'Isn't it? I expect you thought you'd seen the back of me.'

She said it to the fox fur and to her own white bejewelled hand.

'I was just going to say how lovely it is to see you.' I tried to beam at her, but she wasn't looking. 'Have you eaten? What would you like?'

'I'm doing her scrambled egg,' said Howard from the stove. 'Would you care to join us?' He attempted a little chef's flourish, and I was grateful to him.

'Oh, yes! Yes, please. That's so kind.'

'I see you've certainly made some changes around here,' said Celia, her eyes meeting mine at last, and with an undoubtable challenge in them. 'I don't think I've ever seen Howard cooking before.'

'It's the war, not Joy,' said Howard, rescuing me again. 'We've all had to muck in.'

'What about Mrs Bubb? She's still here, isn't she?'

'Yes, and so are two evacuees, Mrs Bubb's son, pigs, a cow, a horse . . . she can't do it all for us.'

'I see.'

Howard placed a plate of scrambled egg on toast in front of each of us, then sat down as well. 'Joy cooks too, don't you, Joy?'

'Oh . . . very ordinary things . . . inedible mostly!'

'Delicious mostly!' said Howard, winking at me.

'Delicious – of course!' said Celia, with an edge of bitterness so slight I tried to pretend it hadn't been there.

Already she was filling me with hurt and panic and a desperate desire to push my scrambled egg into her face. No, wait! This was Celia. She had been ill, and I hadn't been

270

to see her. She was probably still unhappy. James would want me to be lenient.

'Celia, you look quite lovely. How have you been?'

She finished chewing a morsel of toast and said, 'Actually, I was just saying to Howard, I've not been well for years.'

'I'm sorry—'

'Only the usual thing. Anxiety and so on. So anyway, what I *also* told Howard was that I've booked myself into the local nuthouse for a few days for some treatment.'

'Treatment? Nuthouse?'

Celia laughed. She showed all her teeth under her bright lipstick, and looked thoroughly pleased with herself. 'Isn't it a *hoot*? I might even have electric shock treatment or something, although I'm not terribly keen on that idea.'

'Oh, Celia!'

'It's all voluntary. I'm not a registered loon or anything! I must say, it's such fun being mad! You can do anything you like and get away with it!' Her tone was unconvincing and slightly hysterical, and there was that hint of volatility that I realized had always made Celia so alluring. 'I shall have to be careful, though,' she said, delicately balancing some egg on the tip of her fork, 'I don't want to end up like that friend of yours . . . what's-his-name? . . . Philip.'

'How do you know Philip?'

'My friend Beatrice worked at the same airfield as him in Sussex.'

'Oh, I didn't know. She wasn't hurt, then?'

'Hurt? No – in fact she's left now – expecting her first.'

Howard was looking uneasy, and tried to talk about the delicious egg, but his uneasiness only made me more curious.

'What do you mean, "end up" like him? He wasn't mad, you know.'

'Well, maybe not. But let's face it, you're not usually *totally* sane when you commit suicide, are you?'

I dropped a piece of toast and it fell raspberry-jam-side down on the table. I sat staring at it for a moment, with the strange feeling that it had hurled itself face down to hurt me. 'He was killed in a bomb blast. She must've known some other Philip.'

'Oh no, it *was* the one. I remember because James told me . . . Oh no! I wasn't supposed to tell you, was I?' She showed no contrition whatsoever, merely rolled her eyes and feigned a self-mocking half-smile. 'Me and my big mouth!'

Howard sighed and closed his eyes. But she simply shrugged. 'I'm sorry. He must've been a pretty close friend, then, if James and Howard thought it would upset you. An old flame, maybe?'

'No. Not at all. We weren't . . . close.' I piled my used cutlery on to my plate along with my saucer, empty teacup and the wasted toast which left a sticky red mess between us on the table. 'Well . . . do you want to stay here? It's a bit of a squash at the moment. But you're welcome as long as you like.'

She raised her eyebrows at me. 'Are you inviting me to stay in my own house?'

'Celia . . .' Howard looked uncomfortable. 'You're always welcome here, you know that.'

'Am I? Am I? Oh, I'm always welcome in my home – I'm so *glad*. I mean, I turn my back for one moment and suddenly you have a new daughter, a daughter who cooks, a daughter who gets *you* to cook, who transforms the grounds into a market garden, who turns the house into some sort of hotel for waifs and strays, a daughter who has two children – what are they? *Heirs* to the Buckleigh estate?'

'Celia, please—'

'Oh, stop it, Howard. You're spoiling my breakfast.'

'But you left of your own accord. I thought you'd got married to someone.'

'I *have*. I *have* married someone: Larry Ravenhill.'

'Oh, what's he like?' I tried to seem interested, but I could hear how silly and eager I sounded to her. Of course I didn't need her to tell me what he was like. I could picture him quite clearly with his hundred-acre estate, his party-going, horse-gambling, gin-swilling friends called Miles and Giles, an eccentric mother with small dogs named after Greek gods, endless sisters named after Greek goddesses, a younger brother called Ravenhill Two, and a manner of speaking without moving his lips.

'He's absolutely *loaded*.' She waggled her fingers to display the rocks. 'Larry. Two houses, one swimming pool and a prize-winning racehorse *and* his father has a handy little villa in Juan-les-Pins when the war is over.'

I thought she was going to tell me the entirety of his material possessions. 'Any children?'

'No.' She pursed her lips. Then she smiled unconvincingly. 'What would I do with children? Tell me about yours. I suppose you have boys.'

'A boy – Andrew, and a girl, Jill.'

'A boy *and* a girl!' She affected an overly pleased-on-my-behalf tone. 'And how old are *Andrew* and *Jill*?' She said it as if they were names so plebeian she hardly knew how to pronounce them.

'Andrew's four and Jill's one. She'll be two in September.'

'Aha! So Andrew is the son and heir! Does Jill mind?' She put her fork down with a clatter. 'Eldest sons! They have it all, don't they? I expect he's very special, isn't he? *Andrew*.'

I didn't want to speak any more. I looked back at her and willed her to look me in the eye. But Howard intervened.

'Celia, I don't know what all this is about. I thought you *wanted* to live away. You said you'd married someone wealthy, that you never wanted to come back.'

'That's what you wanted, isn't it?'

'I want you to be happy.' She leaned back in her chair, but Howard wasn't giving up. 'And what's all this son-and-heir business? I've never cut you out of my will. Half of everything I have is yours.'

'And the other half goes to the ragamuffin boy!'

'It'll be divided equally between you and James.'

'Why does he get *anything*? You *adopted* him.'

'Like I adopted you.'

There was a silence. Howard swallowed hard. Celia flared her nostrils and her mouth started to wobble and look very fragile.

'But it's James and . . . *her* who get the house, isn't it?' She gestured to me with a flap of her hand. 'They're the ones who get to live here like Lord and Lady Muck with their son-and-heir! And then, *he'll* get the house, this little . . . *Andrew* person, and anyway . . .' Her voice was faltering now. 'And we all know why *she's* so special, don't we!' The wrist did its little flap towards me again, and I couldn't help remembering having held it once, when she'd hissed at me to hurt her. Harder. Harder. Hurt *me!*

I leaned over to take her hand again, but she pushed it away. Howard was already on his feet, trying to put an arm around her, but she stood up brusquely. The chair made a sound that echoed like gunshot on the flagstones.

'Please don't leave like this, Celia!'

'No! No! I'm sorry I came. I've behaved dreadfully – as usual! Please don't see me out.' She wiped her eyes and walked towards the back door, putting on her gloves. 'I'll just have a look round, if I may, then I'll be on my way. Please don't see me out.'

'Let me give you a guided tour,' I tried, thinking of all the changes there had been since she had last seen it.

She turned on me from the door, a contemptuous figure in green from head to toe. 'Please. I don't need to be guided around Buckleigh House.'

And then she was gone, and the kitchen fell silent except for Mrs Bubb who was shuffling about by the sink with some freshly cut flowers.

'I don't understand,' said Howard, sinking back into a chair. 'I haven't cut her out of the will. She said a few years ago she never wanted to see me or this house again.'

'Doesn't know *what* she wants, that one,' said Mrs Bubb, stuffing the flowers into a yellow vase. 'Never did.'

And for the first time I could see that it wasn't Buckleigh House – or any other house – that Celia wanted at all.

57

It was gone midday before we realized he was missing.

I warmed up a vegetable stew from the day before, and all the children had come in from playing or helping outside. They eventually sat around the table after being sent off to wash their hands or stamp the mud off their shoes. All except Andrew, and Jill indicated he was looking at the pigs. It was only much later we discovered that what she'd really meant was he'd been looking at the pigs when she'd last seen him. Not long after breakfast.

When he didn't appear for the jam pudding I went out to call for him, and when he didn't come I went to the pigsty to find him. He wasn't there, and Mr Rollins hadn't seen him since about eight thirty. A rush of nausea gripped me. I began shouting his name over and over, until I was screaming it at the top of my voice, and the children ran out to see what was the matter, and Howard came full pelt from the vegetable garden, running like a giraffe.

'What is it? What's happened?'

We split up: me, Howard, Mr Rollins, Mrs Bubb and the children in pairs, and we searched the grounds. We searched in every shed and in every hedge; Mr Rollins dragged an old horse trough and I closed my eyes in dread; we combed the field and the orchard, emptied every chest in the house, opened every cupboard, pulled everything out from under the beds. Every second was charged so full of fears it bulged into an hour's length. And every moment all I could think was what if we were looking in the wrong place and his life depended on us finding him right now? Time, that had dragged so long and so wastefully throughout the war, now seemed to be priceless. All I could hear was my breathing – quick, heavy lungfuls – and my voice shouting for my lost son. I passed Howard in front of the house. We were both panting, and I could see wisps of his hair stuck to his forehead with sweat.

'It's Celia!' I thought I had just formed the words in my head, but I'd said them out loud.

'Why would Celia want to take him?'

'It's Celia – I know it! Car's gone.'

'Of course it has. She left about nine.'

'Oh, God! She's had him for three and a half hours! Oh, God!'

But I could see he was beginning to panic as well. The children were straggling back to the house.

'Perhaps she took him for a drive,' suggested Johnny. 'I would've gone.'

I started running to the road, and Howard came after me. I looked up the road to the hills and down the road to the village. Which way? Which way? Panting before I started, I began running at full tilt into the village, asking anyone I met en route if they had seen Andrew.

The centre of the village was deserted, except for Vile It who told me to fucking fuck off and stood with her arms out to protect the entrance to her bus shelter. I stood distraught and tried to catch my breath, when the lone figure of Mr Bearpark rounded the bend in the road up ahead, pushing his dear polished bicycle.

'Mr Bearpark!' I screamed. 'Have you seen Andrew or have you seen an open-roofed car with Celia in it?'

'Lord, you're out of breath, young lady. You want to get your breath back. Cycling's done my lungs a power of good, look. You want to—'

'Have you? Have you seen him?' asked Howard, running up.

'Oh, good afternoon, sir. I didn't see you there. Well, now . . . I haven't seen either of them recently . . .'

'Thank you! Sorry to bother you!'

'. . . but what I *did* see earlier this morning was Celia Buckleigh in a car with young Andrew, but that was around about nine o'clock this morning, I'd say . . . maybe more like—'

'Where?'

'T'was going that way, towards the east.' He waved his free arm vaguely. 'Don't know where it goes, don't want to know. Happy here in Woodside, I am . . .'

'Where's the nearest nuthouse?' I demanded.

'Nuthouse?' He looked momentarily offended.

'Mental asylum – we think that's where they're heading.'

'Oh. You'd be talking about the one somewhere out by Dip Woods. What's it called now . . .? Down under the old hill fort . . .?'

'Good Shepherd House,' said Howard. 'It's Good Shepherd House – she said. I'll get the car.'

I stopped breathing. My mouth filled with saliva that tasted of bile. I thought I was going to be sick.

'. . . quite content I am in my . . .' I could hear Mr Bearpark wittering on.

'Joy?' I heard Howard, too. 'Are you all right?' But I couldn't move. Pom pom pom pom pom went my heart. I thought it was going to break out of my chest. '*Joy?*'

I looked at him: 'D'you have petrol?'

He drew his hand across his face. 'Damn and blast! There must be some somewhere! I'll run back and see what I can find. You ask around the village. *Someone* must have enough to get us that far.'

'How far is it?'

'Four, five miles.'

'*Five miles?*' I closed my eyes.

'It's not *that* far!'

'I know.' It was no distance at all. I had been living just five miles away from that terrible place all this time.

I grabbed Mr Bearpark's bike. 'I'm sorry! It's an emergency!' and I started cycling furiously as I let the adrenalin work my legs.

'I'll catch you up!' Howard called after me. 'I won't be long!'

'Use the gear!' wailed Mr Bearpark. I turned briefly to see him standing on the pavement, bereft. 'It's not used to . . .'

58

I cycled out of the village at a fair old rate, and it was a relief to feel my body using up all the energy I had become suddenly endowed with.

It had rained the night before, a heavy summer downpour that had excited all the flowering plants and set them off sending out their pollen, offering themselves to the bees all along the hedgerows. The air was thick with it, sweet and rank and heavy. My own sweat added to the frenzied scent as it prickled on my brow and in my hair, ran between my breasts and behind my pumping knees. I saw nothing, only felt the smell of things, and the heat. I smelt my first baby, awash with sweet, earthy fragrance. I breathed him in, keening for the instantly familiar smell of his head, his neck. I gasped at it, gulped at it, found myself panting so loud I was groaning, pushing on the pedals through the dead weight of the air.

What did Celia want with him? I could see her arch smile: *What would I do with children?* And what would she do? Why would she take him back to Good Shepherd House? I was wasting my time. They could be anywhere by now. Anywhere.

I came to a fork in the road and took the right without stopping. It was a wasted trip, a stupid, futile waste of time, but I had no other ideas and my legs wouldn't stop. If I ever found him again I would hug him and hug him and hug him and never let him go. If I found him . . . I kept finding him and running towards him and holding him, holding him. If I kept thinking it, it would happen.

And why did I think Celia had him, anyway? What if he'd just wandered off away from the house . . . what if someone else, some pervert had lured him away and . . . what if . . .? I was losing valuable time. I was cycling the wrong way but my legs wouldn't stop. There was something about Celia's hostility that I had batted away, because it would hurt too much. But now I let it in. I let her spite wash over me and I remembered it: *We all know why she's so special, don't we?*

I stopped pedalling. Turning, I saw a figure on a bicycle on the long sweep of the road behind me. It was shouting.

'Joy! Joy!'

As he came closer I could see that Howard was exhausted. He had found his old bike from before the last war and his long legs had made up the time between us. Now he was shattered.

'Howard!'

'I'm coming with you!'

We stood in the middle of the road, panting.

'I'm sorry!' he breathed. 'No petrol. Nothing. Everyone's searching. Mrs Bubb's called the police.'

'She thinks he's your *real* grandson.'

'Mrs . . .?'

'*Celia* does.'

We cycled on without talking. I knew Dip Woods because the bus used to pass it on my way home from leave. Passengers got off there. People got on. We turned off down the unsigned lane leading to the woods. I was alert now, looking out for clues, not sure which side it was on, searching for entrances.

And then we saw it.

Two pillars covered in ivy rose beneath the trees at the side of the lane. They were widely spaced, and between them a straight, imposing driveway led up to the porch of a pink-stoned symmetrical building.

I put my bicycle against one pillar. 'I'll go,' I said.

'I'm not letting you go alone,' said Howard, dropping his bicycle. 'That's why I've come – to be with you.'

'There's no need.'

He took my arm and placed it through his, folding his other hand over mine. 'I was insensitive earlier. I completely forgot: this is your nemesis, isn't it? They're your idea of hell, aren't they, places like this?'

'This very one.'

'This one?'

I nodded. There was the same pink-brown façade, like a smear of old blood. It was smaller than I remembered it, but no less terrifying for that. Its tall windows reflected no light from the woods, and stared blackly into the darkness. There were pale quoin stones at the edges of the building, making it look like the piping on Celia's school blazer. There was a smell. A sickly, sweet familiar smell that sent me reeling back in time, and I was walking down this path with someone older, someone taller, someone holding my hand.

I clung on to Howard hard, and he responded with a little pressure on my hand which said he had tight hold of me.

I willed my feet to keep going, but I was wading not walking. We could see Celia's car parked up ahead to the left of the building, and it kept my legs going.

'Can they put me back in?' I asked.

Howard squeezed my hand. 'Why should they? You're just visiting with me.'

'I was signed over to them. Surely they have to take me back if they find me.'

The building was getting larger, we were nearly at the door. 'Don't say who you are.'

As we approached the front door itself there were new

horrors. The musty mix of old flowers and old coats and floor bleach made me freeze. I had scrubbed this porch floor so many times. I flinched at the instant recognition of the tile pattern. Memories I'd thought were dead.

Howard rang the bell. My breathing stopped and I tried to think of Andrew. That hug . . .

A short, grey-haired woman answered the door. I was relieved to see that I didn't know her at all. Howard explained that he had come to see his daughter, Celia, and we were invited in.

But there were more horrors. Standing in the entrance hall I was assaulted by the spiteful shoe-polish smell of orchids. It smacked me about the face like Sister Conceptua had done. It reeked from every outpost of my memories and I wasn't going to let it in. I would find the orchids – there they were in that pot – and I would snap off the heads and stamp on them. I would smash everything, unlock all the doors, set all the inmates free.

But the grey-haired lady smiled pleasantly, the red-stoned brooch of a dove sparkling innocuously from her soft, grey twin-set. I tried to dislike her, wanted her to show something of the horror I'd known in this place, so that Howard would understand.

'We're having a cup of after-lunch tea in the rest room at the moment, if you'd like to join us.' She indicated a room off to the side, where we could see easy chairs and some dazed-looking people, and I realized that 'we' did not refer to the staff. 'Some of the residents like to have a little nap, so we'll keep our voices down.'

We followed her into the long room which I couldn't remember ever having entered before. It was lit at both ends by tall windows, and a dozen or so residents were lolling in chairs, napping or sipping at regulation cups of tea.

I saw him straight away: the top of his little brown head as he read a comic on his lap.

'Andrew!'

'Mummy!'

I ran over to him and he leapt to his feet. I could tell he was pleased to see me, and he let me hug him and make a fuss. 'Oh, Andrew! Andrew!' I began to kiss him and kiss him, and he wriggled free, laughing.

'I've made lots of friends. This is Mabel who plays the piano . . .' A middle-aged woman in girls' plaits stood up suddenly and curtseyed at us. '. . . and that's Mr Man who sings songs and reads me stories . . .' He indicated a man napping in a chair, the *Beano* covering his face. '. . . and this is Aunty Celia and she drives a big car and is Granddad's daughter and she's got loads of *Beanos* and *Dandys* I can have . . .'

I looked at Celia, and she looked down at the cup of tea on her lap.

'Are you the Princess Royal?' asked Mabel suddenly.

'No,' I said. 'I'm sorry.'

She looked devastated.

'Are you the King of England?' she asked Howard.

'Yes. Yes I am, actually.' Mabel genuflected and Howard held out his hand. 'Pleased to meet you. So glad you could be here.'

Mabel beamed.

I wrapped my arms around Andrew again, but once more he wriggled free and went to show Howard his comic. Only then did I become properly aware of Celia and I sat down next to her.

'Tea?' The grey-haired lady held out a cup for me. 'I might be able to find you a biscuit.'

'That's all right. I'm fine.'

She bustled off to fetch some tea for Howard, as bright and as smiley as a fairy godmother.

'Celia—'

'I suppose you're going to accuse me of kidnapping him.'

'You *did*.'

'He wanted a ride in the car.'

She looked at me now with a slow bat of her eyelids, as if it were the only respectable thing she could have done.

'You took him without telling anyone.' I may have said it through gritted teeth, I'm not sure. The man behind the *Beano* was beginning to stir and I was trying to keep my voice down.

'All right!' she hissed. 'So I took him without asking. He's my nephew, isn't he?'

She was trying to pull the rug from under me again. I looked at Howard, but he was deep in a cartoon with Andrew, who was sitting on his knee.

'Have you *any idea* what you've put us through?'

She said nothing.

'*Have* you? You know the police have been called?'

'Oh dear,' she sighed.

'Why did you do it?'

'He's quite a sweet boy, isn't he? Well done you.'

'*Why?*'

She leant back in her chair and turned her head to face me. One of her toffee-coloured curls had come unpinned and fell down the side of her face. Her eyes, as they met mine, filled with tears.

'I wanted to know what it was like to be real,' she whispered.

I watched as a tear spilled over and ran down to her chin.

'But you *are* real.'

'I mean . . . the genuine article.' She dabbed at her cheek with the back of her hand. 'The favoured one.'

'Who? Andrew?'

'Andrew . . . *you*. Andrew *because* of you. You're both real relatives of Howard. I'm just a pretender.'

'I'm no more a real Buckleigh than you are.'

She raised her eyebrows. 'Don't you even know it, Joy? Don't you see? You're his love child. Gracie and he—'

'Celia, I ran away from this place when I was about five. Gracie took me in. I know she's not my real mother. I've met my real mother, and she's dead now.'

Celia sniffed for a few moments. 'So Andrew's not Howard's *real* grandson. I thought . . .'

I put my hand on hers. 'Why does any of this matter? Why do you care about it so much?'

She looked at me in helpless astonishment, her eyes pink and uncomprehending. 'How could you understand? At least you had a mother who loved you!' Then she began to sob, and I was embarrassed and intrigued by her loudness.

'Well, actually . . .' But she was right. I *had* had a mother who loved me. And only now I began to glimpse the atrocities that Celia had known at the hands of *her* mother. For how could it be that Celia, of all people, felt unloved? How could this strong, manipulative, confident child be the same woman who sat before me, crushed and sobbing for someone to say that she mattered in the scheme of things? That without having to comply with a set of requests, without having to supply information, run errands, spy on others, achieve unreachable goals, break unbreakable hearts, look better, smarter, more fashionable, more glamorous than anyone else's daughter, without having to do any of these things, she was lovable anyway, just as she was.

Andrew came over to ask why Aunty Celia was crying and climbed on my knee. As I squeezed his shoulders and breathed him in, I saw something through the tall back window which opened on to the garden.

Howard came and sat next to Celia on the other side of the couch to me, and took her hand in his. At the far end of the long garden I saw a dark figure moving like a phantom among the rose bushes. I knew before I saw the startling band of white in the blackness of her forehead that I couldn't escape her. She was heading this way.

I stood up quickly and grabbed Andrew's hand. 'There's something I need to do. I'll be back.'

59

'Are we going home?' asked Andrew.

'Soon. I just want to . . .' I stood in the hallway and turned to the back of the house. 'This way.'

We stopped by the back door, and I stared at it.

'Come on, let's go and see the garden!' Andrew was pulling at me now, reaching for the door handle, having seen the sunlight through the panes of glass. It was a brass knob, gleaming in places, dull and mud-coloured at its base. The keyhole was empty now, but it was different in other ways, shrunken somehow, less grand and threatening. Andrew had reached up and was turning it. And I had reached up too – to an eye-level handle on a grand, grey, sinister door in my bid for freedom.

The nun was coming for the door and we stood back as she opened it from the garden.

'Hello,' she smiled, a picture of innocence (but I wasn't fooled). 'Are you lost?'

I looked at her pale cheeks marbled with delicate pink threads, her gentle grey eyes gazing expectantly – almost tenderly – at mother and son. I did not recognize her.

'No. No – I was wondering if I could . . . Is Sister Conceptua here?'

'Sister Conceptua?' She looked confused for a moment, and then thoughtful. 'Wait here one moment. Won't you sit down?' She indicated two metal chairs next to the orchid display and I declined. Andrew went to sit down anyway, and lay down on both seats, because he could.

Very shortly the nun returned with another nun.

'This is Sister Frances, and I forgot to introduce myself: Sister Agnes.'

She held out a dry, cool hand, and I felt obliged to shake it, and to repeat the procedure with Sister Frances. 'Joy – Joy Buckleigh.'

'And this must be your little boy! Oh, isn't he a dear!' Sister Frances was already moving herself delightedly towards the seats, but I got there first. I wasn't taken in by any of it.

Andrew showed off a bit and started to shoot us all to get more attention. Sister Frances smiled at me shyly. 'You wanted to know about Sister Conceptua?'

'Yes. Is she still here?'

'Are you a friend?' She raised her eyebrows and smiled, almost defensively I thought, as if to say 'I'm interrogating you but let's pretend I'm not.'

I shook my head, aware from Andrew's fidgeting that my time was limited. 'No. I wanted to talk to her, that's all. There's something I wanted to say.'

Sister Frances and Sister Agnes looked briefly at each other. Sister Frances clasped her hands together and said: 'I'm afraid Sister Conceptua left some years back.'

'Most of the nuns have gone now,' added Sister Agnes. 'We're only here in a pastoral role.'

'And some practicalities.'

'Oh yes! We do plenty of practical things too.'

'But Sister Conceptua left before the others – she was very ill.'

'Ill?'

'She became very . . . her mind, you know.'

'Mad?' I asked.

The other nun nodded, smiling. But Sister Frances continued: 'Let's say . . . mental problems. I didn't know her well, but . . . I think she was quite a force to be reckoned with.'

'Where is she now?'

'She was taken to Coney Hill in Gloucester – you know, the asylum? I believe she died there last year. I'm so sorry.'

'Oh.' To my utter amazement, I felt tears on my face, and my mouth was doing that ugly distorted thing it does when you try not to cry. Sister Frances took my hand in surprise, and the other nun tried to coax Andrew away from the plants whose leaves he was plucking and folding into ammunition.

'I'm so sorry,' she said again.

'No . . . No! It's nothing. I would've liked to . . . ' What? Slap her face, tell her to see how that feels, slap her about a bit generally, stick her head down the toilet, pull her hair, strip her of everything – every last item of clothing – and laugh at her? Even now, when all the cards were in my favour, she had outdone me. Even in dying she had scored a little victory, given me the last stinging blow.

I sighed and reached for Andrew's hand. The nuns scuttled around me as I went back into the rest room, and brought me some tea although I didn't want it.

Howard stood up when he saw us, and swung Andrew up into the air. 'You all right?' he said to me. I nodded. 'Because if you're ready to go, there's a chauffeur coming to pick us up in ten minutes.'

'A chauffeur?'

'Mr Tribbit is bringing his grocery van. I rang Mrs Bubb to let her know we found him. It was Mrs Tribbit who picked up the phone. They're all there – practically the entire village, searching the grounds.'

Now I let myself look at him, because I could pass off the slight redness of eye as stemming from deep emotion at the collective concern for my son.

I noticed that Celia had disappeared. 'Is Celia all right?'

'She's gone for an appointment upstairs.'

'Will she be okay, do you think?'

Howard drew his hands over his face. 'She'll be a lot better now, I think. All that stuff about not being real.' He screwed his face up in confusion. 'I mean, we're all real, aren't we?'

'Goodbye, Mabel!' said Andrew, waving to her dramatically.

'Goodbye!' said Mabel, jumping up. 'And goodbye, Your Highness, so pleased you could come.'

'Goodbye, Mabel, it's been a pleasure.' Howard gave a little royal wave. 'I just happened to be in the area.'

'And goodbye, Mr Man,' said Andrew, lifting the *Beano*. 'Thank you for singing to me.'

'Oh, you off, little man?' I heard him say. And as I turned back to take Andrew's hand I saw Mr Man looking at Andrew, his face lit up with smiles, and then looking at me, his little head cocked to one side in exactly the same way it had been when he offered me the lavender. When our eyes met I had to slide mine away. I couldn't bear to see the look of recognition, that instant of thwarted delight as I turned away.

Moments ago I had stood in the hallway feeling brave and ready to face my demons. Now I stood in the same spot feeling shabby and cowardly. We bid goodbye to the nuns, and they stood in the doorway and waved us off like two friendly but anxious-faced guinea pigs peeking out of their hutch.

We walked together down the drive, the three of us holding hands in a row. Andrew, who walked in the middle, turned round to wave. I turned back too, and saw, to my horror, a face at the front window. His mouth was opening and closing. I couldn't tell if he was singing 'Daisy, Daisy' or shouting it.

I carried on without looking back. Just kept on walking.

60

There was a letter, of course. Howard handed it to me with such painful apology that I touched his arm.

It was, at least, unopened.

Dear Daisy ('Joy'),

I don't know what to say to help you. I can tell from your long silence, that you don't wish to continue our ~~frien~~ contact, and I don't blame you at all. It is important to rebuild your life from the rubble, and I'm so proud of how far you've come.

You wanted to know why she did it. I've been thinking about this a lot, and I can see that it haunts you night and day, just as her making me carry out her wish haunts me. But the thing is, what can I say? That she had lost her reason, after the death of Ivy? That no one could replace Ivy? That she resented you for not being Ivy? That she thought you were simple? That she couldn't cope with another child like Sidney? That she was as poor as a church mouse and had to sacrifice one child so that the rest of us could survive? All of this is true, but none of it is the whole truth.

Daisy, it is harder than I can begin to tell you to know the truth, even when it is not hidden. You see, I hated her for what she did to me. And it is true that it was an evil thing she did. But it is also true that she was a kind woman, who worked her fingers to the bone for us. And she was proud of me. And she was hurt when I didn't want to see her. She could hurt, despite all her toughness. And so what do I know? I know nothing and I know too much. And I can't bear it any more.

But what I do know is this: sometimes there are many, many versions of the truth, and if you want a single truth you may have to settle for a well-constructed lie.

Goodbye, my lovely little sister. I wish I had known you more. There is not one day that has gone by since that terrible parting that I haven't thought of you. I love you so very much. And that is a single truth.

Please don't think I do this because of anything you have done or not done. It is because of what she did, and my own weakness. I'm sorry from the bottom of my heart.

Your loving brother,

Philip x

61

I began to cling to people, Gracie in particular. I had this ridiculous notion that she would go off with Howard and want nothing more to do with me. And yet it was the one thing I most wanted for her in all the world. Poor Gracie didn't know when she was interfering and when she was needed. She didn't know what to do with me any more than I knew what to do with myself. I wanted to know what she was doing all the time, and became terrified she would leave me.

And the children . . . I clung to them for solace at night-time. One night I would sleep with Jill, the next with Andrew. I would close myself around their dear, perfect bodies, breathe in the sweetness of their baby soft hair, and cry silently with love for them. Their little sighs and murmurings would wake me – alert as a cat – when they had bad dreams. Then I would stroke their dimpled hands and their marshmallow arms, and wonder what sort of mother could give away these precious gifts.

Once Andrew asked me to sing him 'Bright Moon'.

'I don't know that one.'

'Yes, you do. Mr Man sang it to me. Bright moon on Charlie Chaplin . . . and baggy trousers. You hum it sometimes.'

'Oh, that one.' So I sang it.

'For the moon shines bright on Charlie Chaplin,
His boots are cracking,
For the want of blacking,
And his little baggy trousers they want mending
Before we send him
To the Dardanelles.'

Sidney had wrapped himself around me like this, had felt my dimples and my night murmurings. We would have learnt each other's movements, rolled over together like clockwork. Sidney had had a warm sleep companion, and then suddenly, without warning, a cold empty bed.

I couldn't name my misery. I would sit and weep for whole mornings without knowing why. I would turn the wireless off for some peace and quiet, and then feel injured because the newscaster had stopped speaking to me in mid-sentence. I thought I overheard Howard say, 'Don't tell Joy' again on the phone, or 'Don't tell her yet.' I felt negligent, feeble, and I had the ominous sense that there was no good left in the world, and that no one was safe. The sound of a bird squawking could make me jump and break out in a sweat. I was terrorized at the thought of Andrew or Jill cutting themselves with a knife, spilling hot tea over themselves, being spat at by the fire, not seeing a barbed wire fence in time, catching their fingers in a door, playing with matches, stroking a mad dog or choking on apple skin. And yet I couldn't bring myself to sing to either of them with any cheer in my voice, or tell them a story that was not a glum monotone. I could hold them very close – so tight that Jill's arms hurt and she wanted to wriggle free – but I couldn't give them the tenderness owed to two small children whose accidental death was just around the corner.

I was convinced my disquiet would end when James came home, but James would not be back until the winter if he was lucky. As the months went by, however, I grew more and more introverted. I found myself staring out of windows for half-hours at a time, or unable to get up in the mornings and face the day.

In November 1945 the air smelt of winter: cold lungfuls bereft of pollen but with a hint of woodsmoke. The trees grew thin and ragged, fluttering their last remaining leaves like tiny items of washing on a line. Mist turned the hills into looming clouds. The blackberries shrivelled on the hedgerows, dry and rotten, and everything seemed attached to something else by strands of cobweb. I took the children into the village for a walk. The walk was for my benefit: Jill and Andrew sat at each end of the pram, even though Andrew was strictly far too big for it.

I was making my way to the corner by the memorial cross – because that was where the fish van stopped on Fridays – when something very queer happened. Suddenly I became aware of two huge sheep blocking the pavement up ahead. They were making their way towards us, slowly at first, but then at quite a sinister trot.

They came right up to the pram, and one of them leapt up on her hind legs and put her trotters on the side. Jill screamed. Andrew giggled. I tried to shoo them away. There was no one around at that moment, and I found my pulse racing in silly terror. They were only sheep, and with a couple of big shoves they trundled back down the street and stood looking hurt and bewildered by the green.

I remembered then that Miss Wallock had died last year, and these were probably two of her old lambs: they'd seen the pram and thought she'd come back for them. They stood longingly by as I purchased four tails of cod, occasionally putting one hoof tentatively forward as if to make another run at the pram, then thinking the better of it as I caught their eye.

I felt oddly moved by those two old sheep, lost without their dear Miss Wallock, but with no real place in the sheep world after so much Wallock-love.

I felt increasingly isolated and introverted. I couldn't seek advice from the one person who might have helped me, because I felt the burden of Gracie's sacrifice for me. If I asked one more thing of her it would plunge me into a deeper self-loathing. One evening, when Howard was painting a cluster of orange rowanberries in the drawing room and I was watering the plants, I asked him quite suddenly, 'Am I mad?'

He looked up briefly, and then stroked his fine paintbrush over a square of watercolour in a metal tin. I supposed it was too much to ask of him to talk about emotions. One whiff of feeling and the Englishman retreated swiftly into his impenetrable shell. But I was wrong. Howard was just biding his time. It seemed my madness or lack of it was not as clear cut as I had hoped.

'Well,' he said, not looking up, 'I suppose guilt and regret have their uses in the short term . . .' He put his brush into a jar of water, and we both watched as the orange colour streamed into it like a rescue flare. I waited, not at all sure he would continue. 'But long term, they're absolutely useless. They'll destroy you if you let them.'

He squeezed the water out of the brush and refined the tip. I waited, but there was nothing more.

'So . . . am I mad, do you think?'

I watched as he painted another whole rowanberry, painstakingly dipping and stroking and blotting. I'd given up waiting for a reply when he said:

'When you're in the trenches, you have to stay alert. If you let yourself sink back, the rats'll get you.'

I closed my eyes in exasperation. This was so typical of Howard: one hint of emotion and he retreated into trench warfare. I sprinkled the remaining water on a rubber plant and went towards the door.

'Stay alert,' he said to my back.

I turned around to face him. 'Alert to what?'

He looked up from his work and in a rare moment of eye-to-eye contact he said, 'Loveliness. Lovely things . . .' He looked awkwardly at his rowanberries. 'Moments of joy.'

And that was it. His head was down over his work, and I was left, mouth ajar in the doorway.

62

Late that November I had a letter that made me cry. I cried so much that Andrew ran over to me and started stroking my hair.

'What is it, Mummy? What's the matter?'

'Daddy's coming home!'

I squeezed him very tight, but he backed off and looked at me earnestly. 'Never mind, Mummy,' he said. 'Don't cry. If we don't like him, we can always send him back.'

But Daddy didn't come home. Not straight away, at least. It would take six weeks for his voyage from India, and then there would be some disembarkation leave before being posted to Aston Down to await release from the RAF. Those six weeks passed slowly. I went to his wardrobe and took out his old clothes, opened his old stamp books, smelt inside his shoes. But nothing smelt of him, and I couldn't conjure him up.

I made myself a new dress and new outfits for the children. I went to the hairdresser's in town and bought myself lipstick and a pair of shoes with little heels. I sat in front of the mirror at my dressing table and held my hair in different shapes, inspecting my skin, my smile, my eyebrows, wondering if he would find me different to the woman he had fallen in love with. I didn't like my nose. I inspected it in profile in the three-way mirror. There it was, that image I so rarely looked at because it confused me so much: Joy into infinity.

At first I couldn't think how he would fit in. We had our routines now, our patterns. The children had become children without him: he wasn't a part of anything they did or thought. I had my things to do each day. There just wasn't a place for him. Before I'd had vague imaginings of him taking me to town in the cart, of me ironing his shirts while he smoked a pipe, or chatting to him as I knitted by the fire in the evenings. But it was Howard who took me to town in the cart, I liked to listen to the children play whilst I ironed, and I chatted with Gracie or Mrs Bubb by the fire in the evenings.

'It's always hard at first,' said Mrs Bubb, helpfully. 'My friend Pam's daughter took one look at her husband when he came back and told him to clear off. Told him he wasn't the man she married he was so changed.'

'Did they work it out?'

'Hang! No! She's seeing the postman now. Then there was Mrs Alma – you know Mrs Alma with the ears? – her husband came back to find she'd put a smile on the face of every man this side of Gloucester. So *he* walked out. Then there's Mrs Davies – you know, with the blue door – and *she* had her husband come back with bits missing, so that can't be easy. Well, I suppose it depends which bits. I wouldn't mind the odd leg off, but there's bits I would mind, I don't mind saying.'

In the second week of January I was in the garden on the far side of the house pruning some fruit bushes. Andrew and Jill were helping me make a big heap of twigs for a bonfire, and kept getting distracted by interesting-looking cuttings that turned into swords or walking sticks or cigarettes with real smoke as we sent coils of dragon breath into the jagged cold of the air. Suddenly something leapt from behind a bush and scampered up the greengage tree. It was Tigger, son of Digger, sleek and beautiful, trying to enjoy our company, trying to show me something, perhaps.

'Look!' yelped Jill, as if she had never seen our cat before. 'He's right up high.'

'He's amazing,' I said.

'No,' Jill frowned. 'He's a cat.'

I smiled, noticing how simply the little furrow between her brows disappeared when she settled on an idea.

'You don't get mazings round here.'

'I see,' I said. 'Where do they live, then?'

'In the jungle.' Then she bubbled over with laughter as Tigger made a branch wobble up and down. Her head went back and out it came: long, uncontrollable chuckling, and her eyes disappeared in the wideness of her smile. I held on to the loveliness of it, and the moment opened like a parachute, billowing and floating and holding me gently in the air.

Suddenly I heard Andrew's voice near the front of the house speaking in unexpectedly stern tones.

'No, I'm afraid you can't,' he said.

Looking up, I could see him standing, arms akimbo, and addressing someone out of view around the corner of the house. Then I heard a male voice, and then Andrew planted his feet firmly apart and said: 'She doesn't speak to strangers and neither do I!'

I ran around to the front of the house, expecting to see James. But the person standing there was indeed a stranger. His face was gaunt with sunken, hooded eyes and his skin was so brown that the whites of his eyes seemed luminous. I stood, startled, a few yards away from him, and put my arms automatically around Andrew's shoulders.

'It's all right, Mummy. I've told him to clear off.'

I couldn't take my eyes off him. At this last comment his gleaming, sunken eyes welled up and he looked at Andrew in disbelief. He looked back at me and smiled: a tentative, apologetic smile that didn't seem to know where it was going. Seeing my recognition, it grew and covered his whole face, the teeth glowing brightly against the tanned skin.

I ran towards him and embraced him. But even in that moment of elation I felt the strange bones in the lean body, and he seemed so frail and unfamiliar I didn't know how hard to hold him against me, and I wondered if we would ever truly fit together again.

63

The feast laid out in the dining room seemed ridiculous: Victory Jelly with flags in it. A monstrosity.

The Mustoes were there with George and their youngest Emily (Robert, Mo and Tilly weren't demobbed until later in 1946), Mr Rollins and his family and Mrs Bubb. I could only think that I didn't know my lines. I felt nervous, unhinged, and a little stupid. It was easy enough to step back from things with all the noise and laughter and congratulations. It wasn't until they had all gone home, when the children were put to bed, that James and I had to confront who we had become.

I found him standing outside the orangery, looking up at the stars. The realization that he would not slot into place either, that he too was adrift, gave me an unexpected jolt. I stood next to him and he held my hand. We said nothing for a long time.

'This must all seem very trivial to you,' I said at last.

There was a long silence, and when he turned his face to mine I could see his eyes glistening. 'This is what we were fighting for. This is what it was all for: you, the children. I've missed so much of it – their childhood, I mean. I didn't want to miss it.'

'I'm sorry.' I squeezed his hand, not expecting his tears.

'There were times I wished I was fighting,' I said hopelessly. 'It's been such a long, long war just waiting.'

He put his arm around me and rested his head on mine. I could hear him sniff and swallow. 'I've done things . . . I've done things I'm not proud of in this war.' His voice faltered at the end, and I didn't know how to react to this new version of James.

'You're home now. It's over now.'

'Who knows how many other women and children, waiting for the war to end . . . innocent people just caught up . . . just in the wrong place . . .? We . . . I don't know if we'll ever be able to forget what we did.'

I burst into tears.

'I've upset you – I'm sorry! I'm so sorry, darling.'

He took me in his arms and we buried our heads in each other's necks, but I felt treacherous. I wasn't crying for those other women and children, I was crying for myself, crying because my saviour was just another human being racked with guilt, surprised not to find what he thought he'd find, and all at sea.

As the days went by we tried to draw closer together, remembering what we had been before so much stuff got in between us. I brought him breakfasts on trays, posies of flowers, drawings by the children. He made me sketches of birds, took me and the children on walks, and I would pass through kissing gates bordered with holly berries and through bright fields of sheep with buzzards flying overhead under windswept clouds and see nothing. The children would laugh about something he said or did and I wouldn't notice. Sometimes I watched him from our bedroom window walk to the end of the garden, and would see him stretch out like a cartwheel, whispering to the moon or listening to the trees. I was struck with the awful possibility that he didn't feel the same about me either.

At night we couldn't touch because Andrew would come and sleep between us. Neither of us took him back to his room, because we knew there was something else in the way, something huge and growing: an incubus that wouldn't go away.

On the fifth morning of his leave I was awoken by the wireless on loud downstairs. There was no one else in the bed, so I put on my dressing gown and went down to the kitchen. The wireless was not on. No one was about, but the music was very loud and clear. I followed it to the orangery and there, with his back to me, was James playing his cello. The sunlight made the tips of his ears glow, and I watched the dear point where his hair reached his tanned neck. His right shoulder moved slightly under an old cotton shirt, and I could see the fingers of his left hand making confident, magical movements on the strings.

Jill and Andrew were sitting on the floor beside him, dipping bits of toast into boiled eggs.

'Have you had enough?' he asked Jill, stopping his playing when she reached up with eggy hands.

'I've had a little nuff,' she said, her head on one side, 'but not a very big one.'

James threw his head back and laughed. I caught the moment just there, and it opened like a falcon's wings, spreading his laughter through the air, wider and wider until it soared.

He saw me and smiled.

'Our daughter needs a bigger nuff!' And I saw him again, for an instant, the same man who'd gone away.

'One more nuff coming up, then.' I went back into the kitchen and Andrew followed me.

'Daddy's going to get me a go in a Spitfire. Only I need to sleep in my own bed because fighter pilots aren't allowed to sleep with their mummies. Do you mind? I'll still look after you.'

'That's fine. How exciting! A ride in a Spitfire!'

'I know. I'm going to . . . Mummy . . . why are you smelling inside Daddy's slippers?'

64

Despite the confusion of his presence, when James went back to Aston Down I missed him.

The following weekend I walked the grounds wondering if he would make it back for a visit. When I reached the beech tree at the far end of the paddock I stopped suddenly, startled by a stream of smoke rising from the chimney of the empty cottage. At first I thought it was on fire: it had been derelict for years. But it was definitely coming from the little chimney stack and, now that I studied it, the roof seemed in unusually good shape for a wreck.

Something brushed my shoulders and I looked round. There was nothing there. My hair seemed caught on something, and I swept it aside. I felt uneasy. There was a presence somewhere near.

Suddenly my hair was caught up in a hand and lifted on to the top of my head. I gasped.

'You have remarkably beautiful shoulders.' I looked up to where the voice was coming from and saw James lolling from a branch. 'I've never looked at you from this angle before.'

'You scared me half to death.'

I made to climb up as well. He reached out an arm and pulled me up. As soon as I was beside him he looked at me intently, and stroked the side of my face.

'There's someone in the cottage,' I said awkwardly.

'I know.'

He lay back on the branch and fiddled with a twig.

'Who?'

'Gracie and Howard.'

I let out a disbelieving snort before catching his eye and seeing that he wasn't joking.

He looked out towards the cottage and said, 'They've been doing it up for years. Always planned to live there when I came back.'

I stared at him, but his eyes were still fixed on the horizon. I gave an embarrassed little laugh. 'I think Gracie would've told me.'

Now he turned and looked directly at me. 'Perhaps you just didn't notice. Perhaps she didn't want you to know.'

I felt a quiver of shock and disbelief. But his face was serious. 'Why not?'

He frowned a little. 'An instinctive thing, maybe.'

I was beginning to panic. There had been a plan, and everyone had known about it. Even James, thousands of miles away. But I had been left out.

'Well, from what Dad said in his letters, you hadn't really picked up on it, and she didn't want to seem happier than you were. She couldn't bear to see you sad. She wanted to wait for your happiness before she announced her own.'

My throat was beginning to swell.

'How long . . .?' I whispered. 'How long has it been going on?'

'Since they first set eyes on each other, I think.' He smiled at me and continued to fiddle with the twig.

I closed my eyes at what I had caused: all the love I had stifled.

'I would've been so happy for them! I can't believe they've held back because of me.'

He reached out and took my hand. 'I don't think they held back that much,' he winked.

'Are you sure?'

'Pretty sure. You mustn't worry about it. She wanted you to be happy. The important thing is that you are loved. She did it out of love.'

Somehow I felt the thought of it like a burden, another wrong I was responsible for. My face ached, every feature straining against an expression of pain.

Tigger bounded into the tree and James glanced skyward to the thick mesh of branches. 'Look at that. We're so busy watching the leaves falling off we don't see these buds – they're already starting – look. Growing already.' I looked up, but all I could make out were a few dogged yellow leaves hanging on by a thread. 'You know, for the last few years, I've been horrified by what people can do to each other. On the boat on the way back there were a load of children picked up from a Japanese camp.' His voice faltered a little. 'You've never seen anything like it. They were so thin, so alone.' He reached a hand up and tapped an overhanging branch. 'And I've been dwelling on that: a human being's capacity for cruelty. It's terrifying. It really is terrifying.'

His eyes were glistening with tears and I was beginning to feel panic-stricken again. Just when I'd hoped for some solace, it seemed he was heading for the abyss and he would take me with him.

'But then I've been sitting here and thinking.' He propped himself up on an elbow suddenly and looked out across at the cottage again. 'I've been thinking about a human being's capacity for love. Look at it. It's even more amazing, isn't it?'

I knew he meant Gracie. I knew he meant that I didn't know how lucky I was, and he was trying to make me see it. And it was quite true: I had been so wrapped up in what one woman seemed *not* to have felt for me, that I had failed to enjoy all the love I had. I knew this was right, I knew I was ungrateful and I knew my perspective was all wrong, but that one thing kept pulling me under like a giant weight attached to my ankle.

'I know I have so much to be grateful for.' Tears sprang from nowhere and dribbled down my cheeks. 'I just feel so . . . trapped. Not by you. Not by anyone. Just by thoughts in my head that won't go away.'

He pulled me towards him and the branch swayed a little as I lay down on his chest.

'Well, I think that's my job, isn't it; getting you out of traps?'

'I don't think there's a way out of this one.'

'Look at me.' He lifted my chin gently, and I repositioned my head. His green eyes were gazing so deep into mine that I felt like one of his hypnotized rabbits. 'Don't forget the gypsy soul in me.'

He continued to gaze at me.

'You know, when animals are trapped, you sometimes have to mesmerize them before you can set them free. Otherwise they get frightened and pull away so hard they can take a leg off.'

He ran his hand down between my shoulder blades to the small of my back, and rested it there. He was very quiet and still, but did not take his eyes off me. After some time like this he said, 'Come with me to the house.'

I felt a rush of longing for him. He slipped down from the tree and let me slide down into his arms, and every part of me wanted him. But he was wrong if he thought this would solve things. It was a lovely idea, very animal, very instinctive, it appealed to the feral girl inside me. Even so I knew then that no amount of lovemaking would rid me of this demon. The cat, black and white like his mother, bounded on ahead of us.

'I may be wrong,' he said, as if he read my mind, 'but I don't think so. I'm going with my instincts on this one.' He slipped his hand around my waist and hung it on my hip as we walked. 'Do you trust me?'

I nodded, feeling suddenly heavy with desire. I longed so much to believe in the magic he had conjured up that I let myself believe, I let myself follow him like someone under a spell.

When we entered the hallway he looked about furtively.

'Wait here.'

He disappeared into the kitchen and I heard him say something to Mrs Bubb.

'Come on,' he said, when he reappeared, and he led me up the stairs.

On the first landing he stopped and faced me, taking my waist in his two large hands, as if it were a child's.

'Be still, and let things come to you.' He took a stray strand of my hair and pushed it gently behind my ear. 'Try to trust me on this.' Then he led me further up the stairs and said, 'There's someone I want you to meet.'

I followed him up to the next landing, torn between disappointment and intrigue. He pushed open Jill's bedroom door, and I heard a low murmuring. The cat went in ahead of us.

There, slumped on the bed, was a man in his early thirties. Jill's arms were draped about his neck, and Andrew lay curled on his chest. He stopped singing 'For the moon shines bright on Charlie Chap . . .' and looked at me, his tiny head cocked to one side, and he gave a shy, apologetic smile. Both children were fast asleep.

65

And then the birds came. The starlings had been singing softly to themselves in hedges all winter through but I hadn't noticed them. It was the mistle thrush I noticed first, its short garbled verses ringing out on a bright morning that January. Then the tsee tsee of the robins, the high-pitched bluetits, the explosive, jubilant little wrens, a dunnock or two and a song thrush, could all be heard limbering up for the spring if you only listened. In February and March they were joined by tree-creepers, nuthatches and woodpeckers, and a few keen blackbirds joined the swelling chorus of impending spring. By April, great arrows of summer visitors arrived, until in May there was a flood of song: a kee-kee-kee, su-su-su, tyu tyu, tuk-tuk-tuk, teee-ip teee-ip, tyup tyup tyup, tissik tissik, chee-chee-chee-chee-chee, tooey tooey, liddle-iddle-iddle-iddle, dzwee dzwee, hoo-ee hoo-ee hoo-ee, choodle-oodle-oodle-oop, chip-chip-chipper-chip, haw . . . haw . . . haw, chook-chook-chook as every bird alive joined ranks and heralded the sunshine with such urgent, boundless rapture that you couldn't help but be carried along in their joy.

Everything started to grow again. By the spring of 1946 our family had doubled in size like the hedgerows: the children had a father, a new uncle and two old Wallock sheep pets. Were they happy? Their childhood had been spliced by the war. Half of it without a father, half of it with one. Half with their mother's sadness, half with her joy. How did we fare, then, as parents? What phantoms or pleasures dance through their memories? Only they can tell you that.

And what of us? Young people say that our generation had it easy with love: we *had* to stay together, so it's no wonder we celebrate the anniversaries they will never reach. But when we got to the bottom of that curve, we clung on to the moments of joy, and we just kept on going until we came up again. Love hangs constantly in the air between us, gentle and warm as cow's breath. We cannot disappoint each other. We know too much. Although sometimes, when the moon has risen and the stars multiply softly on a balmy summer night, we can still surprise each other.

Out now in Robinson paperback

Tommy Glover's Sketch of Heaven
by Jane Bailey

In 1944 eight-year-old Kitty is placed as an evacuee in a Gloucestershire village with a cold, unhappy couple, Joyce and Jack Shepherd, who seem to find her cockney chirpiness and comic observations repugnant. Neither of them approves of Kitty's friendship with Tommy Glover – an older child from the boys' home – and even seem to nurse a mysterious hatred of him.

Kitty's relentless curiosity slowly transforms the strangely troubled marriage of Joyce and Jack, and when she exposes a terrible secret, the lives of nearly everyone in the village are changed forever.

£6.99

Why not try the Amelia Peabody murder mystery series?

No. of copies	Title	Price (incl. p&p)	Total
	Tommy Glover's Sketch of Heaven	£6.99	
	Crocodile on the Sandbank	£6.99	
	The Curse of the Pharaohs	£6.99	
	The Mummy Case	£6.99	
	Lion in the Valley	£6.99	
	The Deeds of the Disturber	£6.99	
	The Last Camel Died at Noon	£6.99	
	The Snake, the Crocodile and the Dog	£6.99	
	The Hippopotamus Pool	£6.99	
	Seeing a Large Cat	£6.99	
	The Ape who Guards the Balance	£6.99	
	The Falcon at the Portal	£6.99	
	Thunder in the Sky	£6.99	
	Lord of the Silent	£6.99	
	The Golden One	£6.99	
	The Children of the Storm	£6.99	
	Guardian of the Horizon	£6.99	
	The Serpent on the Crown	£6.99	
	Tomb of the Golden Bird	£17.99	
	Grand Total		£

Name: _____

Address: _____

_____ Postcode: _____

Daytime Tel. No. / E-mail _____
(in case of query)

Three ways to pay:
1. **For express service telephone the TBS order line on 01206 255 800 and quote 'EP2'. Order lines are open Monday – Friday 8:30am – 5:30pm**

2. I enclose a cheque made payable to **TBS Ltd** for £_____

3. Please charge my ☐ Visa ☐ Mastercard ☐ Amex ☐ (Switch issue no.____) £___

    Card number: _____

    Expiry date: _____ Signature: _____
                                  (your signature is essential when paying by credit card)

Please return forms (*no stamp required*) to, Constable & Robinson Ltd, FREEPOST RLUL-SJGC-SGKJ, Cash Sales/Direct Mail Dept., The Book Service, Colchester Road, Frating, Colchester, CO7 7DW.

Enquiries to readers@constablerobinson.com.
www.constablerobinson.com

Constable and Robinson Ltd (directly or via its agents) may mail, e-mail or phone you about promotions or products.
☐ Tick box if you do not want these from us, ☐ or our subsidiaries.